CALLER 26

By J.P. Pellegrino

Copyright © 2014 by Jeffrey P. Pellegrino
Published by Jeffrey P. Pellegrino
Cover Image and Design by Jeffrey P. Pellegrino

All Rights Reserved

This is a work of fiction. Names, characters, businesses, organizations, places, events, and incidents are either the product of the author's imagination or are used fictitiously. Any resemblance to actual persons, living or dead, events, or locales is entirely coincidental.

To my wife:
This was hard. Thanks for the support. I love you.

To the reader:
Evil wins when we do nothing to stop it.

Chapter 1

Dr. Susan Stein drifts into a nauseating and distorted world. Her mind is a foggy swamp, her body drowsy and queasy. A dizzying haze dominates everything... everything except the itch in her crotch. *My panties are wrong,* she senses. *They're scratchy... and twisted...*

While needles of itchy sweat move across her crooked and aching body, a dull thump, like a fist on a wooden table or a sneakered toe steadily kicking a hollow wall, resonates throughout the blackness of her twirling, floating world. Clarity slowly emerges, and after a few bewildering moments, she perceives this rhythmic thumping is her own skull bouncing against the stiff surface on which she lies. She tenses the muscles in her neck in a vain attempt at stabilizing her grainy head, but it isn't enough. Listlessly, rhythmically, her head bounces as her black world twirls. She feels her body lift, float, and then slam against the surface below her. Sound and a distant but present pain intertwine with the awful blackness.

A train, she thinks, her body again floating and then slamming, her head bouncing off the surface, the dull pain rattling her brain. Float. Slam. Rattle. Float. Slam. Rattle. *I don't remember taking a train.*

A wave of pressure cramps her stomach, and she senses she might throw up, but like her itchy crotch, something's not right with her mouth either. There's something there, binding and restricting.

Oh God. Fear seizes her core. *I can't move my lips. I can't open my mouth!*

She swallows hard, forcing a creeping stream of fierce bile back into her stomach. Her eyes water as a few burning drops of acid drip from and then tickle her nose. She coughs, but the sound muffles inside her restricted mouth, making her gag and cough again. A tear creeps across her burning cheek as panic overwhelms her in a sudden wave of heat. *Oh please, don't let me drown!*

As her awareness untwists into five separate senses, confusion pervades. It's not until she manages to hold her heavy eyelids open for a long count to five that she begins to comprehend her reality.

With every ounce of will, she attempts to call to her husband, but she can't move her lips. Tears flood her eyes, and panic shakes her body. Her head throbs as she strains to keep it from bouncing against the hard surface.

As lines of tears tickle her cheeks, she struggles to wipe at them, but she can't do that either. Her hands are numb, and they are secured behind her back. Terror seizes her, and acidic pressure begins to fill her stomach once more. The tickle on her cheeks is maddening, and the fact she can't scratch at it makes it even worse. She shakes her head and screams, but no sound escapes.

Acid creeps from her stomach, a slow-moving river burning its way toward her mouth. She starts to sob. For the life of her, she can't understand why her head will not stop banging against the damn floor. She struggles to call her husband once more, but it's useless. Her breathing labors as her nose clogs with mucus.

She pulls against her restraints, desperately trying to free her hands so she can wipe her nose and scratch the tickle from her cheeks, but the effort is useless. Panic overwhelms her common sense. The acid in her throat burns unbearably. Her right nostril is completely clogged, and despite the rattling of her surroundings and the loud rhythmic banging of her head, she hears the bubbling noise that life-sustaining air makes as it tunnels its way through the tiny opening that remains in her left nostril.

Terrified of drowning, she flails her body in jerking twitches as the twirling darkness accelerates. She fights to fend off an inescapably intense and horrifying death as she slowly chokes on her own snot and vomit.

Visions flash in the darkness. A portrait of her husband and her son; a photograph of her home and its view, sunny and open and free; the anticipatory smile on her son's face before he leaves for chess camp. She feels the touch of her husband's beard against her cheek. She tastes his kiss, its familiar warmth, and these visions comfort her while she lies in the nauseating blackness, awaiting death.

But as the seconds pass, she realizes death has passed too. She forces herself to swallow even though a lack of saliva makes it impossible. She can both hear and feel her head whacking the surface below her, but she can do nothing to stop it, and it drives her insane.

She again struggles against the straps that bind her hands, but the effort is futile as the straps tighten even more. She puckers her lips in an attempt to free her mouth but quickly understands whatever is covering her lips is not coming off.

Closing her eyes and tightening her neck muscles, she finds mild success in stabilizing her bouncing head, and this momentary sense of control allows her a brief period during which she can focus. She forces herself to concentrate.

She remembers being picked up for work, and she recalls stopping to help a man on the highway, a blond-haired man whose blue car had been blocking the road.

The choppy scene plays out in her mind. She sees her Hummer lunge to a stop, and then she watches her driver climb down from his door. But then he's lying on the road, and the man from the other car, the one with the blond hair is jumping and yelling for her. She sees herself climbing out of her door and running to help…and then the movie ends.

Reality overwhelms her confusion.

Oh my God, she thinks, before sobbing uncontrollably. Acid resurges. She urinates on herself. Her fear-engulfed body shakes uncontrollably. She screams, but all that escapes is a muffled, high-pitched squeal that is smothered by the constant rattling of her blackened surroundings.

As her chest tightens, the rapidly rising vomit again works its way toward its wonted freedom. Mucus bubbles her nose causing her already dark world to close in again. She strains to breathe, and although her single free nostril struggles to provide enough air, it can't.

One Week Earlier

Chapter 2

Her contract read, "...no less than twenty-five (25) callers per day...no less than five (5) days per week...no less than forty-five (45) weeks per year..." As a way of preserving her own sanity, Dr. Susan Stein, host of *The Dr. Sue Radio Show*, kept with blue ink on a yellow legal notepad, a written tally of the day's callers (in between doodles of hearts, hairdos, puppy dogs, and overlapping concentric circles). Although she was on the verge of wrapping up her twenty-fifth call of the day, and that meant she could, if she so desired, end the show, her internal clock was telling her too many agonizing minutes still remained, and there were no more commercial spots to take up the remaining time.

Dr. Sue took a deep breath, closed her eyes, and rubbed her pasty temples with her extended thumbs as she rested her numbing head on a bridge of interlaced fingers. It was Wednesday, and she had been taking calls for nearly three hours. Both physically and emotionally drained, she battled the familiar squeeze of her headphones as she retraced the words *New Headset!!!* on the yellow notebook that lay atop her tiny work area.

Forcing herself to concentrate, she took a small sip from her third bottle of Dasani water, burped silently into her clenched left fist, and then wiped the dampness from her lips with the back of that same left hand.

"Well Sheila," she said after clearing her throat and releasing the cough button, "there comes a time in a person's life when he or she has to take responsibility for what they have done. You are thirty-two years old, but it sounds to me like you're acting like a twelve-year-old. I know this is probably difficult for you to hear, but you really need to grow up. You can't have it your way all the time. As soon as you learn that, you'll see that your life will become a lot happier, and things will run a lot smoother. And that is how we, *grown-ups*, like things to be."

From her seat inside the production booth, she stared through the partitioning glass at Howard Thorsen, her producer. He was giving her his familiar *you're-treating-your-listener-like-she-is-a-child* look, the most annoying one where he mashes his mouth into an inverted U and then silently shakes his head back and forth, eyebrows raised, nose crinkled, as if something stinks, at a rhythm that is directly timed to each of her pronounced words. She forced herself to look away, and instead, concentrate on the reaction of her caller. It was obvious to Dr. Sue *this* caller had needed an on-air ass-chewing, and it was her job to do just that.

"You're right Dr. Sue," the distant sounding voice whispered into her headphone-covered ears. Had Dr. Sue not been wearing the headphones, and had she not been sitting enclosed inside her glass cubical but instead out with Howard and the rest of the production crew, she would have heard the caller's hushed response as it resonated from a round metal speaker that hung flush against the wall just outside of the booth. "I know what I need to do," the voice said.

"I know you do Sheila, and I know you can do it. Stop being a brat, and go conquer the world."

"Okay. I will Dr. Sue. Thank you. B' bye."

"Bye."

Dr. Sue inhaled deeply. She felt the impending approach of another hot flash and suspected the amount of Dasani that was present inside her tiny cube was insufficient to douse the ensuing flames. The small muscles that sat beneath the larger ones at the base of her spine were beginning to spasm, and her toes were getting hot.

She glared at the clock again while inhaling deeply. She could feel her face getting flush, and she could see by the squint on Howard's face he knew she was frustrated at what the large red numbers were yelling. By contract, she could end the show right then, but as she had suspected, too many minutes remained, and things would be awkward.

Thankfully, the hot flash appeared to have missed her. Wiggling her cooling toes, she exhaled quietly before deciding to plug her fundraiser once more. Then if there was time for one more call, she would take it.

"Just a reminder folks," she said into the oversized felt-covered microphone that hung from the top of the broadcast booth, directly in front of her face. It was through this portal that she was able to convey her solicited advice to the millions of listeners who tuned into her syndicated daily show, all across the nation. "We will be at Disneyland all day on Saturday. So if you're not too busy, and you want to have lots of fun, and also help a worthy cause, you can join us. Disneyland has promised to match the proceeds raised dollar for dollar, and they are going to give to the Dr. Sue's Children Fund three dollars for every ticket sold. The weather looks great, surprise, surprise. I promise. It'll be a lot of fun. So come join us. It's for a great cause."

She glanced at the clock again. It was getting close. Looking toward Howard, she saw he was giving her the signal, his thumb and pinky held parallel to the deck and rocking back and forth, that it was her decision whether or not she would take a twenty-sixth call. She saw the names on her monitor were still flashing, and that meant there were callers on the line.

"Okay," she said into the microphone. "It looks like I have time to take an extra call today." She noticed Howard clap silently in his patronizingly annoying way. She smiled, flipped him the bird, and then said, "Amy. You're caller twenty-six. Welcome to the Dr. Sue Show. What can I do for you?"

"Hi Dr. Sue. My name is Amy."

"Yes dear. I know."

"Sorry. I'm...I'm just a little nervous."

"Don't be nervous. What's up?"

The hot flash sparked to life from Dr. Sue's right foot at the end of her middle toe, and it quickly traveled up her right leg where it paused in her tensing lower back before exploding like an atomic fireball throughout the rest of her body. Sweat beads formed on her face, and the tiny five by seven foot booth suddenly felt like a one by two foot coffin. To top things off, the caller, the extra one, the one she went above and beyond to help, suddenly erupted into an unintelligible staccato of broken sentences and teary gibberish.

"I grew up without a dad," Dr. Sue heard as the caller rambled, "and I didn't want my son to too...and his daddy is a bad man...and my mom warned me...and my friends did too...but I didn't listen to them...and I think he does bad things to little..."

Unable to withstand both the blistering heat and the indecipherable gibberish, Dr. Sue mashed the button labeled *CALLER MUTE* with her left index finger while simultaneously chugging a fourth bottle of Dasani water. She pressed the button with such force the tip of her finger turned red and then white before going numb. When the water was gone, she let the plastic bottle fall to the floor before snatching her notepad from her desk so she could fan her face.

Finally, after a few eternal seconds, the wave passed, and she could feel the conditioned air begin to cool the sweat on her forehead. Following a few deep breaths, she returned the notepad to her desk and reopened her eyes.

She zeroed in on Howard and mouthed the words *thank you* at him. He looked like a stunned mullet complete with bulging eyes and gaping mouth, and Dr. Sue knew he foresaw her wrath over his gross mismanagement of the show's time.

Silence dominated the phone line. Not sure if the caller had dropped from the line, Dr. Sue composed herself by clearing her throat and then releasing the mute button.

"Amy? Are you still there?"

"Yes. I'm sorry."

"Okay. Well, that was way too much for me to digest all at once. I don't have a lot of time so I need you to calm down, *slow* down, and talk in complete and coherent sentences."

She noticed Howard was mimicking her again. *The nerve!* He was a dead man.

"Okay. All right. I'm sorry," Amy said weakly. "I'll try to calm down. I'm sorry."

"Thank you," Dr. Sue said, feigning a smile. "Now, let's start over. *Amy*, how can I help you?"

"Well," Amy paused and then said, "I need to leave my husband, and I want you to say that it's okay."

Eyes glued to Howard's, she relaxed her jaw long enough to let out a deep breath and then say in slow, short, annunciated phrases, "I think — I'm going — to need — some background on this one." No mimic this time from Howard. Obviously, her glare indicated she was far from amused. "Can you hold it together long enough to *clearly* tell me why you think you *need* to leave your husband?"

"I'll try."

"No Amy. *Try* won't work. Do."

"Okay, I will," Amy said between swallows. "I can do this."

"Great," Dr. Sue said, shifting her stare from Howard to the clock's red digital numbers. This was going to be close.

"Well, I've been listening to you for about eight months now, and I really respect your opinion."

"Thank you. How long have you been married?"

"Seven years."

"And how old are you?"

"Twenty-six."

"Yikes. Did I hear you have a son?"

"Yes ma'am. He's seven."

"I see. And it's his dad?"

"Yes ma'am, but he hasn't been with us the whole time."

"Okay. Well how long has he been around?"

"Umm, just about a year. He got out of prison ten months ago."

"Prison? What did he do?"

"Well, that's one of the reasons why I called. He went to prison for involuntary manslaughter. He killed a man's wife one night when he was driving drunk, but that was before we met. And now I found out something else, something much worse…"

"Wait. Hold on. Do you mean you didn't know him *before* he went to prison?"

"No ma'am. We met *while* he was in prison."

With a wrinkled forehead, Dr. Sue looked at Howard. He shrugged at her. "I don't get it," she said. "How did you meet *while* he was in prison?"

"We were pen pals. I started writing to him when I was sixteen. It was a class project. We had to write to someone in prison. Part of a social studies project."

"They *made* you write to someone in prison?" Her head throbbed.

"Yes ma'am," Amy said, sighing.

"Go on," Dr. Sue said, afraid to hear the rest of the story. She could see where it was going.

11

"Well, my mom wouldn't let me go visit him. She said it was dangerous. But I wanted to anyway. So I tried to go once. I told my mom I was going to visit UC Davis to check on my application and talk to the dean, but I really went to Folsom Prison. They wouldn't let me in though since I wasn't eighteen, and I couldn't prove that I was related to him."

"Okay. So that's good."

"Well, when I turned eighteen, I went back. They let me see him. He had a special pass so we were able to be alone, with no chaperone."

"And you had sex."

"Yes ma'am," Amy said through a quaky voice.

"And he knocked you up."

"Yes ma'am." She was barely audible.

"I'm sorry." Dr. Sue could hear a faint sob on the other end of the line.

"Me too," Amy said weakly. "It was my first time."

"We do stupid things when we're young," Dr. Sue said, refocusing the call. "I think I heard you say there was something worse?"

"Yes ma'am. A stranger called me yesterday. I don't know how she found me, but she said my husband molested her daughter eleven years ago. That means it would have happened before he went to prison."

"Okay. Is that true?"

"I think so. I mean...yes. It's true. It's all true. I'm tired of lying to myself. He was molesting little girls. And he has a temper..."

The bumper music for the end of the show started to play. Dr. Sue looked toward Howard who was giving her the *thirty-second* warning.

"Amy. I only have thirty seconds so I'm going to say this quickly. Rarely, and I mean *rarely*, do I advise someone to get out of a marriage, especially if there are children involved. But, this is an absolutely cut and dry situation. Now I can't tell you how to live your life, but if I were you, I wouldn't have ever let that man into my house to begin with, whether he was the father of my child, or not. So it's up to you. But I think you already knew the answer before you called, and I think you know what I am going to say. If I were in your shoes, I would leave."

"Thank you Dr. Sue. That *is* what I thought you'd say."

"I'm sorry Amy. I wish I could do more. Go stay with family somewhere and raise a child who will grow up and conquer the world."

"Okay. I will. Good-bye."

"Bye Amy."

The bumper music terminated, and Howard said through a small microphone from the production booth, "Okay, that's a wrap."

Dr. Sue sighed and removed her headset before setting it atop her notebook. The door to the soundproof booth opened with a pop, and Howard walked in.

"Sorry about that," he said. "I had no idea."

"Poor kid. I thought *I* had a headache."

"Saw you had a hot flash right there at the end. Nice recovery."

"Easy for you to say. I can't believe you did that to me. You've gotta manage my time better. That's your job. No more long delays and no more extra callers. And quit goofing off in the booth, or I'll find someone else. Got it?"

"Yeah. Sorry."

She shook the nearly empty bottle of Dasani before swallowing the last few drops. "Don't let it happen again. I mean it." She could see Howard knew she was serious.

Chapter 3

"Patricia Marx. Detective. One of LAPD's finest, or should I say *spineless*?"

Although her back faced the comment, Patty Marx recognized the familiar voice as well as the irritating sarcasm. She contemplated ignoring the remark and venturing farther into the darkness of her crime scene, but she completely understood the idiot attached to the voice was not going to vanish simply because she chose to ignore him.

Stifling both anger and frustration and doing her best to maintain her composure, Patty slowly turned and responded by saying, "Greg Riley. Asshole. *Los Angeles Times* reporter extraordi-*not*."

"Ooo. Good one," Greg Riley said, clutching his shirt in front of his chest with his right hand, as if he'd been shot in the heart. He dropped his hand and said, "*Lead detective*. Not bad. I guess the city's quota policy is still in effect."

Patty gritted her teeth. Despite the night's cool, damp air, she could feel a swath of sweat forming above her upper lip, which she knew to be an irrational reaction that always occurred when she was nervous or upset. Patty could see the tall goof was staring at her sweaty lip as his trademark smirk nestled into the right corner of his mouth, and that made the sweat bead even more.

Damn it, she thought. She refused to let him win. Through clenched teeth, she said in a barely audible voice,

"Look dipshit. Just because you couldn't make it on the force and now have to rely on other people's bad luck to enhance your own sense of self-importance, don't knock me for what I do. At least I'm trying to help, and I'm not some…highbrow media hack who's so…"

She turned away not bothering to finish her sentence. After two deep breaths, she wiped her lip with the back of her right index finger and forced herself to concentrate on anything but the idiot behind her.

"Hey there. Take it easy," Riley said. "I didn't come here to fight."

Patty spun back around. "Yeah, well. Why the hell are you here then? And, don't give me that *to bring the truth to the people* bullshit again. I'm pretty freakin' busy."

Riley smirked again. "Do I annoy you?"

"Now why would you think that?" Patty asked, doing her best to sound in control.

"I guess that's a *yes?*"

"You suck Riley. You know that?"

"Then that's a *no?*"

Patty tilted her head slightly, shook it, and then let out a cluck from the side of her mouth. "You are unbelievably dumb," she said.

The smirk turned into a smile. "You really do like me. Don't you?"

"Go away."

"Admit it. Come on. You like me."

"Yeah Riley. I like you," Patty replied, looking down at her black flats. She noticed a scuff on the inside of her right shoe and tried to buff it out by rapidly rubbing it on the inside of her left pant leg. Using the pause to regain her composure, she looked up at the tall, blond-headed reporter and smiled. "I like you like I like a good case of diarrhea. Out of my system and flushed away." She could hear herself stammering, and it frustrated her.

"Now that's not very ladylike," Riley said.

"I'm sorry *madam*. Did I offend you?"

"Okay. All right. Truce. I'm sorry. Jeez. I'm just trying to get a story. What do you say? Can I get an exclusive?"

Patty stood looking at the gangly reporter. Her conscience, aligned with every thread of common sense, was screaming *NO!*

"Why should I?" she asked.

"Because you just said you like me," he offered from beneath raised eyebrows.

Patty shook her head. A tiny smile broke across her lips. She couldn't help it. It just kind of popped out. She knew she'd regret it.

"Fine you big idiot," she said. "Come on. Just don't *touch* anything. This is my first case as lead, and if anyone can find a way to F it all up, it would be you."

"Great," Riley said, bending forward at the waist and slipping underneath the familiar strand of yellow crime-scene tape. "And don't worry. I won't touch anything."

Riley surveyed the small moonlit park that sat sandwiched between an all-night Laundromat and a doughnut shop. He could clearly hear the waves as they crashed against the silver shore across the street despite the constant din of the slow-moving traffic that inched its way along the road directly adjacent to the park.

Waiting for Riley to finish the seemingly daunting task of tunneling under the tape and walking the difficult six steps to where she was presently standing, Patty could not help but wonder how she had ever trusted such a clumsy goof. She nodded her head toward the center of the park, where a group of uniformed police officers were talking to a woman and a teen-aged Hispanic girl in the gray darkness of a three-quarter moon. "Let's go," she said. "Over there."

"What do you think?" Riley asked, walking beside the detective. "Same guy as last week?"

"Appears to be. M.O. fits. Young girl. Quick snatch. Ski mask. Looks like she got away before he could do anything to hurt her though."

"Lucky," Riley said, walking beside the shorter detective.

"Damn lucky."

"Any clues yet?"

"Nope."

"Any theories? Ideas? Anything I can print?"

"Nope."

"Okay then, let's see. Six kidnappings. Zero fatal. This one got away before he could 'do anything.'" Riley made quotations with the index and middle fingers of both hands out in front of him. "She was 'lucky.' No clues. No theories or ideas, and nothing I can print. When do you think you're finally going to catch this jerk?"

Patty stopped and looked up into Riley's face.

"Sorry," he said. He could tell she wasn't amused. "I mean…I didn't mean that you…well, what I meant was…"

"Shut up."

"Right," Riley said, clearing his throat before fishing a notepad from the inside pocket of his camel-hair sport coat. He unsheathed a small ballpoint pen from its top. "What I meant was, is there anything new in the case?"

Patty ignored him and started walking again.

Riley inhaled the salty air, racking his brain for something clever to say in order to break the obvious tension. *Nothing.* Instead, he cleared his throat and continued to walk beside the detective. He was relieved when he and his escort finally reached the group of other officers.

Riley smiled at the young girl. She didn't smile back. He could tell she had been crying.

"Hey Carl," Patty said. "What's up?"

One of the uniformed officers looked at Riley and then at Patty.

"It's okay. He's with me. Reporter. *L.A. Times.*"

Carl nodded at Riley who detected a bit of annoyance in the officer's glance. He was used to receiving such looks, especially from cops.

"Paramedics are on the way," he said. "She's not really hurt, but her mom wanted someone to take a look at her anyways. She seems to be a pretty strong girl.

"Broke loose from his grip over there and then ran back over here, back to the Laundromat." Carl motioned toward a group of buildings behind him.

Riley could barely make out a dark area behind one of the buildings. He jotted a few words onto his notepad.

"She said she saw him walking out with his laundry, and just as he left, she saw a couple of dollar bills fall to the ground. She waited for a while and then went out to pick them up. That's when he grabbed her and dragged her out back, into the alley. Looks like she got one arm free and was able to scratch his face. Then she said she jammed her thumb into his eye. I guess that's when he let her go. She ran back this way. He ran down the alley, the other way. She never saw his face. There's no description."

"So no rape," Riley asked while furiously scratching notes onto his tiny pad of paper.

"No rape," Carl said.

"That's lucky," Riley said as he continued to scribble into his notepad.

"Yeah. Lucky."

"I mean, she could've been raped like the rest of 'em. I guess he messed with the wrong girl. Pretty much went Patty Marx on the guy."

Patty elbowed him in his ribs.

"Sorry," Riley said, flinching at the sharp pain. He rubbed at the spot with his notebook. "That hurt," he whispered to Patty.

Patty shook her head. "You're an idiot," she said. "Okay Carl. Thanks. Keep the scene secure until the forensic team gets here. Maybe we can get some DNA from under her nails. Also, put the word out to all of the ERs in the area. Ask them to be on the lookout for a man with a laceration to his cheek and an eye trauma. Maybe we can get lucky. Maybe he'll try to get some help." Patty reached underneath her glasses with her right thumb and index finger and rubbed the bridge of her nose. "We'll catch this asshole. Maybe tonight we caught our break."

"Roger that," Carl said. "Do you want to talk to the girl?"

"In a bit," Patty replied. "First, I have to escort this dumb idiot back to his car."

"Roger that," Carl said again, this time smiling.

Riley and Patty walked quickly back to where Riley had entered the crime scene. Neither of them said a word until they reached the area where the yellow tape divided the park.

"That's a tough little girl," he said, shaking his head. His ribs still smarted.

"Yeah. It sure seems that way."

Riley watched as Patty coughed a vanishing cloud of breath into her clenched right first. He stuffed the notebook back into his pocket. "I'd ask you to get a drink," he said. "But it looks like you're going to be here for a while."

"Sure looks that way, though I could use a drink."

Riley glanced at his watch. It was only nine fifteen. "I'll tell you what. I'll leave a light on and my door unlocked. There'll be an apple martini in the freezer. Wake me up when you get there. You know the code…"

Patty looked at Riley. *How could such a goof be so confident?* He had no self-awareness whatsoever. In fact, she could see he was completely oblivious to the fact that although he was talking, she wasn't really listening to a single word he was saying. He just…talked.

But his goofiness controlled her, and for some obscure reason, despite her education and what she had always thought to be an elevated level of good judgment and common sense, his huge blue eyes mesmerized her. It was as if he owned her, and when he spoke, he held a trance over her, and despite her best efforts, she simply could not resist him. Ever.

The worst part was she knew he had played her…made her look like a fool, in front of everyone, and she had let it happen. She could feel the perspiration forming above her lip again, but she dared not wipe it, not in front of him, not right now.

"Riley," she said, raising a hand to interrupt him. "Can you just shut up for a second?"

Riley flinched and then stopped talking. Patty perceived his surprise and grasped at the advantage. Taking a deep breath, she said, "I'm not just going to stop by your place tonight so that I can wake you up and have a drink. You're going to have to work a lot harder than that to patch things up, after what you put me through. And it's not like you even live close." She noticed an unexpected look of surprise in his eyes, and this small victory thrilled her. "I'll tell *you* what," she continued, trying not to gloat at, for once, having the upper hand. "Call me tomorrow. Not too early though. Around noonish." She sighed. "This is going to be a late night. Call me around noonish, and maybe we can get a bite. Then, *maybe* I'll listen. But tonight? You can forget about tonight, okay?"

"Okay. Whatever. Noonish. I got it."

Riley slipped underneath the yellow tape. It was clear to Patty he wasn't pleased, and that was just fine with her.

"Hey Patty," he said as he reached his car.

"Yeah?"

He made a few quick circles in front of his nose with his right index finger.

Patty wiped at her lip and shook her head as Riley climbed into his white Honda Accord. It was a cheap shot, and she knew he knew it too. She nodded once as the small white car slipped into the slow traffic, but she did not see him wave back. She'd won, and she knew he knew that too. She'd let him patch things up tomorrow.

Taking a deep breath, she turned and made her way back toward the group. She wanted to get a statement from the victim before heading back to the office to start the endless paperwork that no doubt would be awaiting her upon her arrival at the station.

As she hurried toward the center of the park, a tickle sparked to life at the base of her spine just above her waistband and then slowly slithered its way up her back. Finding herself alone, she suddenly felt vulnerable, and conscientiously fought an overwhelming desire to run. Jerking at the collar of her dark blue sport coat, she blew warm air into her right fist and hurried toward the men in the middle of the park. Someone was watching her. She could feel it.

Patty fought the urge to trot. Her heart thundering in her ears, she reached down with her left hand and touched the heavy bulge of her pistol with the tip of her left thumb. The strong feeling of the polyester-covered steel that hung at her side a tad below and slightly behind her left breast provided modest comfort as she quickly crossed the dark park.

Just prior to reaching the group of officers, Patty detected movement near a tree toward the back corner of the park, near the doughnut shop. Although the shop was closed, light reflected from its giant front window and illuminated the otherwise dark area directly in front of the store.

"Hey Carl," Patty said in a hoarse whisper. She could feel herself shivering. Beads of perspiration covered her upper lip.

"Yes Detective," the large police officer said without looking at her.

"Don't ask why. And don't move just yet." She paused and took deep breath. "You know that saying about the suspect always returning to the scene of the crime?"

"Yes," Carl said, still looking at his notepad but wanting desperately to look up.

"Well," Patty whispered. "I think there is someone off at the corner of the park, by the doughnut shop…over my left shoulder, standing behind that big tree. It just doesn't feel right. You know what I mean?"

Carl slowly rotated his head to the right so he could look past Patty's left shoulder and off into the distance. He scanned the area, squinting, attempting to focus his eyes despite the darkness.

"I don't see anyth…wait. Yeah. I see someone. He's not doing anything. Looks like he's just standing there. Could be a bum. They like this park. Could be waiting for us to leave so he can get back to his stuff. Can't be too careful though," he said.

Reaching with his left hand, Carl grasped a tiny black box that was clipped to his right shoulder and spoke into a miniature walkie-talkie. "Unit six; King here. We have an unidentified person in the northeast corner of the park, under a tree. He could be our perp or maybe a witness. Either way, we'll need to talk to him. Be prepared to cut off the alley behind the doughnut shop, in case he runs."

"Unit six copies," a voice scratched from within the radio.

Carl reached down with his right hand and undid the latch that held his flashlight.

Patty's heart pounded. She tried desperately to catch her fleeting breath. Although technically she was in charge of the crime scene, she had no idea what to do. She wiped the sweat from her lip.

Carl could sense Patty was nervous. "Easy, Detective. Let the cavalry do our job."

"Right," she whispered quickly. "What are you gonna do?"

"Six is in position," she heard from Carl's radio.

"Okay Detective," Carl said. "Listen to me. When I say *move*, you run toward the alley behind the Laundromat. I don't think he'll go that way since it's pretty far. But just in case, I need you there. He's probably just a bum, but just in case. Ready?"

"Wait. What do I do when I get there?" Patty heard herself ask. She wasn't ready. Not for this. Everything was moving way too fast.

Carl looked up at her. She could see he was annoyed. "Just stand there. He won't go that way. I need you there, and I need you to be in control," he said. "Are you ready?"

No, Patty thought. She wanted to run away. She wanted to quit. Riley was right. She wanted to be anywhere but in this dark, damp park, but she was trapped, and there was nothing she could do.

"Yeah," she whispered between deep breaths. "I...I think I'm ready." She wiped at her lip again.

Carl reached out and touched her arm. "You can do this," he said.

"Thanks," Patty whispered. She took a deep breath, held it, and then exhaled slowly. Smiling uneasily, she nodded and then said, "I'm ready. I can do this."

"Okay," Carl smiled. He removed the flashlight from its holder and pointed it in the direction of the doughnut shop. With his right hand holding the light, he squeezed the talk button of the walkie-talkie with his left thumb and forefinger. "Move," he said into the tiny black box while simultaneously flipping the light's switch, the bright beam hitting its target.

Things happened too abruptly for Patty. There was no *ready, set, go*. No *take your mark*. Just "move." That was it.

Patty looked over her left shoulder and saw a man standing, staring at the group of police officers. He held a white handkerchief up to his left eye, and Patty immediately understood the gravity of what she saw.

"Go Detective! Go!" Carl yelled as he charged at the startled man.

Out of the corner of Patty's eye, she saw Carl dart toward the figure. She in turn dashed, as instructed, toward the dark alley behind the Laundromat. Sprinting as fast as she could and pumping her arms like she used to while competing on the track team in junior college, she could feel her flats beating against her heels as she fought to keep them from flying off as she ran.

She glanced over her shoulder at the scene that was unfolding to her left while running at full speed toward the alley to her right. Like viewing a choppy black and white movie, she saw Carl fall a millisecond before hearing a deafening boom.

Patty stopped running. Her surroundings slowed. She could not believe her eyes. With insufficient time to make any kind of sense of what was happening, she saw the suspect first look over his right shoulder at the alley behind the doughnut shop and then take off running to his left, directly at her!

"Freeze," she heard a frightened female's voice scream, realizing it was her own. Her heart was pounding, its volume overriding all other sound.

Her training must have taken over because she found herself mindlessly fumbling at the holster that clung to her sweaty left side. The choppy movie kept playing. Soundless. Endless. The man was running at her and pointing in her direction. He kept flashing a light at her. All reason ceased to be. There was no further sound. Like looking through a soda straw, everything except that which was directly in front of her was a blur.

As if in slow motion, out of the bottom of her field of view, she saw a small silver semi-automatic pistol rise up in front of her. Still perceiving no sound but feeling the pressure of blood pulsing in her ears, she saw the front of the pistol kick up with a flash, and then she saw the suspect drop to the ground. She stared at the dark lump as it lay on the asphalt six feet from her trembling shoes.

Her hearing returned first, slowly. Nausea overwhelmed her, and she gagged, but nothing came up. Her feet were cold. She gagged again, and this made her eyes instantly blur. She could clearly discern the beating of her heart in her ears as its rhythmic palpitations suddenly turned into the sound of shoes striking the asphalt. Something was off-kilter though. The sound of shoes striking the ground was too loud and too close. She blinked her eyes and managed to focus on a pair of darkly dressed figures as they ran toward her. She could not understand why they were running sideways. She heard herself cough, and then she raised her shaking palm to her forehead. *Blood.*

Someone was bleeding. Someone needed assistance. She wanted to scream for help, but her world was spinning and she felt like she was going to vomit. She began to sob instead as fiery pain engulfed her left shoulder. *Why are my feet so cold?*

"You were right Riley," she whispered, blinking. "I shouldn't be here." And then she blacked out.

Chapter 4

I pick at my thumbnail until it bleeds, but I don't care. Sometimes my bottom bleeds, but no one seems to care about that either. Afterwards, I can't sit down for a long time. I lay in the backseat of the car, on my side, my back toward the front, and pretend like I'm asleep.

My Uncle Kent (he's not really my uncle, but I still call him that so he won't hit me) makes me dress weird. I cried the first time, and he slapped me. But that was okay because I got a black eye, and that black eye saved me for a few weeks. My dress is scratchy, and it smells. I pop my gum and wait in the car until it's time to go inside.

Soon, we'd be making lots of money; that's what Uncle Kent says. But until I turn eleven, I have to pay my dues. After that, once I am eleven, we'll be rolling in the dough, at least that's what he says...

Orlando Price took a long drag from his menthol cigarette. He held the biting smoke in his lungs for a few seconds and then exhaled white wisps through flared nostrils. Glancing down at his grease-smudged digital watch, he saw it was 4:25. Only thirty-five minutes to go.

His cigarette smoldered between the dirty index and middle fingers of his left hand. Holding the cigarette in place, he hefted a sweating can of Diet Coke to his lips with that same left hand and took a large swig of warming soda before wiping the moisture from his mouth with the back of that same hand. He sighed before letting out a tiny burp.

"Hey Orley," a voice said from behind him. "Here comes another one."

Orley glanced over his right shoulder and saw a yellow pickup truck driving slowly toward the shop.

"All right. I'm coming," he said, finishing the last sip of Diet Coke and throwing the empty can toward the trash bin. He watched it miss its mark. Dropping the cigarette butt onto the ground, he mashed it with the toe of his brown steel-toed work boot.

"Nice shot," the voice said. "Ain't ya gonna pick it up?"

"Fuck it," Orley replied. "The Mexicans'll get it tonight. It'll give 'em something to do."

"Ain't you Mexican?"

"Blow me."

"Man, you been in a sore mood all day. Sorely Orley," the voice said. "The Mexican."

"Tiny, I said blow me, you big black jackass."

Tiny dropped his smile. He could tell Orley was serious, and despite Tiny's 7-foot, 400-pound frame, he was deathly afraid of the smaller man. He'd known Orley in prison, and he had seen him work over his fair share of guys. "Sorry man," he muttered. "I was just kidding."

"Yeah well, I'm not in the mood," Orley replied, motioning to the driver of the truck he wanted him to pull his vehicle into bay number two. "I know that bitch is up to something."

"Afternoon fellas," a voice called out from the driver's seat. "Got a few?"

"What's up?" Tiny asked.

"She's running a little hot. I think it's the thermostat."

Orley looked at his watch again. With a clenched jaw, he exhaled through his nose. He hated his damn job. "Can you bring it in tomorrow? It's getting kinda late ya know," he said, but he knew the answer before he even asked the question.

"Naw," the driver replied. "I need it first thing in the morning. Gotta go out to the Valley. Check on a transformer."

Orley snatched a red handkerchief from the back left pocket of his faded blue coveralls and then wiped the greasy sweat from his upper back and neck. Scratching his nose, he snorted the dirty, dry Los Angeles air.

"Terrific," he said. "Go take a seat inside. We'll check the damn thing out."

He glared at the driver who smiled, hopped out of the truck, and then made his way over to the waiting room near the soda machine.

"Little faggot," Orley mumbled. It didn't take a genius to understand another long day of unpaid overtime had arrived. "Fuck," he muttered as he walked toward the truck.

Orley had taken his current job at the county garage when it was offered to him as a condition of his parole. He had agreed to work five days a week for a set salary so he could move down south to be with his family. He didn't necessarily hate the work itself as he had always been a rather good auto mechanic, even before he had gone to prison. But he hated days like this one, when he was forced to work long hours of overtime without getting an extra dime for the effort.

But what could he do? The terms of his probation dictated he remain employed at the garage for a period of five years, after which, if he behaved, he could look for another line of work, should he choose to. Today though, he would choose anything to not fix the slowly dying truck of the pencil neck geek who had just dropped it off. He had to get home, and he had to get there soon.

Orley watched the truck tilt considerably to the left as Tiny squeezed his large frame into the vehicle.

"Hey," he yelled. "Go easy man. I don't want to have to change the shocks, too."

Tiny responded by thrusting a melon-sized middle finger into the air while expertly driving the pickup truck onto the lift.

A child's cough grabbed Orley's attention, and he shifted his gaze from the pickup truck to the parking lot adjacent to the garage. *Not now*, he thought, as a ball of heat suddenly formed between his legs.

He tried to focus his attention on Tiny and the truck, but a dark blue minivan in front of the *Chuck E. Cheese* pizza restaurant across the parking lot dominated his control. The sight of a slightly overweight woman stepping from the driver's door made his crotch burn. "No," he mumbled, noticing the woman was about his age. He could feel his pulse as it pounded in his groin. His saliva thickened, and the heat began to radiate down his left leg. He wiped his mouth with the back of his right hand.

"What's that?" Tiny asked from inside the bay.

"Uh…nothing. Just talking to myself."

Although he wanted to look away, his insatiable demon would not let that happen, so he continued to stare, contemplating his options. Suddenly, two blond-headed boys jumped from the van's sliding door and darted toward the restaurant. The fire in his crotch cooled, and he exhaled loudly enough for Tiny to notice.

"You sure you're all right man?"

"Yeah. I'm all right. Thought I saw someone I knew. Wasn't her, though."

"Oh, okay," Tiny replied. "You ready to lift?"

"Yeah. Go ahead."

"All right. Coming up."

Orley heard the hydraulic motor whine while the vehicle lift raised the truck into the air.

"Cover me," Tiny said after the lift had come to a stop. "I'm going in."

"Don't get stuck."

"Ha ha motherfucker," Tiny said as he disappeared into the space below the vehicle.

Exactly an hour and twelve minutes later, Orley shook the last cigarette from the foil-lined pack and brought it to his lips. He crinkled the empty package into a small ball and tossed it into the trashcan. Digging a lighter from his pocket, he flicked the flint roller twice before it actually produced a flame. He lit the cigarette and then returned the lighter to the same pocket.

"See you in the morning," Tiny said as he walked toward the bus stop at the corner of the strip mall's parking lot.

"Yeah," Orley replied. "Don't eat too much." He saw the melon once more as Tiny shot it up to his side without even looking back.

Orley glanced at the *Chuck E. Cheese*. A few more cars had pulled into the parking lot, and he saw the mini-van was still there.

A tinge of heat tickled his groin, and although he knew he should leave, immediately, he couldn't move. He knew he needed a release. But, he also knew standing in a parking lot after dark, across the street from a kid-dominated restaurant was not a grand idea. Realizing if he did not drive away soon, something bad was going to happen, he walked quickly to his car, fishing his keys from his pocket on the way, but it was too late.

Orley's eyes locked onto the heads of three young girls as the car in which they sat pulled into the parking lot. The oldest girl looked to be about fourteen. He saw her lips purse just before blowing a pink bubble from what looked to be a perfect little mouth. His throat dried. He puffed on his cigarette.

Despite the evening's cool air, a single bead of stinging sweat slid from his forehead into his right eye. Enormous pressure built in his groin as his erect penis strained against his coveralls. Somehow, he managed to make it to his car, and before he knew it, he was speeding away from the parking lot. He had no idea what happened to his cigarette.

He could barely breathe as he pulled onto the freeway and into traffic. His demon demanded a release. *Why couldn't the bitch have had a daughter,* he thought. *If only she'd had a daughter, his life would be okay, and so would everyone else's in the area.* He wiped sweat from his forehead with his left forearm and contemplated his limited options. It had to happen before he got home. The desire was inescapable. He needed a release.

He scanned his surroundings, his eyes darting, searching for a target, something, anything. It was dark, and he knew it would be difficult to find someone the right age right now, especially on a school night.

Tingling pricks of itching sweat spread across his back. He needed a plan. Getting caught was not an option. He could not afford to go back to prison. Too many enemies. Too many debts. He would be hard-pressed to survive long. *Get a grip man.*

The fear of getting caught must have overwhelmed his demon because the burning began to leave. He didn't know why, and he didn't really care. The cloth in his crotch loosened, and his heart rate began to slow. He wiped the sweat again from his brow this time with his right sleeve, inhaling deeply and then exhaling noisily. The demon was gone, for now.

"That was close," he said aloud.

Orley knew seeking to feed the demon right now would have been risky. He had no plan and no gun. He was sure he would have slipped up and left a clue. Things would have been too rushed. They would have found him this time.

Not like three weekends ago though. That had been perfectly planned and perfectly executed. His demon had been pleased.

He'd seen the ad on Craigslist. *Girls' clothes for sale: ages 2 to 9*, and that had meant only one thing, a young girl for the taking. After staking out the house for a few days, Orley learned no man was present, even on the weekend, and as he had suspected, the girl was the perfect age.

So he waited until dusk, when things were the most chaotic in a normal world. He made the call indicating he was interested in the clothes and was given the green light to "come on over and see if there is anything you like." So he did.

Orley found it amazing how trusting people were, especially when a potential profit existed. The woman opened the front door, and he immediately jabbed her with the cattle prod. She went down quickly, and he hit her again, just to be sure. After that, it was quick. Ski mask on, grab the girl, and go. Drop her at a park a few hours later. No evidence. No ill feelings.

But tonight, he wasn't prepared. Tonight would have been a mistake. Of that he was sure.

Orley finally pulled into the parking lot of his apartment complex. It was well after seven o'clock, nearly an hour and a half later than normal. *Where's her car*, he thought, noticing his wife's space was empty. He had a hunch something was up. She usually had Joel bathed and in bed by 7:30. Hopefully it mean she'd run to the store. He needed more cigarettes. He only had one pack left. But something in the air told him he was not going to be happy.

Orley killed the ignition and then stepped out of the car. He could see the lights of Disneyland off in the distance, and he could hear the noise of the traffic from the freeway that paralleled the apartment complex.

Closing the car door, he followed the grease stains along the faded yellow walkway, up the steps and to his apartment.

Yeah. Something's not right, he thought as he unlocked and then opened the door. The apartment was silent and dark. She was definitely no here. Neither was their son.

Orley flipped on the light as he walked through the doorway, dropping his keys onto a chipped wooden end table to the right of the door. The atmosphere in the apartment felt wrong. Although fully furnished, the space felt empty, cold. He walked straight into the tiny kitchen and opened the refrigerator. No dinner. *Something's definitely not right.*

Snatching a can of Busch beer from a half-empty twelve-pack, he popped it open and took a long drink. A wet and foamy burp followed. He turned away from the refrigerator and kicked the door closed with his heel. *Maybe she went to pick up some Chinese food or a pizza*, he thought. *She better have picked up another carton of cigarettes too.*

Orley let out a smaller burp before walking into the bathroom to take a leak. He continued to drink the beer as he urinated, not caring his urine was splashing onto the seat. That last job had made him pretty greasy, and he needed to take a shower. Hopefully, the bitch would be back by the time he was finished. He was starving.

Reaching between the plastic curtain and the wall, he twisted the silver handle until he heard the water begin to splash against the floor of the tub. After removing his clothes and leaving them in a pile in the middle of the bathroom floor, he grabbed the beer can off of the toilet tank, pushed the peach curtain aside, and stepped into the shower.

Orley took a long final chug and then threw the empty beer can toward the matching peach wastebasket that sat next to the toilet. The sound of the rushing water overrode the clatter of the can as it clinked along the orange and white linoleum floor. *She'll pick it up*, he thought.

He felt much better after cleaning his greasy hair and body. *Maybe the bitch will get some tonight*, he chuckled. If not, he would consider other options. After turning the water off, he stepped out of the shower and grabbed one of two peach-colored towels that hung symmetrically from a rack on the back of the tiny bathroom's door.

Ten minutes after stepping into the shower, Orley walked back into the small family room wearing light-green hospital scrubs and a yellow t-shirt, expecting to either see his wife or hear the television. Instead, he walked back into the same quiet semi-darkness from which he had left. It was then he spotted the note on the kitchen table.

Chapter 5

Icy cold stars freckled the cloudless black sky, and except for the barely audible, evenly spaced breaths of her small son who stood next to her, Amy Price could hear nothing. Fear had eaten at her for most of the terribly long day, but now, a crushing exhaustion was producing a blanket of ambivalence that seemed to be making everything seem okay.

"There's so many of 'em Mom," Joel said, pointing a tiny gloved index finger toward the dark sky.

"I know," Amy said, trying her best to sound chipper. "You're really gonna love it here. When I was your age, Aunt Meg and Gramma and I used to come up to this cabin all the time. I tried to count the stars once. I think the highest I got was three hundred and twenty-seven before I got confused." She smiled at her seven-year-old son. "Come on. Let's get inside before we freeze to death."

"'kay," Joel said still gazing up at the night's sky. As he stepped forward, his toe caught the edge of the sagging wooden porch causing him to stumble slightly. She could tell he was exhausted too.

Amy inserted and then twisted the key while simultaneously nudging at the wooden door with her left hip. It finally opened, its bottom scraping noisily along the cabin's wooden floor.

"Oh shoot," she said after stepping into the darkness and flipping the light switch next to the door. "I'll be right back. I have to turn the power on. Stay here."

She slipped back outside and darted around the corner to the rear of the cabin. Using the beam from a tiny flashlight that dangled from her key chain, she spotted the metal door of the small breaker panel that sat at eye level on the cabin's back wall. Using a smaller key from that same key chain, she unlocked the latch and then opened the small door. It was freezing, and she was pretty sure there would be no spiders in the box, but she swept the light across its confines anyway, just to be sure. All was clear.

She pushed the red lever marked *MAIN* down to the *ON* position. Instantly, a rectangular square of yellow light appeared on the dirt next to her as light from inside the cabin shined through a curtainless window to the left of the breaker panel. Amy closed and locked the door and then swiftly returned to the front porch. Her heart jumped into her throat.

"Joel," she yelled.

"What's wrong, Mommy?" he asked from within the cabin.

"Uh...nothing, hon. I'm okay." She swallowed and then shook her head. *Damn it*, she thought. *I can't leave him alone, ever, not even for a second.* She scolded herself while scanning the dark area that surrounded the cabin. She knew they were alone, but it didn't matter. She was going to have to adjust the way she conducted her business, and leaving Joel alone for even the briefest moment was not an option. She swore to herself to never do that again.

Upon entering the cabin, she pulled the heavy wooden door tightly behind her. After that, she secured both the lock on the door's handle as well as the deadbolt that sat above the handle, and she even considered sliding a chair in front of the door, just to be sure, but she dismissed the idea. *There's no way he'll find this place*, she thought. *Not in a million years*. She almost believed herself.

Amy closed her heavy eyes as she exhaled loudly. It had been quite a few years since she'd visited the cabin, nearly ten to be exact, but the smell of the dusty wood and dry air was all too familiar. Although the cabin was now completely silent, in her mind she could hear wood popping in the fireplace and pots clanging in the tiny kitchen. Each piece of furniture was original. The large brown corduroy couch. The dark brown coffee table. The tilting Lazy-boy. All of it was exactly as it had been when she was little.

She glanced around the small room. *Oops. Still no TV*. That was going to be a sore subject with Joel, but they would have to make do with the radio for now.

A tiny spark of naïve excitement crept into her, and she almost felt free again, and it was a good feeling, if only fleeting.

She yawned and stretched. Her body ached. She was beyond exhausted. In the morning she knew the all too real battle against real fear would dominate as a gnawing sense of doom would once again take full force, but right now, all she craved was sleep, and she knew Joel needed it too.

"There's a bed in the room right over there," she said to Joel, pointing to one of the cabin's two interior doors. "Why don't you take your suitcase in there and unload your things into the dresser. I'm gonna start a fire. Okay?"

"'kay."

She watched her precious son roll his multi-colored suitcase toward the bedroom, and then she saw him disappear into the dark room just before it threw its own rectangle of light onto the dusty wooden floor.

Amy plopped onto the sofa and sighed. Had it only been a day? She glanced at her wristwatch. It was nearly three in the morning. She'd been up for almost twenty-one hours. It felt like an eternity.

Amy was positive Orley had known something was up. She hoped it was just paranoia, but she could tell he knew she was keeping a secret. It had taken every ounce of will to keep from falling apart while waiting the eternal hour that it took for him to eat, dress, and then finally leave for work, especially since it seemed he was in an exceptionally foul mood.

Luckily he hadn't asked her anything. She wasn't sure what she would have said. She had been so nervous she barely remembered kissing him on the cheek and saying bye. After that though, the details were crystal clear.

She crept into Joel's bedroom and peeked through his curtains so she could watch Orley's car back out of its spot and then leave. Once the car was gone, she acted quickly. She packed their things, stuffed them into her own car, grabbed her son, wrote the note, and then left.

She and Joel had driven for hours, and during those long drives, she had explained as best she could to Joel why they had to leave his daddy. It had been more difficult than she expected, but she knew, in her fractured heart, leaving had been the right thing to do for the both of them. Maybe someday he would understand.

Amy took solace from Joel's reaction he was not exactly disappointed, and that helped. Intellectually, Joel's indifference made complete sense. He had only met his daddy twice before Orley moved in with them. Orley *had* taken him fishing and camping in his motorhome a few times since his release, a thought which now made her blood chill with horror, but there was not, as far as she could see, a strong or even mediocre father/son bond forming between the two of them. And, although she tried to encourage this relationship, in the end, thankfully, she failed. But in so doing, in her mind, she also failed her son, and that crushed her. She had vowed to bring him up in a two-parent household, unlike the home in which she was raised, but now that was not possible.

After escaping from their apartment, she and Joel had driven seven hours north, from Anaheim to Monterey, to pick up the cabin's key from her mom. She and Joel stayed at her mom's house only long enough for Amy to tell her mother she had left Orley and she wished she could stay there with her but she knew he would first drive to her mom's house to look for the two of them. She told her mother she had withdrawn forty thousand dollars from the couple's savings account and could live off of that for a while, until she figured things out. Before she left, she warned her mother under no circumstances, should she *ever* tell Orley where she and Joel were located.

"In fact Mom," Amy remembers saying, "if he does come here, tell him you haven't seen me since Christmas, and I called and told you I was going to Colorado or something like that. He doesn't know about the cabin, and he'll never find it."

Her mother hated Orley. She hated him with a passion. So it was no surprise she had ecstatically agreed to keep their secret. Amy had never seen her mother so happy. Her mother offered Amy additional money, but she turned it down.

"Keep it," Amy said. "Maybe in a year or so, when things blow over, we can move home with you."

And so, after that quick hour of hugs and tears and assurances everything was going to be okay, Amy and Joel climbed back into their car and drove back down south to the cabin.

The cabin itself was completely hidden, unless someone knew exactly where to look. It sat on the backside of a rolling hill about a half mile off of a two-lane highway called San Francisquito Canyon Road near the small town of Green Valley which was located in the hills north of Los Angeles, just south of Palmdale and Lancaster. The tiny structure could not be seen from the road as it was hidden by a combination of rolling terrain and a mix of tall pine trees and small shrubs. It rested at the end of a narrow winding dirt trail that ran from a parking lot behind a small convenience store. From that lot, the trail looked just like one of many firebreaks that traversed the dry hills, so unless someone knew there was a cabin at its end, that person could look twice at the winding trail of dirt and think nothing of it.

Amy took a deep breath. She had loved the cabin growing up, and she was glad her mother had kept it. This would be a new home for her and Joel, at least while she thought things through. This had been where her mom had taken her and her sister when they were even younger than Joel, right after her dad had been killed in a helicopter crash off the coast of Japan. It had been the perfect place for her mom to mourn, think, and then get on with her life, and Amy was determined to make it work for her as well.

But her fear pervaded. There was something about the look Orley had given her that morning, a look that said, "I know what you are going to do, and you know I will find you." She dismissed the thought as irrational, but try as she could, she had this sinking feeling he *would* somehow track her down, and that feeling was unbearable. In fact, during the entire fifteen-hour ordeal, she had found herself continually looking in her rearview mirror, expecting to see his face, his icy gray eyes, his tattooed forearms, his goatee, his flattop, his devious smile. She was deathly afraid of his temper.

She forced herself to calm down as her heart, once again, began to pound against her chest. She could feel tears well in her eyes, tears she could have sworn she had run out of earlier in the night. Panic surged as reality congealed in her throat and remained lodged like a lump of dough. Her racing heart overwhelmed the deafening quiet of the isolated cabin.

"Relax," she whispered. She had made it this far, and although she was scared, she sensed the cabin's location would provide a safe place for her and her son.

Swallowing, she took a deep breath, ran a twitchy right hand through her hair, and then hefted herself from the sofa. She needed to get her mind off the subject.

She wiped at her nose with the back of her right hand and then tiptoed the few steps to the tiny bedroom before peeking around the corner and seeing her son's freckled face as he lay, sound asleep, on top of the bed silently breathing through his open mouth, his left hand still clutching the handle of his suitcase.

Amy smiled weakly. Seeing him lying there so innocent and sweet confirmed to her she had done the right thing. She walked to the bed and slid his tiny boots from his even tinier feet, setting them on the floor next to the headboard's post. She could feel the damp warmth his feet emitted as she removed each boot.

Next, she pulled his hand away from the suitcase and then unzipped his jacket before quickly slipping it off of his still sleeping body. Amy pulled his black fleece hat from his small head revealing a twisted matt of dark brown hair and then moved him slightly toward the center of the double bed. She spotted a gray wool blanket on top of the room's only dresser, grabbed it, and then spread it over him. He looked so sweet. She bent forward and kissed him lightly on the cheek. This caused him to sigh and roll over onto his right side, away from her.

"I love you, honey," she whispered into his ear and then stood up, stretching. She was very tired. Although she had gotten out of bed at her usual six in the morning, she had not really slept the previous night. *The fire can wait until tomorrow*, she decided.

Stripping to just her sweatshirt and panties, she silently slid onto the cool bed next to her son and snuggled him close to her body. After that, she reached over and turned off the bedroom's light, leaving the light on in the main room.

The entire cabin was silent and cold. The tiny bedroom was freezing, and the skin on her legs quickly sprouted a rash of goose bumps. Slowly though, she could feel the tiny bumps disappear as the air beneath the thick scratchy blanket rapidly warmed. Her body released a final shiver as the heat from Joel's small body made the temperature beneath the blanket just right.

Tomorrow, Amy thought. *It will all begin in the morning. Everything would be all right. I will make this work. We will be okay.* But, even as she repeated these positive thoughts, she was even more positive something terrible was going to happen

Chapter 6

"I'm starving," Dr. Sue announced as she emerged from the women's restroom. "Who wants to get a hot dog?" She exaggerated a frown when she saw only six small hands rise into the air.

Bending at the waist and resting her hands on her knees, she stooped her five-foot frame forward and said, "Wait, wait. Did I say *hot dog*. Nobody wants a hot dog at Disneyland." She paused with giant eyes for dramatic effect. "What I meant to say was, 'Who wants cotton candy and ice cream?'" She watched all fifteen hands thrust high into the air. "That's what I thought," she said. "Follow me."

Straightening, she rubbed the front of her thighs with her hands before walking toward a refreshment stand in Tomorrowland. The group followed. "Anything they want," she said to one of the teenage girls that was helping to control her group of young children.

"What about you?" she heard a familiar voice say from behind her.

"I could really use a hot dog with the works and a large diet soda," she said to Howard, who suddenly appeared next to her. Her own stomach was growling as well.

"Jeez, let's see," Howard replied, counting on his pudgy fingers. "That would make it a grand total of three hot dogs, with the works, in a grand total of six hours. At that rate, even you, *Ms. Stomach*, should gain about twenty-nine pounds by the end of the day." He feigned a frown and thinned his lips. "That's not a very good example to set for these young minds of mush."

"Hey," she replied. "I'm just working on my winter layer. Can't you see I need it?" She swept her hand at the clear, warm, late-winter Southern California air.

"Well, in that case, I'll take two," Howard said. "I'll flip you for 'em."

Dr. Sue smiled. "Two out of three," she said. "No cheating. Loser flies *and* buys."

"You're on," Howard replied, digging a quarter from the pocket of his khaki Dockers.

Five minutes later, Dr. Sue watched as Howard returned with a box holding three hot dogs, with the works, and two large wax-covered cups. "How much did this set you back?" she asked, grabbing one of the cups of diet soda. She took a sip.

"Well with what you pay me, about two weeks' salary."

Dr. Sue chuckled. "Get me a memo," she said. "We'll talk about a raise. I can't have my producer starving on me so close to retirement."

"Seriously," Howard said. "Today's been a huge success. You must've raised a half million bucks." He nodded toward the group of red-shirted kids who were smiling and gorging themselves on what seemed to Howard as every kind of sweet in existence.

"It's the least I can do to help them," Dr. Sue said. "Heck. After today, it looks like I'll need most of that money to pay for dental bills."

Howard chuckled. "I still don't see how you can only weigh a hundred pounds, the way you put food away." He motioned toward the crinkled-up hot dog wrapper.

"Strong metabolism," she replied with a mouthful of hot dog. She swallowed and then took a sip of soda through a clear straw. "And, it's only about ninety pounds, thank you very much."

"Oh. Sorry. My bad. Only ninety pounds."

Howard and Dr. Sue sat silently as they munched on their meals. After a few minutes, Dr. Sue noticed that one of the red-shirted helpers was motioning the group was ready to go. She nodded back.

"I think it's time to ride the tea cups," Howard said. "We *weak* metabolizers need a way to keep our weight down too."

"Maybe in a little bit," Dr. Sue replied. "I promised them we'd go on the Peter Pan ride next. Then we can go on the spin and puke if you'd like."

Howard bowed slightly giving an exaggerated air of mock respect. "You're the boss," he said. "Whatever thy highness commands."

"You said it, not me," Dr. Sue replied before straightening up and walking toward the group.

"That's $4.25," the pimply-faced teenage boy said from behind the refreshment counter.

"Four and a quarter, for a cup of Diet Coke?" Orley said digging into the right front pocket of his jeans. "Not to mention the ninety-two bucks it cost to get in this place. Happiest place on earth, my ass." He threw four singles and a quarter onto the counter before turning away and scanning the area.

From beneath black sunglasses, he watched the small group of red-shirted youngsters as they followed the tiny waif of a matching red-shirted woman away from another refreshment stand and toward a group of rides.

Although he had recognized Dr. Sue immediately, he had pictured her as being much taller, probably because that's how he'd seen her on a few of the area's billboards. But, as he had suspected, she was not larger than life. Instead, she was a tiny creature, an easy target.

He sipped at his drink while he eyed the group, the cool liquid keeping the anger-inspired acid in his stomach. Orley was still pissed, but now at least he had a plan. All he needed to do was to bide his time and wait for the right opportunity.

He was not too concerned about the man who appeared to be tagging along with her as it was clear he was incapable of performing the duties of a bodyguard. The guy was plump and slow, pasty and bald. Orley seriously doubted the man could stop anything from happening. He was weak. He would be easy to deal with when the time came as long as there was nobody else.

Chance brought him to Disneyland after he had heard a commercial on the radio mentioned a fund raiser at the park. That was right before he had gone into a fit of rage and smashed his small radio against the workbench in his garage, just before devising his current plan.

He continued to scan the area. No one else stood out as security. It seemed to be just her, the fat guy, and a bunch of teenaged helpers. *Piece of cake.*

Orley took another sip from his drink. One thing he did notice was he'd had none of his *cravings* since before arriving home and finding the bitch's note two nights ago. Never, in his wildest dreams, had he imagined he could actually be in a place like Disneyland without going absolutely out of his mind. Little girls everywhere. His demon should be roaring, but it wasn't. So, for now, he socked the location away, for future use. Because eventually, he knew he would be required to feed the beast.

As he stood in the middle of the park and eyed the many young girls, he wondered where the demon had gone. Right now, he felt absolutely nothing except pure hatred. He guessed he could only satisfy one craving at a time, and currently anger was controlling everything. His plan was all that mattered.

Orley shadowed the group, creeping along at a distance, watching the tiny crimson wave of kids follow the little monster through the park, and waiting for his chance to approach her. He needed to control his anger long enough to complete his mission and then leave without causing a disruption. He could not afford to alert the park's security. The conditions of his probation dictated he remain well clear of any place such as this. Going back to the joint for being at Disneyland was not an option.

He finished his soda and then let out a four dollar and twenty-five cent burp. "Sorry," he muttered to a hunched over Japanese woman who was inching her way forward in a line next to him. He returned her offended stare with another small burp and then smiled as she shuffled past him.

Orley watched the fat guy walk away from the group so he decided to make his move. Taking a deep breath, he approached the tiny woman, and straining to keep his anger under control, said, "Excuse me. Dr. Sue?"

"Yes," she said, turning toward and looking up at her inquisitor. "Can I help you?"

Orley was immediately taken aback. Dr. Sue looked much older in person than she did on the billboard signs. The depth of her wrinkles, the sharpness of her crow's feet, and the hollowness of her cheeks actually surprised him. Her skin appeared impossibly thin. In fact, she looked frail and almost…*human*. He stood there silently staring, temporarily frozen from acting by a force he could neither identify nor control. Only after hearing the bitterness in her voice was he shaken from his trance.

"I said *hello. Can I help you?*"

Orley reached into his right rear pocket and withdrew a folded piece of notebook paper. He forced himself to smile even though he really wanted to snap her sarcastic head from her tiny shoulders. He took a deep breath instead.

Dr. Sue, seeing the piece of paper emerge from the back pocket of his faded jeans, said, "I'm sorry, sir. I don't give autographs."

She turned her back to him to face the group of kids, but before she could say anything to them, he grabbed her thin arm and spun her back around with a violent jerk, his anger invigorated by the startled look of fear in her pale blue eyes.

"I don't want an autograph lady," he said still holding her arm. "I just want you to sign this." He held the folded piece of paper directly in front of her surprised face.

Dr. Sue attempted to yank her arm free, but he squeezed it even tighter. "What's that?" she asked through deep breaths. "You're hurting my arm."

Orley released his grip, satisfied he had her attention and not wanting to cause a stir. He noticed some of the kids were starting to look scared.

"Sorry," he said. He saw her slowly rub her upper arm. "I don't want any trouble."

"Well, that's not the way to *not* look for trouble," she said, taking a few small steps away from him. "What do you want?"

"What do I want? Well, my wife left me, after she called you, and I want you to sign this note saying you made a mistake, and you should not have told her to leave me."

Orley saw Dr. Sue's forehead wrinkle.

"Wh...what?"

"Just sign this note. That's all I want. I don't want any trouble." He shook the paper in front of her face.

"Is there a problem here?" Orley heard from behind him.

"Howard," Dr. Sue said, letting out a deep breath. "Call Brett. I'm scared."

Orley forced the note into Dr. Sue's hand. "Just sign the fucking note, lady," he said. "I don't want any trouble."

"I'm not signing anything. I've never told anyone to *leave* anyone unless they deserved it." She looked up at the taller man. Feeling empowered by the sudden presence of another grown-up, she said, "And from my limited dealings with you, I'm sure I gave sound advice." She dropped the note to the ground. "Now, if you don't get out of here, I'll call security, and they can help you find the exit."

Orley, filled with an intense rage, took a step forward.

"Hey," Howard yelled, putting his right hand on Orley's left shoulder.

Orley spun to his left, knocking Howard's hand away. "Don't fucking touch me man," he said, sliding his sunglasses back up into place with his left hand.

"Sorry," Howard whispered, visibly shaken by Orley's sudden move.

Orley turned back to face Dr. Sue, but she was gone. He bent over and picked up the note. Jamming it back into the right rear pocket of his jeans, he turned around and walked away from the red-shirted group, knocking Howard's shoulder with his own as he went by.

Orley was so enraged he could hardly see. His instinct demanded he pursue Dr. Sue, but he knew the best thing to do was to leave.

Taking deep breaths, he forced himself to calm down. After a while, he would devise another way to get what he needed. But not right now. Right now, he needed to get the hell out of Dodge. He knew he'd caused quite a stir, and he really couldn't afford any trouble. As he reached the end of Disney's Main Street, he started to calm, but then, out of the corner of his eye, he noticed a pair of men walking toward him. As he hurried toward the gate, he judged the distance between the exit and the men and quickly determined he would make it out before they could reach him.

"Excuse me sir?" he heard one of the men say as he slipped out of the park through a one-way turnstile. He ignored the man and sped up his pace. "Sir?" he heard the voice say again a little louder. "Sir!" Orley continued to hurry away from the park, not looking back until he reached the parking lot. When he managed to take a peek, he saw one of the men talking into a small walkie-talkie and the other scribbling something onto a small notebook. After a few minutes, he saw them both disappear into the park.

He found his car and climbed inside.

"Fuck," he said, slamming the steering wheel with the palm of his right hand. "What now?"

"Is he gone?" Dr. Sue said from inside the ladies' room.

"Yeah. Coast is clear," Howard said. "I called security. They're going to make sure he leaves. I also called Brett. He'll meet you at the gate when you're ready to leave, just to make sure that guy doesn't give you any grief in the parking lot or something like that."

Dr. Sue emerged from the ladies' room.

"You okay?" Howard asked.

"Fine."

"He had some evil eyes, huh?"

"Yeah. And those tattoos."

"Any idea who he was?" Howard asked.

"No," Dr. Sue said. She reached up and rubbed her left arm. It really hurt. She could tell there would be a bruise in the morning. "I mean, you know. Twenty-five calls a day. I can't remember them all. I don't know. Maybe I should have signed his damn piece of paper."

"I think you handled him fine. He obviously has problems. You know you can't sign any random thing. Who knows what some nut might do with your signature? Next thing you know, it's on the internet and all that."

The two walked back toward the group. Dr. Sue noticed a couple of her teenaged helpers were comforting a few of the children who looked like they had been crying. And, she could tell her helpers were also scared. She was disappointed, but who could blame them? She was pretty shaken too.

"This is supposed to be a fun day," she said to Howard. "I can't let that jerk ruin this fun day." She paused and then said, "Wait. I've got an idea."

"Anything to help," Howard replied while following her.

"Okay gang. Listen up," she said. She saw the kids look up at her. "How about a trip to the arcade? I have one hundred dollars' worth of tokens. That should keep you guys busy for a long time."

She was rewarded with a sea of blinking eyes and smiling faces, and this made Dr. Sue smile back.

"It's amazing how resilient they are," she said under her breath to Howard as the group began to move again.

"Definitely impressive," he replied.

Dr. Sue followed them to the arcade. Although her heart was still fluttering a bit, and she was sure she was visibly shaking, she was determined to make today a special one for her kids. She was prepared to do anything to pull that off, but she had a horrible feeling things were only going to get worse.

Chapter 7

Dr. Sue was exhausted. Although the day had been a monumental moneymaker for the charity, she was thankful it was over and she was finally able to leave the park. She had forgotten how tiring it was to shepherd a child around an amusement park, let alone a whole flock. It had been more than ten years since her son was the same age as those five and six year olds. Her feet hurt, and her legs ached. She desperately needed an aspirin and a hot bath.

"You okay?" Brett Nelson, Dr. Sue's driver and bodyguard, asked. "That guy never came back. Did he?"

"Ugh. Yeah. I'm okay. He was just some weirdo."

Brett sighed. "Well, I'll keep an eye out for him. You said he's got brown hair, a flattop, and a goatee right?"

"Yeah," Dr. Sue said yawning. "And tattoos. A lot of tattoos. All over his forearms." She shook her head and shivered.

"You sure you're okay? I told you I should have gone in there with you guys. I don't do you any good in the car."

"I know. I know. I'm still trying to get used to this whole armored car, bodyguard thing," she said, flipping her right hand in front of her face as if swatting a fly.

"Hey. You gotta do what you gotta do," Brett said. "Especially when you do, you know, what *you* do."

Dr. Sue shook her head. "No. I refuse to accept that. This day was not about me. It was about the kids. I didn't want them wondering why I needed a bodyguard while I was at the happiest place on earth. You know what I mean."

"Yeah well."

"Yeah well nothing. I'm okay. Everything's okay. Let's just drop it."

"Fine. Sorry. Consider it dropped."

Dr. Sue patted Brett on his steely right thigh. "No, I'm sorry. I'm okay. I'm just tired. I'm going to close my eyes and take a snooze. I know I'm safe with you here."

"All right," Brett said. "Traffic's pretty light. We should be to your house in about an hour or so."

"Okay. Wake me up before we get there. Like before we go up the hill. I love to see the city lights, and it looks pretty clear tonight."

"You got it."

"Thanks."

"Not a problem."

Dr. Sue leaned her head against the passenger door of her yellow Hummer H2. She stared at Brett for a few seconds before closing her eyes.

Brett had been her bodyguard for the last four months. He seemed so much older than his young thirty-two years. She had hired him two weeks after he left the Navy SEALs. His qualifications were impeccable, and she felt totally safe around him.

At first she had not been too thrilled about the prospect of hiring a bodyguard. But she had come to realize, in general, people did not really want to be told how they should live. And although the advice she gave was totally solicited and rarely of her own volition, she had received her share of threats from both individuals and special interest groups. Her stance on homosexuality had caused an enormous stir, and her views on stay-at-home moms made her target number one on the feminist movement's hit list.

Not only did she now live under a microscope with all of her enemies hoping, praying she would somehow slip up so they could label her a hypocrite, but ever since her show had made it into syndication, she, her husband, and her son had actually received threats of physical violence.

They had tried to simply ignore the threats at first, but an altercation in front of her home involving her husband and a lesbian had proved to be the catalyst that made her family pack up their belongings and move to the *fortress* in which they now lived on top of a hill overlooking the San Fernando Valley. They moved to their isolated home and hired Brett in the same week. Ever since then, life had been pretty good, save the few threats a week via social media and e-mail. But they had learned to cope, and things were going all right.

Dr. Sue could feel the Hummer gently rolling along the freeway as she drifted in and out of sleep. She dreamed about her husband and her son who were at her son's chess camp in San Jose. Though the two were supposed to return late next Sunday evening, she wished they could have been at Disneyland with her today.

She was beginning to take notice of how much she was missing time with her family now that her work had become more demanding, and her ability to devote time to her son had become a little less abundant. She wondered if she was, in fact, being a little hypocritical in some of the advice she was giving since she could see her work was starting to interfere with her family. The only counter-argument she could make against that line of reasoning was she was doing something good for society. She clung to that explanation hoping someday she would believe it.

"Dr. Sue...Dr. Sue," she could feel a slight nudging on her left arm. "Dr. Sue. We're going up the hill."

Dr. Sue awoke with a start, blinking the dark, headlight-illuminated scene into focus. She yawned and then shook her head. "Thanks. That was pretty quick. It feels like I just fell asleep."

"You were snoring."

"I don't snore," she said, smiling at Brett and batting her eyes like a sorority girl.

"Oh yeah," Brett said. "You're right. I must've been the one snoring, and you must've been the one wishing I would shut the hell up."

Dr. Sue punched Brett in his rock solid triceps.

"Oh yeah," he said. "I think there's a fly in here, too. I just felt one land on my arm I think."

Dr. Sue chuckled. "I'm glad I hired you," she said.

Turning her head to the right, she rested her right ear against the headrest while staring out of the passenger door's window. She focused on the lights of the valley as her gently ascending vehicle slowly made its way up the steep hill to her home.

"What a beautiful night," she whispered.

Orley followed the yellow Hummer until it transitioned from the main highway to a secondary road. Unlit, this narrow street had only two lanes, and it appeared to lead into an area of isolated and exclusive homes. Until this point, he had been able to blend in with the rest of the cars as they sped along the crowded highway, but when Dr. Sue's vehicle exited the freeway, it was just his car and the Hummer. Despite his obviousness, he chose to follow the Hummer until it suddenly slowed to make a left turn onto a dark road. Unable to surreptitiously tail the car after it made that turn, Orley continued driving straight ahead. He was sure Dr. Sue's driver would notice his car if he also made the turn, and he was quite certain his Chevrolet would draw unwanted attention around here.

He had to assume Dr. Sue's house, probably more accurately *her mansion*, sat somewhere on the street onto which he had seen her Hummer turn. He just hoped he could determine which one was hers when the time came.

After continuing for about a minute, he slowed and then swung his car back around so it faced the opposite direction and then slowly and quietly returned to her street. When he was about a hundred feet shy of the corner, he stopped the car on the dirt shoulder and looked at his watch. Twelve-thirty.

Killing the car's engine, Orley pondered the situation. He was fairly confident her driver doubled as her bodyguard. The kid looked pretty big and pretty hard. In a fight, one on one, he would probably give Orley a run for his money, though Orley had never been one to fight fairly. His cunning and his level headedness allowed him to survive in prison. He was pretty sure he could take down the big man when the time came. He just had to figure out how.

Taking a moment to check his surroundings, Orley noticed a severe bend in the highway that curved sharply to the left just prior to reaching the road onto which Dr. Sue's Hummer turned. He had seen the Hummer's brake lights illuminate for some time before the truck could actually negotiate the turn onto the street, and this revelation allowed the seedling of an idea to pop into his head. Rubbing at his goatee, he squinted at the road and massaged the thought.

After sitting in the dark and contemplating his options, Orley read his watch again. More than ten minutes had passed, and no other cars had appeared. Finding that odd, he wondered if anyone else lived out here. The area was silent and dark. He decided to check it out on foot, to see if it was secluded enough.

Quietly, he reached up and slid the interior light's small switch all of the way to the left so the light would not illuminate when he opened the door. He knew in such intense darkness, light could be spotted from long distances, and he did not want to draw any attention to his car. Hopefully, no one else would drive by, especially the highway patrol. If a cop did happen to appear, Orley was sure the officer would see the car and assume it had broken down, or it had been stolen and left after a joyride. Either way, it would be a few more hours before anyone returned to take any action. He probably had a few minutes to investigate. It was worth the risk.

Stepping from the car, he quietly closed the door and then darted around to the shoulder. It was cold, and Orley shivered despite his black leather jacket. He jammed his hands into his coat pockets, and turned his collar up against the dry, biting air. Taking a deep breath, he hurried toward the dark road. He could hear his teeth chattering.

Trotting, Orley covered the distance rather quickly, his feet crunching against dirt and rocks of the road's shoulder with each step. His heart was beating rapidly, and he could hear himself breathing against the otherwise total silence of the area. When he reached the intersection, he scurried around the corner, away from the main road.

Blackness continued to dominate. He moved slowly up the street and noticed the incline began to steepen rather quickly. In fact, it inclined so much he could reach forward and without bending too much, almost touch the asphalt with the tip of his middle finger.

He continued to hike up the steep hill until the scene opened up to his right revealing the lights of the San Fernando Valley. The view was impressive. As he continued along the constantly bending road, he noticed a yellow sign about a hundred feet ahead. It wasn't until he was five feet away that he could actually make out the black letters: *PRIVATE DRIVE. TRESPASSERS WILL BE PROSECUTED.*

Winded, Orley rested against the sign's wooden post. He needed to get into shape. He had seen no other houses so he wondered if hers was the only one on this street. After pausing for a minute to catch his breath, he became aware of the openness of his surroundings and despite the darkness, suddenly felt vulnerable. He hurried back down the hill toward his awaiting car, thankful the descent was much easier than the climb as gravity aided greatly.

In no time, he found himself at the intersection of the private road and the highway. Glancing left and right, he saw no evidence of anyone else so he trotted back to his car. His antenna was free of orange tags which meant no police officers were waiting to haul him away.

Adrenaline pumped in his veins, and butterflies tickled his stomach. He yanked the door open, slid in, and then slammed it closed. His seedling of an idea rapidly germinated into a full fledge plan.

Taking a deep breath, he started the ignition and smiled as he continued to develop his idea. *Perfect*, he thought. He slid the transmission into drive and pulled out onto the highway. As the road curved to the right, Orley started to grin. His idea was perfect indeed. All he needed now was to pick the perfect day.

Tuesday, he decided. Tuesday, he would retrieve his wife and son.

Chapter 8

"Hello Mickey," Amy Price said, smiling at a short middle-aged man who looked even shorter standing behind a chest high wooden counter. She placed her items: instant hot chocolate, oatmeal, toilet paper, and a gallon jug of nonfat milk, onto the worn-out counter. "You don't remember me. Do you?"

Mickey Michael, the proud owner of Mickey's Mart, stared at the pretty young lady who was addressing him.

"Well," he said rather shyly, "you do look somewhat familiar to me. Let's see…"

After a few seconds, Amy decided to let him off the hook. "It's me, Amy Nicholes, well, Amy Price now." She detected a twinkle of recognition in his pink eyes.

"Why yes, Amy. How the hell are you?" He quickly covered his grinning mouth in embarrassment when he saw the little boy move next to her. "Sorry," he said quietly.

Amy chuckled. "Don't worry. He's heard a lot worse than that. Believe me."

"Well, Amy…Price is it? I haven't seen you in, let's see, about…"

"Thirteen years," she interrupted. "I haven't been up here since I was fourteen."

"Well. You still look the same. Cute as ever. And who's this?" he asked as he handed a piece of red licorice over the counter.

"Tell him honey," Amy said, looking down at her son who had reached out and quickly snatched the candy.

"Joel," he mumbled, before jabbing the thin piece of licorice into his eager mouth.

"He's my son," Amy said. "He's a little quiet. He said his name was Joel."

"Hi there Joel," Mickey said. He looked up at Amy. "I've been seeing smoke up the road for the last couple of days. Thought maybe your mom came up again. She was up here last month. First time I saw her in a few years too."

"Yeah. She let me have the place for a while, until I can get my feet back underneath me."

Mickey watched Amy throw a lump of thick, dark hair over her head. He thought he saw a tear drop onto her left cheek as the hair split into tiny wisps that slowly descended back into place on either side of her small face.

"Everything okay?" he asked, seeing things were not.

"Yeah," she replied after taking a deep breath. She smiled a tight-lipped smile at Mickey and then nodded at Joel. "I left his daddy a couple of days ago."

"I'm sorry."

Amy sniffed wet air through her nose. "Not me. He was a bad man," she said, wiping her left eye with the back of her right hand. She took a deep breath and nodded twice. "Things'll be better now."

Mickey heard her exhale through her mouth. "Well, if there's anything I can do, anything at all, just let me know."

"Okay," Amy said, smiling weakly. She coughed an embarrassed laugh and then sniffed loudly again. "I'm sorry."

"Don't be," he said. The compressor inside the beverage cooler kicked on. Other than its buzz, an awkward silence dominated the small space. Looking down at the counter, Mickey interrupted the uneasy quiet by clearing his throat and saying, "Let's see. We're running a special on, well, everything you bought here. We'll call the damage…uh…five and a quarter." He looked up and smiled.

Amy recognized that familiar concentrating-eyeballs look as his small watery eyes stared at her from between a familiar set of horn-rimmed glasses and a dominating hair-arch near the bottom of his wrinkled forehead. As if whisked back in time, she realized Mickey had not changed a bit and his presence provided her with a feeling of security. She smiled and handed him six dollars.

The small wooden cash register dinged loudly in front of him as its wooden drawer popped open. Barely turning his head, he looked down, dug three quarters from the drawer with his left index finger, and then slammed the drawer closed with his right palm. Amy estimated the entire exchange took less than six seconds.

"There's seventy-five," he said, handing her three shiny coins.

"Thanks," Amy said turning around and walking toward the door. Joel followed her.

"Good-bye Joel," Mickey said as the two reached the door. "I'll see you later."

"Bye," Joel mumbled.

Amy paused before pulling the door open and looked over her shoulder. "There's one thing," she said.

"What's that sweetie?"

She turned to face him. "If anyone comes looking for me, tell them, well, *him*, you haven't seen me in a long time. Not since I was a little girl."

"Okay. Should I be expecting him to come here looking for you?"

"I hope not. He shouldn't know about this place, but you never know. Orley…he's my husband…he…well let's just say he has a very bad temper. I don't know what he's going to do. I just left him."

"Don't worry about me," Mickey said, smiling in a reassuring grandfatherly way. "The Chinese couldn't get this old Marine in Korea. No bad-tempered jerk is going to get me here either. Your secret is safe with me."

"Thanks Mickey," she said. "I knew this was the right thing to do." She slid outside, and pulled the door closed behind her.

Jason Frank had finally arrived. He had hit it big, really big. His boring life as an assistant manager at his neighborhood Dollar Store had instantly changed exactly six weeks and five days prior when his seven numbers hit, and he won half of the California Lotto.

"Just sign here, Mr. Frank," the man in the nice-looking gray suit said, offering a pen from behind the marble-topped desk.

Jason took the pen. "Right here?" he asked.

"Yes sir. Right there, and then that'll be it."

Jason scratched his name on the line and then handed the pen back to the smiling man.

"Congratulations, Mr. Frank. You are now the proud owner of a new Jaguar XJR."

Jason smiled and accepted the salesman's outstretched hand.

"You wanna go get the car?"

"You bet," Jason said, rising in unison with the salesman. "Where is it?" he asked, looking around.

"Should be right out front. Can I get you an espresso or some tea?"

"No thanks. I just want the car." Jason smiled shyly at the salesman. "You know."

"Certainly sir," the salesman said. "I understand completely. Let's go get it."

Jason followed the short salesman through the showroom, expecting to awake at any moment from this dream. The two men walked out of a glass door and onto the dealership's front lot, and there, sitting under bright white lights, shining in fluorescent glory, was his brand new, midnight-blue dream car.

"Go ahead. The doors are unlocked. It's really yours."

Jason turned and grabbed the salesman's hand, pumping it a few more times. "Thanks again Ron. Thank you."

"No. Thank you Mr. Frank."

Smiling, Jason let go of Ron's hand and walked eagerly toward his new car. He slowly opened the door and slid inside.

"Oh yeah baby," he said softly, inhaling the new car smell. He reached down with his right hand to turn the key. Only there were no keys. *Oh, that's right*, he thought, before pushing the ignition button. He'd have to get used to that too. The engine started right up, and for the life of him, he couldn't stop smiling. He still couldn't believe this car was his.

He had purposely chosen the Jaguar and not a Mercedes or a Beamer. They were too trendy. A Jaguar said *class*, and he needed to exude that classiness now that he was a rich and distinguished man.

He fastened his seatbelt, tuned the radio to the classical music station, put the car into drive, and then slowly, cautiously, drove it off of the lot and toward his new palace overlooking the Valley. He could not wait to show Raymond and the boys his new ride. They were going to love it, and he was going to be the hit of the town.

Chapter 9

Patty Marx squeezed her already closed eyes when she heard the unmistakable voice that was talking, rather loudly, in the hallway.

"There she is," Riley said, walking into the hospital room. "Come on. I know you're awake."

Patty cracked open her left eye, hoping to see the voice was just a drug-induced nightmare. No luck. Just Riley's goofy smirk partially hidden by a huge bouquet of balloons.

"Damn it," Patty said. "I told them not to let you in here."

"Come on now. You can't keep the press out," Riley said, looking around the tiny room. "Where can I put these?"

Patty stared at Riley for a few seconds. "You don't really want me to make a suggestion. Do you?"

"Nice one," Riley said, walking across the small room. He set the basket of balloons on a chair that sat beneath the room's only window.

"Now, all you need to do is sit down, and you'll have read my mind," Patty said.

"Well, it's good to see you smiling at least. You didn't look too good on Friday."

"You weren't worried about me. Were you?" Patty asked mockingly.

"Of course I was."

Patty blushed slightly and smiled. "That's sweet."

"I didn't want to have to invent the rest of my story," Riley said, reaching into the inner pocket of his camel's-hair coat and withdrawing a small notebook and pen.

"Asshole," Patty said. She turned her face away from him and secretly wiped the sweat from her lip.

"What? Come on. I was just kidding."

Riley saw Patty slowly turn her face back toward him. "I was really worried about you, especially the night of the shooting. I didn't think I was going to have you around to bust on anymore."

"I should be so lucky."

"Seriously," Riley said. "The doctors gave you about even money on whether you were going to make it through the night. You lost a lot of blood, and they were really concerned about infection. I mean they were seriously worried. Not me, though. I knew you'd pull through. You're a fighter, whether you believe it or not."

"Yeah? Thanks," Patty said, smiling. She could feel her face getting hot.

"There's way too much piss and vinegar inside that hard body of yours to let a little infection take you down. Way too much."

Patty giggled. "Asshole," she said again. "How come I can't seem to shake a little gnat like you then, huh?"

"Well that's obvious," Riley said.

"Oh yeah. How?"

He smiled. "Because I smell good. I have great hair, and let's face it, you just plain old like me. Admit it. You're attracted to me."

Patty closed her eyes and shook her head. "Yeah well, you're lucky I can't get out of bed today, or I'd show you how attracted my fist is to your chin."

"Grrrr," Riley said. "You are so sexy when you act tough. So, how long until you can leave?"

"Well, today's Sunday. Hopefully, I'll be able to go home on Tuesday."

"When do you have to be back at work?"

"The department is giving me a month of convalescent leave. My shoulder doesn't really hurt that much. Maybe it's just the drugs. Doctor said it went right through the meaty part on the outside. No bone damage or anything like that. Just the blood loss. I told the Captain I could be back at work sooner than a month, but he said it's pretty standard to take that much time off when you are shot in the line of duty. I don't know."

"I think it's going to take them that much time to get your commendation ready," Riley said. He saw Patty blush again.

"I don't think I deserve any kind of recognition. Heck, I was lucky. Besides, I was just doing my job. No different than anyone else."

"Be that as it may, you spotted the guy and then finally took him out. If it weren't for you, they'd still be looking for that idiot. And a kidnapper slash rapist would still be on the loose. A little congratulations is in order."

"Thanks Riley. That must've killed you to say that."

"Yeah well. I mean don't let it get to your head or anything. The community says thanks. Me? I'm still waiting for an apology..."

Oops.

Riley saw the beads of sweat.

Here it comes, he thought, cringing. He had once again stepped over the line, and he knew there was no going back to the other side. He racked his brain for something clever to say, but nothing came to mind. He squinted instead.

"*Me* owe *you* and apology...You are an *asshole*! How can you actually think I need to say *sorry* to you for *anything*? And why can't you say anything *nice* to me without being a smartass?"

"Look Patty. I said I was sorry. I've said it a thousand times. I'm sorry for what I did. I'm sorry. I'm sorry. I'm sorry. Okay, I crossed the line. And I do think you're a hero. I thank you. Everyone thanks you. You did great. You're the greatest detective in the LAPD, hands down."

"Now you're patronizing me."

Riley shrugged his shoulders. "I don't know what else to say. I can't talk to you. It's obvious you're in one of your moods."

Patty squinted back at him and clenched her jaw. "You are such a jerk Riley. I'm, I'm speechless…no wait. I'm not speechless…forget it. You don't want to hear what I really want to say. Just go away. Take those damn balloons and stick them up your ass. Straight up your ass Riley. Good-bye."

Fighting the urge to wipe at her lip, Patty instead closed her eyes and folded her hands on top of the tan blanket that covered her stomach. The pain in her shoulder throbbed rapidly.

"Come on Patty. I'm sorry. I was just kidding."

Patty remained silent.

"I really do think you're a hero, okay. I really do."

"Go away Riley."

"You're serious," Riley said, still standing in front of the bed. He was amazed at how she could be so hot and then so cold in such a short period of time.

"You're not going to talk to me?"

"No."

"Really?"

Silence.

"Patty? Hello?"

More silence.

"Fine," he said shaking his head. "I'll go. Sleep well. I'll tell the department to pick you up on Tuesday. You can ride home alone."

"Thank you," Patty said, eyes still closed, hands still folded on her stomach, shoulder still throbbing at a ridiculously rapid pace.

"You're welcome," Riley snapped as he turned and walked the few steps to the doorway. He paused at the threshold and then turned back to face her. "You know. Once you learn to lighten up, you'll realize the world isn't out to get you and there are people out there that really do like you as a person. Pretty soon, though, those people will be gone, and then all you'll have is your job and your badge, and those can get pretty cold over time." Riley paused a moment before leaving.

Patty squinted through her left eye as Riley exit the room and then disappeared. She waited a couple more seconds before fully opening both eyes, and through her tear-blurred nearsighted vision, she noticed the big silver balloon in the middle of the bouquet read, in giant red letters, *I LOVE YOU!*

Chapter 10

Uncle Kent (he's not really my uncle) teaches me what to do. It's gross. He slaps me because I'm getting older.
"Don't start men-stating yet." That's what he's always saying when he slaps me. I don't know what that exactly means, and I don't ask him because he gets mad, and it hurts when he slaps me.
I need to learn and to shut up. The big payoff is getting close; at least, that's what he says...

Orley slid the shower curtain aside and grabbed a towel from the rack that hung above the toilet. The small bathroom was a cloud of steam, and although he stood in front of the mirror, he could not yet see his reflection. Having just bleached his hair, he leaned his nude belly against the slippery white sink and stared at the foggy mirror wondering if he would be able to recognize himself. He contemplated the last two days while waiting for the mirror to clear.

After following Dr. Sue home and then checking the area near her house, he had come up with a pretty good idea. The long drive home provided him ample time to create a rough timeline and then to refine the plan. By the time he pulled into his parking spot, he had a clear idea of what he was going to do.

Exhausted, he slept like a rock until ten in the morning. After that, he dragged himself out of bed, threw on some sweats, and then headed to the RV storage facility where he kept his 36-foot motorhome. Once there, he spent most of the day modifying the inside of the large rig.

The following morning, on Monday, he awoke bright and early, well before sunrise. After leaving a message on his boss's answering machine that he would not be in because his whole family was sick, he drove his motorhome in the predawn darkness to a Wal-Mart parking lot in the San Fernando Valley. From there, he took a series of buses back to his apartment in Anaheim, exhaustedly making it home before 7 AM, which was his goal.

Although he was dead tired, he packed a cooler with a couple of peanut butter and jelly sandwiches and the last four Diet Cokes from his refrigerator, bought a carton of cigarettes and a bag of chips from a liquor store near his home, and then made the infuriatingly long drive back to the Valley and to the secluded road that led to Dr. Sue's mansion.

The abrupt bend in the road just prior to her intersection made it easy for him to recognize the turn onto her street. To say the least, the area was isolated and sparse, especially in the daylight. He drove past her street, just as he had done on Saturday night. Only this time, he didn't turn around and then head back. Instead, he continued until he reached a small dirt path that intersected the highway.

Seeing the trail led to a firebreak, Orley quickly glanced around to verify no one was there before making a right turn onto it. After driving for about twenty seconds, he reached another intersection of trails, which enabled him to turn right again and onto a path that paralleled the highway back toward Dr. Sue's street. This new trail was perfect. It was tucked into a shallow gulley that sat behind a scattering of small shrubs and low trees, and it allowed Orley's car to remain hidden from anyone on the road, not that anyone, it seemed, ever really drove out here. He parked in a spot where he had a clear view of her intersection.

Satisfied with his concealed location and confident he could not be seen from the road, Orley rolled the windows down, killed the ignition, and then checked his watch. It was just shy of a quarter to nine. He hoped he was not too late.

I should be fine, he thought, reaching into his cooler and snatching a dripping Diet Coke from the slushy ice. He remembers taking a long swig which felt good against his dry throat.

Since her show did not start until noon, Orley guessed Dr. Sue would probably wait until after the morning rush hour before leaving for work. He knew traffic could be horrendous between seven thirty and nine thirty. In fact, just that morning, he made sure he left early enough so as to miss the daily jam. If he hadn't, his one and a half hour drive would have most certainly turned into a two hour and forty-five minute nightmare, and he never would have made the rendezvous.

Betting she would wait until traffic died down before making her way into the city, Orley sat in his silent car, sipped at his soda, and waited to see if he was right. His estimate was dead on.

He saw the nose of the yellow Hummer poke out from the intersection, delay for a few seconds, and then make a right turn to head down the highway away from him and toward the freeway that led to the city. He remembers looking at his watch and reading it was nine thirty-three. He had been correct to the minute.

Orley figured Dr. Sue was pretty demanding and her schedule was unceasingly structured. He guessed they would, every day, leave her house at precisely nine-thirty and it would take three minutes to get off of her property and down the hill. It was just a hunch, but once again, he was willing to bet his plan on his hunch.

After the Hummer left, Orley remembers having waited an extra ten minutes and noting not one single car passed that stretch of isolated highway. In fact, he hadn't seen another car all morning. Satisfied, he started the ignition and put the car into reverse. He slowly backed down the dusty road until he hit the intersection that led to the main highway.

He remembers bouncing back onto the asphalt and making a left turn onto the same road on which the yellow Hummer had just driven, the road that led to the city.

As he passed Dr. Sue's street, he glanced to his right and saw the ascending lane. As expected, nobody else was there. He slowly navigated the highway's winding road as it curved gently to the right and then sharply to the left, confirming it was in fact a blind curve.

Perfect, he'd thought as he accelerated through the turns. On his way home, he made one more stop, at a drug store in the Valley, to pick up the remaining elements of his plan.

Now, as he stood in front of his mirror, towel wrapped around his waist, he could begin to make out an image as the steam slowly dissipated, and just as he suspected, he could not recognize the man that stared back at him. Although the eyes were the same, he found himself looking at a slightly younger, clean-shaven man with really short, bleached-blond hair, and he couldn't help but think he looked pretty damned good.

Nodding at himself in approval, he brushed his teeth, flossed, and then unwound the towel from his waist. He tossed it onto the curtain rod where it dangled helplessly for a few seconds before falling into the tub. *Fuck it*, he thought as he walked into the bedroom to get dressed. *The bitch will pick it up when I bring her back.*

Hanging in his closet, wrapped in plastic, was his best suit, the same gray suit in which he was sentenced to and eventually released from prison. Dressing in a pair of blue jeans and a dark gray sweatshirt, he slipped on his running shoes and then grabbed the suit, a pair of black loafers, and a heavy duffle bag from the closet. He slipped on his wristwatch and looked at the time. Seven PM. *Ahead of schedule.*

Edward Michael followed the slow-moving line of people as they made their way from the airplane, up the jetway, and to the gate. He emerged from the tunnel and noticed a sign to his right that directed him to the baggage claim area. Following the signs through Los Angeles International Airport, he eventually found himself at the bottom of an escalator and in front of a large silver machine that was spitting suitcases from its elevated opening. He watched the large machine as it launched bag after bag down a long slide that led to a rotating belt. He nudged his way toward the trough of bags so he could shamelessly wait for his own suitcase to emerge.

He matched the flight number on his boarding pass with the numbers on the screen. Satisfied he was in the right place, he shoved the stub into the back pocket of his khaki pants and then rubbed the back of his neck with the same right hand.

"Hello Edward," a man's voice said from behind him.

"It's Eddie, Uncle Mickey," Edward said as he turned to meet his greeter.

"Well, your mom wants me to call you Edward while you're here. She thinks Eddie makes you sound like a kid."

Edward shook his head. "Mom," he said looking down at his brown shoes. "Why the hell does she care?"

"Hey. Whatever. Edward. Eddie. It doesn't matter to me. Just give me a hug, huh?" Mickey bear-hugged his nephew, lifting the taller boy off of the ground. "Hell, it's been more than a few years since I've seen ya. It'll be good having some company around." He set Edward back onto the ground.

Edward regarded his uncle. *Poor little guy*, he thought. It was true. Edward had not seen his uncle since his aunt died almost six years ago. That was when Edward was fourteen. To Edward, his uncle appeared much older now, compared to six years ago.

"Well, I guess it'll be okay," Edward said, trying his best to sound serious. "Not really how I wanted to spend my spring break though. But Mom said I needed to come out and see you. Thinks you can straighten me out or something."

Mickey chuckled. "Yeah. It's either me or the Marine Corps. I know your mom doesn't want you going to the Corps. I don't know why. Worked for me. Either way, you're here. It'll be fun. I promise." Mickey giggled. "You're gonna love Green Valley."

Edward rolled his eyes and then turned his attention toward the turnstile, immediately spotting his maroon suitcase. He watched it ride along the conveyer belt before finally reaching out and grabbing it with two hands. Setting the suitcase onto its two wheels, Edward looked at his uncle and sighed. "This is it. Let's go see beautiful Green Valley."

"Well all right. Truck's in the lot just outside."

Riley opened his front door and was immediately greeted by the familiar beeping that told him his alarm system was armed. Yanking the keys from the green door, he kicked it closed with the heel of his left foot, hurried across the small foyer to the alarm pad, and then typed in his code. The beeping stopped. After dropping his keys onto a small dry-sink that sat directly beneath the alarm pad, he slid into the kitchen and grabbed the last can of Diet Coke from the refrigerator. He popped the top and then took a huge cold slug, exhaling and burping loudly.

"What a day," he said softly before turning and looking at his answering machine. He noticed the little red light was blinking. A closer look showed he had four new messages as indicated by the small red number 4 in the dark window adjacent to the tiny blinking light. He hit the play button.

It's me. Sorry I was such a bitch today. You're right. Thanks for the balloons. I can't say I love you yet. There's still a lot we need to work through. If you get this, and you still want to pick me up tomorrow, call me back. If not, I understand. I don't know. I guess I hope you call. Bye. Beeeeeep.

The remaining three messages were just dial tones, but he could see by the caller ID they were from the same number as the one that left the message.

He took another gulp of Diet Coke and then looked at the clock. It was nearly ten thirty. *A little late to be calling the hospital*, he thought. Finishing his drink in one final gulp, he dropped the empty can into the white wastebasket next to the white stove and let out one final burp.

"I'll just surprise her tomorrow," he said, walking out of the kitchen, flicking the light off as he exited. He verified the door was locked before turning off the lights in the foyer and heading upstairs for bed.

"Yeah. She'll love that."

Chapter 11

Sometimes they're rough. It hurts most of the time, but I'm not allowed to cry. One time, one of the dads sat on the bed and read to me. He bought me pancakes and hot chocolate. He said he would save me.

Then he told me to take a shower. He watched me wash my hair while he did it to himself. When I left, he was sitting on the back of the bed and crying. The pancakes were really good though...

Orley stepped from his car in the dim parking lot of a Days Inn. It was dark, and thankfully the lot was empty of any other people. He reached down behind the driver's seat and pulled on the latch that allowed him to fold the seat forward, exposing the rear bench. Reaching into the darkened car, he removed a black duffle bag and set it gently onto the blacktop next to the car. Taking a deep breath, he forced himself to relax. "Just a walk in the park," he said softly before unclipping the plastic-covered suit from the hook adjacent to and slightly behind the driver's door.

He held the suit in his right hand and threw the seat back to its upright position with his left. Then he locked the door before slamming it shut. Instinctively, he surveyed his surroundings but saw nobody else. Still holding the suit in his right hand, he reached down with his left and carefully picked up the duffle bag, its contents clinking against each other in the still air.

Orley wiped the sweat from his forehead with his right shoulder, grateful for the chill. He forced himself to relax by unclenching his jaw and taking two deep breaths. The bag jingled again as Orley threw its carrying strap across his shoulder before stepping off toward the Wal-Mart that was located adjacent the motel.

Over the sound of his heart thudding in his ears, he could hear that traffic was pretty heavy on the highway in front of the motel, so he took a circuitous route that led him away from the motel and into the back of the Wal-Mart parking lot. He needed to be seen by as few people as possible.

Reaching the expansive parking area, Orley noticed three other motorhomes had joined his own near the back corner of the lot. He expected company as RVers often slept in their rigs in Wal-Mart parking lots while traveling. He knew there was a risk in parking his motorhome where he knew others would be, but he figured an isolated coach would draw more attention than just another motorhome amongst a cluster of three or four. Fortunately, he did not see any people outside of any of the motorhomes so he pulled the brim of his Detroit Tigers baseball hat down to shadow his features and hurried toward his rig.

Orley could feel his heart rate increase as he quickly slipped the key into the deadbolt and then unlocked the aluminum door. He ducked inside and slammed the door behind him. His heart was pounding in his chest, and he could feel the tickle of sweat as it trickled down his back. Despite his nerves, things were going great.

He checked his watch. It was a few minutes past midnight. Turning to his left, he stepped into the motorhome's small back bedroom and hung his suit in the mirror-covered closet that dominated the left wall of the tiny room. After that, he set the duffle bag onto the queen-sized bed, which sat opposite the closet, and unzipped it. He withdrew a couple of items he knew he wouldn't need that night, and laid them next to the duffle bag. Satisfied, he zipped the bag closed.

"All right, let's do it," he said softly. Leaving the zipped bag on the bed, he turned around, and once again, pulled the brim of his ball cap down to hide his features before ducking back outside. He trotted quietly away from the ad hoc campground and was relieved to hear nobody emerge from any of the other motorhomes in the group.

Down the street from the Wal-Mart was an AM/PM mini-market with attached gas station. He had scouted the area earlier in the evening and decided the location of this station would fit his plan perfectly because of its vicinity to both the Wal-Mart and also to the upper-class neighborhoods that dotted the nearby hills.

Thirsty, he was tempted to duck inside the store to buy a Diet Coke. He fought the urge, though, knowing he could not risk being seen. He had to remain calm, and he needed to be patient in order to pull off his plan.

He surveyed the cars presently fueling at the station, but none of the models were adequate for his need. He glanced down at his watch and saw he had plenty of time. In fact, he thought, the more time he took, the better.

Ding. "Low fuel," the female voice said from inside the car. Enjoying the cool grooves that had been purring from his stereo system for the past three hours, Jason Frank looked down and saw his fuel gauge was between the quarter and empty tank lines. He glanced at his clock. Two-thirty. He had seen signs indicating there were gas stations at the next exit. Hopefully, one of them would be a twenty-four hour station.

Jason's eyes were tired, but his heart was still racing in his chest. He had taken a few hits from a joint before leaving, and although the joint calmed him down slightly, the effects of the eight Red Bull and vodkas with which he began the evening's festivities were continuing to override the marijuana's dulling buzz. He could not complain, though, as the booze, the weed, and the night's sexual pleasures left him feeling tired but pleasantly awake. His new car had been a hit. He could not wait to see the reaction of his friends up north.

Although he was only a few miles from home, he thought it better to fill the tank tonight before his long drive to San Francisco in the morning. It would save time in the morning. Plus, he had a fierce case of the munchies, and he really had to take a leak. *A quick bag of Doritos should cure that problem*, he thought, as he pulled into the gas station's driveway.

Orley was getting desperately cold. His entire body shivered, and he could actually hear his teeth chattering. He glanced at his watch. *Damn.* He could not take the frigid air much longer. He decided to give it another ten minutes before he would have to duck inside for a cup of coffee and a new plan.

He blew warm damp air into his hands before stuffing them back into the pockets of his dark coat. A few more minutes, he decided. A few more minutes and then he would need to do something to warm up.

In the darkened distance he noticed a glow that eventually pierced the blackness with two pinholes of light.

"Come on baby. Come on," he said over and over, hoping it would stop, pleading it would be the right kind of car. He let out a sigh that sounded more like a moan and then stamped his feet on the ground to keep the blood flowing into his toes. Blinking the cold from his eyes, he watched from the shadows as the dark-colored vehicle pulled next to one of the station's eight gas pumps.

This might work, he thought.

He saw a tall black man step from the driver's seat of what appeared to be a brand new dark-blue Jaguar.

"That's perfect," Orley whispered as he watched the driver hook the nozzle into the gas tank. From the shadows, Orley stared at his prey. His first choice was not to confront the man as he looked pretty gruff, but he would do what he had to in order to stay on his schedule. "Come on. Go inside," he whispered.

Jason hooked the hose's nozzle onto the car's gas tank receptacle, and then he set the lever on the handle so it would provide a steady flow of gasoline into the thirsty tank. Satisfied the nozzle was secure, he walked out of the chilly night and into the warm mini-mart.

Orley could not believe his luck. Someone or something was definitely looking after him tonight. He counted quickly to one hundred to ensure the big man was not going to immediately return to his car. Satisfied, he scanned his surroundings and then quickly approached the vehicle.

Heart pounding in both his chest and his ears, he carefully tried the door. He was greeted with a pop as the door cracked open. Careful not to open the door too far so as to prevent the illumination of the car's interior light, he glared through the window but saw no keys.

"Damn it," he hissed before noticing the ignition button to the right of the steering wheel and a set of keys sitting in one of the cup holders between the two front seats.

"Wait a second," he said quietly as he quickly yanked the nozzle from the tank and jammed it back into the pump. He screwed the gas cap back into the car and then slammed the tiny hatch closed. In a matter of seconds, he smoothly and deliberately, opened the door, slid onto the driver's seat, pushed the ignition button, and was greeted by the starting of the car. He eased the vehicle into reverse, and keeping the lights off so as to not attract attention from the inside of the store, he slowly backed away from the pump. Satisfied with the distance traveled, he put the car into drive, and lights still out, drove out of the parking lot, onto a service road, and then eventually, onto the main highway.

Applying slow but steady pressure on the acceleration pedal, he allowed the car to speed up without squealing the tires. He did not bother turning the lights on until he could no longer hear his heart beating in his ears. After a few eternal minutes, he checked his rearview mirror to verify he was not being followed before turning off of the main highway and onto a state road that led into the hills overlooking the valley.

Jason Frank emerged from the men's room, letting the door slam behind him. He walked over to the display of potato chips and grabbed a medium-sized bag of Cool Ranch Doritos. He could smell the coffee and determined a cup o' joe was in order. He poured himself a cup of coffee, added a splash of French Vanilla creamer, grabbed the bag of chips, and then headed to the cashier's counter.

"Is that it?" the Middle Eastern man asked from behind the register.

"Yeah," Jason said yawning. "Oh. And gas…uh…number 7, I believe."

"Okay. That's thirty-two thirty-seven."

Jason pulled a fifty from his front pocket and set it on the counter. "Wait," he said. "How much?"

"Thirty-two thirty-seven, please."

Jason squinted at the small man. "What?"

"Thirty-two thirty-seven. Four dollars and seven cents per gallon. Seven gallons. Chips. Hot coffee. Yes. Thirty-two dollars and thirty-seven cents, please."

Jason was confused. How could it only be seven gallons? The gas tank was nearly empty.

Panic immediately overwhelmed the munchies. "I'll be right back," Jason said, leaving the chips and coffee on the counter. "It must've clicked off." He sprinted toward the door, knocking over a tall sunglasses display case on the way. "I'll be right back," he yelled over his shoulder as he slipped outside.

Orley parked the car on a dark street in a residential neighborhood that was situated adjacent to the state road. It had been about twelve minutes since he had stolen the car. He withdrew from the left breast pocket of his dark blue t-shirt a notepad-sized aluminum container with a long chord protruding from one of its ends. Plugging the chord into one of the car's outlets, he set the small rectangular device onto the dashboard.

He put the car into drive again and continued through the neighborhood until the street intersected with a larger road that eventually led to the 101 Freeway. He stayed on that freeway for about six miles and then took the exit that led toward Dr. Sue's house.

Orley patted the little device that sat on the dash of his new car. He hoped his little electric friend was working correctly and blocking the LoJack signal he knew was emanating from somewhere inside the car. Hopefully, the tiny device would keep the cops away. He looked at his watch. It was nearly three. All he needed was about six and a half hours.

Chapter 12

Uncle Kent says we're getting close. I don't know what he means so I smile a lot. I hope it's good. I'm tired of crying...

Orley awoke with a start. It took him a few confusing moments to remember where he was. His eyes snapped to his watch. Eight twenty. *Okay.* Through quick, vertical strokes, he rubbed the sleep from his face with his left hand and then shook his head a few times, blinking repeatedly until his bright dusty world came into focus.

Clearing his dry throat, he sat straight up and then stretched his tired torso by hunching his shoulders forward and twisting his head from side to side. The sun was shining brightly through the car's non-tinted windows, and the temperature was rapidly rising inside the vehicle. A Styrofoam cooler sat on the floor in front of the passenger seat so Orley lifted its lid and extracted a dripping bottle of lukewarm Frapuccino from a puddle of warming water that used to be a bag of ice. Twisting and removing the cap, he slugged down the entire bottle in less than five seconds. He opened the car's door and then tossed the empty container into the brush next to the car.

After a few moments, he realized the one drink wasn't going to do it for him so he retrieved the last Frapuccino from the cooler and downed it with the same ferocity, tossing the empty bottle next to the first one. Satisfied, he pulled the door closed, lit up a cigarette, and then recalled the previous evening's events.

After stealing the vehicle, he made it most of the way to this spot before realizing he needed to go back to the motorhome to get his suit and duffle bag. He had cursed himself for being so careless. In fact, he almost ditched the plan entirely for fear of being caught. The only thing that kept him going was the fact that the car was perfect, and there was absolutely no way he was going to force himself to freeze through another night in order to steal a similar one.

So, instead of calling it off, he decided to take the risk and returned to the motorhome to get his things. He moved quickly and deliberately and was able to retrieve what he needed and then make it back to his current location without a hitch. He patted the LoJack jammer that was plugged into his lighter. *Definitely worth the investment*, he thought.

While at the motorhome, he took a little extra time to prepare the rig for a rapid getaway. He had also taken the time to change into his suit, minus the coat and tie. He figured attempting to dress in or near the car in its current, dusty location might prove to be tricky, and he didn't want to get dirt on his suit as details were going to allow him to pull this off. So, he dressed in his pants, shirt, socks, and well-shined shoes and drove to this pre-staging area, where he could remain out of sight of any traffic that might happen to travel on the lonely road until he was ready to put his plan into action.

He could feel his heart rate increase when he looked at his watch. *It's time*, he thought. He was banking everything on the fact that Dr. Sue would leave her house at exactly nine thirty, and he was relying on the fact that no other car would use that isolated road.

Using the rearview mirror, he threw a half-Windsor knot onto his necktie, and then slipped on his suit jacket while remaining seated in the driver's seat of the Jaguar. He did not want to get his shoes dirty just yet.

At exactly nine twenty-five, he started the ignition and slowly inched the car from the dirt trail onto the highway. Satisfied he did not kick up too much dust, he accelerated, driving past Dr. Sue's intersection and toward the blind bend in the road. He was wide awake now, and his senses were alive.

Brett Nelson drove the short distance from the garage to Dr. Sue's circular driveway at 9:25. As always, she emerged from her giant wooden door at exactly 9:30, this time dressed in a nice, fire-engine red, short-skirted business suit. He saw her hair was pulled up and back so it sat in a disheveled, tiny, wispy bun on the top and back of her head. He could not help but admit she was a knockout, even for a woman in her mid-fifties.

As she reached the yellow Hummer, she popped open the door and heaved herself into the front passenger seat.

"Good morning Brett," she said with a red lipstick smile.

"Good morning Doctor. You're dressed up today."

"Got a meeting with the mayor this afternoon, after the show. Gonna talk about some concerns and issues. You know. The usual stuff. Keeps wanting me to run for office."

"Why doesn't he just call the show?" Brett asked while slipping the massive vehicle into drive and slowly exiting the property.

Dr. Sue giggled. "I never thought of that. I'll mention that to him."

"No names. I mean, I voted for him and all. But I don't want him to think I put him on the spot, you know. I don't need him coming after me or anything…"

Dr. Sue laughed. "Relax Brett." She patted his hard knee.

Brett fought hard to ignore the electric twinge that shot down his belly every time she touched his leg. He looked at her from the corner of his eye. If she only knew what he was thinking, she would fire him for sure. He forced himself to concentrate on something else. *It's Dr. Sue, for Christ's sake*, he thought.

He guided the Hummer down the narrow, winding lane until he reached the stop sign at the end of the descending street. Looking both ways, he saw the highway was empty, as usual, so he turned onto it.

Out of the corner of his right eye, he saw Dr. Sue slowly remove her smooth, nylon-covered right leg from atop her left one and lay it down next to its match. He could barely see the gap between her thighs. He felt himself becoming aroused and forced himself, once again, to concentrate on the road.

Taking the gentle right turn, he glanced down once again and saw Dr. Sue slowly throw her left leg over her right. But, before it found its destination, he heard her voice pierce the tense silence.

"Look out!" she yelled, as he slammed on the brakes.

Earlier, Orley determined he needed just about three minutes. He had driven to the blind bend in the road where he stopped the car so it sat facing away from Dr. Sue's street, slightly straddling the double yellow centerline, and angled toward the opposite lane. He opened the driver's door and stepped out. He could hear the faint hum of an approaching vehicle and hoped it was the right one. So far, the goddess of good luck hadn't let him down so he was feeling pretty comfortable.

Taking a deep breath, he turned so his back was to the oncoming traffic and pretended to be pushing the car toward the left side of the road. His left hand was on the open door and his right was gripping the steering wheel.

He could feel his heart pounding in his chest as the noise of the approaching vehicle was getting louder.

What if it doesn't stop, he thought. He had not considered that. For a moment he contemplated jumping into the ditch next to the road, but he fought the urge to run. Instead, he used his anger to push away his fear. He gritted his teeth, closed his eyes, and held on tightly to the Jaguar. *This…might…hurt…* Startled from his trance by the staccato chirping of tires, he slowly turned and found himself looking directly into the large and shiny grill of the yellow Hummer.

"Whoa. That was close," Dr. Sue said, blinking. Mouth agape, she exhaled loudly.

"Sorry," Brett said. His face was flush with embarrassment. He looked up and saw a well-dressed, blond-headed man who looked like he was trying to push a brand new Jaguar to the side of the road.

"What's he doing here?" Dr. Sue asked.

"I don't know," Brett replied. "I haven't seen anyone on this road, well ever, except maybe a few."

"What should we do?" Dr. Sue asked.

"Well. He looks harmless. Probably made a wrong turn or something." He looked at Dr. Sue and then asked, "Want me to see if he needs a hand?"

"You're the trained eye. You tell me."

Brett studied the situation. Nicely dressed. Nice car. Nice neighborhood. Seemed okay to him.

"I'm going to help him move his car. You stay here and lock the doors. Does your phone work here?"

"Sometimes," she said. She removed her small Motorola phone from her matching red purse and read the words *No Service* in the tiny window.

"Where's your satellite phone?" Brett asked.

"I forgot it at the office. Don't look at me like that. I had to charge it up. It was dead. I'm sorry."

"Well, he looks okay." Brett turned his attention back to the man who was staring, obviously startled, at the Hummer. "I'm gonna give him a hand."

"Brett."

"Yeah."

Dr. Sue grabbed his right forearm. "Be careful."

"Relax," he said, opening the door and stepping down onto the road. He slammed the door behind him, and Dr. Sue locked it.

"What's up?" Brett said, walking toward the man.

Orley shook his head. "I don't know. It just stopped. I'm pissed. It's brand new. Still has paper plates."

"Yeah. I see that."

"Damn it," Orley said, rubbing his stubbly hair. "Hey, can you help me push it off to the side of the road. I've got On Star. They're on the way."

"You bet," Brett said. He turned toward Dr. Sue and gave her a thumbs-up.

"That your wife?" Orley asked, nodding toward the Hummer.

"Something like that."

Orley grinned. "Right," he said.

"What do you want me to do?" Brett asked, changing the subject.

"Well, no need for you to do the heavy work. Why don't you steer, and I'll push."

"Deal," Brett said, assuming the position Orley previously owned.

Orley walked to the back of the car. "Ready," he said.

"Yup."

"Okay. One. Two. Three."

Orley pushed the car and Brett maneuvered it the short distance across the road and onto the left shoulder so it faced in the direction that was opposite traffic. Once it was on the shoulder, Brett expected the car to stop, but Orley kept pushing.

"Stop pushing," Brett called out.

"I'm not," Orley lied, still pushing the car. He saw it heading toward the brush next to the side of the road. "Must be going downhill."

Brett instinctively jumped into the driver's seat and pressed the brake pedal. The car came to a sudden stop about a foot from the ditch that paralleled the road.

Perfect, Orley thought. Without hesitating, he made his way to the driver's open door. "Thanks," he said bending down to talk to Brett who had plopped down onto the driver's seat. He noticed Brett looking at the interior of the car. "Nice, huh?" Orley said, slowly reaching into the backseat.

"Not bad," Brett agreed.

"Drives nice too," Orley said, grasping the cattle prod that was lying on the floor behind the driver's seat. He glanced over his left shoulder and could see Dr. Sue, who was still in the Hummer, had no way of seeing, from her vantage point, what was about to happen.

"Looks like it's a nice ride," Brett said. "Might have to get me one someday."

"Yeah. Me, too," Orley said, grabbing Brett by the upper arm and yanking him out of the car.

"What?" Brett managed to say before Orley jabbed him in the side with the cattle prod and released a burst of electricity.

Brett flopped to the ground, and Orley hit him again with another burst. He tossed the prod into the backseat and then turned toward the Hummer to yell for help.

Dr. Sue caught the thumbs-up from Brett and then stuck the phone back into her small, red purse. She attempted to close the latch, but before she could, the purse slipped from her hand and fell to the floor, its contents spilling out next to her feet.

"Great," she whispered. She looked up and saw Brett move to the driver's side and the blond-haired man move toward the rear of the dark blue car. *This shouldn't take long*, she thought, bending over to retrieve the items from the floor.

She picked up the purse and held it in her right hand. Then she grabbed the phone, her lipstick, and a compact mirror and fed them into the purse. Reaching under her seat, she located her mascara, a small notebook and pen, and her wallet which she stuffed into her purse as well. After straightening up and carefully snapping the opening together, she let out a sigh and looked out at the scene ahead of the Hummer.

What she saw did not register at first. The blond man was waving his arms over his head and yelling something. Panicking, she looked around for Brett and then spotted his blond hair beneath the car's door. He was lying on the side of the road, and he was not moving.

Dr. Sue immediately began to panic. She yanked open her purse and snatched her phone from the bottom, flinging out most of the recently retrieved items in the process. She stared at the tiny window on the phone. *No Service.*

Damn it, she thought. She looked up at the man once again. He appeared to be bending over Brett. She saw him look up in her direction and yell something that could not be heard through the bullet-resistant glass. She wanted to roll down the window, but she couldn't since the glass was designed to stop a round from a medium caliber weapon, not to actually be opened.

A little voice in her head was screaming at her to stay put, but she had to do something. It looked like Brett needed some help, and she was a doctor after all. She took a few deep breaths before finally opening her door. She stared at her phone once more. *No Service.* Tossing the phone onto the seat, she jumped out of the Hummer and trotted toward the scene.

***

"Come on. Come on," Orley kept saying, waving his arms at the Hummer. "Come on, you little bitch." He heard the driver stir on the ground behind him. He could not have him wake up now.

Returning to the car, and using the vehicle to block the bodyguard's body, Orley reached behind the driver's seat and grabbed the cattle prod. He had enough power left in the stick for one more hit before it was out of juice. He quickly looked back at the Hummer and determined to anyone in the car, it would look as if he was just trying to revive the man who was lying on the ground.

Orley blasted Brett one last time, and he saw the driver go limp. Once again, he tossed the cattle prod into the backseat. Then, he leaned over the bodyguard and counted to six before straightening up. Sweat was beginning to bead on his forehead. His wool suit was getting hot.

He stood up, once more, and waved his arms in the direction of the Hummer. He knew this was his last shot. The man would be awake in less than five minutes if he did not act fast.

Just when he was about to give up, Orley saw the passenger door to the Hummer pop open, and he saw Dr. Sue jump out and make her way toward him.

"He just passed out," Orley yelled as she trotted in his direction. "Just keeled over and passed out. Grabbed his chest. I'm totally freaking out."

"Does he have a pulse?" Dr. Sue asked as she took a knee next to Orley. She thought she recognized him from somewhere.

"I don't know. I'm...I'm...an agent. I represent writers. I'm not a doctor. I don't know much."

Orley watched Dr. Sue reach down and put her finger on her driver's right wrist. "You a doctor?" he asked.

"Yeah. He's got a pulse," she said, looking at Orley. She could have sworn she knew the man. She placed Brett's arm back onto the ground. "You said he just keeled over?"

"Yeah. He was lookin' at the car and bam. Just went down." Orley made a tumbling motion with his right hand. "I called On Star. They're sending someone out. I got a first-aid kit in the trunk. Hold on."

Orley reached into the driver's door and punched the trunk release. He quickly walked around to the back of the car and opened the trunk. A plastic zip-lock bag with a chloroform-soaked rag was sitting atop his duffle bag. He pulled the rag from the bag and then looked over the trunk lid at Dr. Sue who was still kneeling next to the bodyguard.

Without closing the trunk, he stepped around the car and lunged for his prey. Grabbing her around her tiny shoulders and chest with his left arm, he pulled her in tight and cupped the dripping rag over her mouth and nose. He felt her struggle against his grip, but surprise coupled with his overwhelming power enabled him to keep her still until he felt her go limp in his arms. He kept his grip tight and left the rag over her mouth while he counted an extra ten seconds just to be sure she wasn't faking.

Satisfied she had passed out, he lifted her limp body and carried her to the back of the car where he gently set her down inside the trunk. Opening the duffle bag that lay next to her head, he withdrew a set of plastic zip-ties and a roll of silver duct tape. He ripped off two long sheets of the tape and pressed them tightly on top of her closed lips. After that, he rolled her over onto her stomach, and pulling her arms behind her, inserted her wrists into the zip-ties before tightening them snuggly together. He took a deep breath and stared at his catch. *Bitch*, he thought. He slammed the lid of the trunk.

Grabbing the wet rag from the ground, he walked to the driver and covered his mouth and nose for a long count to forty-five. He wanted to make sure the man did not wake up unexpectedly in the next few minutes.

"Now for the hard part," Orley said quietly as he bent over and grabbed the man's right arm. Lifting the bodyguard up so he was in a limp, seated position, Orley put his own head into the man's armpit and then slowly used his smaller body to leverage the large man into a semi-standing position. From there, he lowered his head toward the man's waist, and with a loud grunt, picked the solid man up so his waist rested on Orley's right shoulder.

Orley staggered with the bigger man on his shoulder the long forty steps, slightly uphill, to the Hummer. When he reached the rear door on the driver's side of the vehicle, he leaned the man against it and then opened the driver's door. Thanking physiology that the adrenaline was still coursing through his veins, Orley hefted the man into the driver's seat and then let out a sigh. He bent over for a long twenty seconds to catch his breath. He thought he was going to vomit.

After the short rest, Orley stood straight up and nervously scanned his lonely surroundings. Although he suddenly felt vulnerable, he heard and saw nothing unusual, and he was grateful for the highway's isolation. His breathing nearly back to normal, he reached into the Hummer and turned over the ignition. Jamming his left arm into the high-sitting Hummer, he held down the brake with his left hand while he grasped the shifter and put the car into drive with his right hand. He let go of the brake, and the car idled forward.

Orley jumped out of the way of the large vehicle as it rolled past him, but before he was totally clear, he grabbed the steering wheel and gave it a quick shove, rotating it slightly in a clockwise direction, causing the truck to slowly turn to the right. After a few dramatic seconds, the Hummer reached the right shoulder of the road where it rolled off of the pavement and careened into a small gulley. After a muted thump, Orley could hear the engine still idling. Satisfied, he trotted back to the Jaguar, jumped into the driver's seat, started the car, and then sped off, careful not to leave any tire marks on the road.

"Okay, you bitch," he said. "You'll be giving no more bad advice. Let's go get my wife and son."

Chapter 13

Howard Thorsen first peeked into the break room before actually stepping in and looking around. *Empty.* A huge lump formed in his throat. Squeezing his eyes shut, he prayed his instincts were wrong.

"She in here?" a female voice asked from behind him.

Howard shook his head. "No," he said, slipping his thumb and forefinger under his glasses and pinching the bridge of his nose. "She's not here either."

"Well, I'm sure she's around somewhere," the voice said again. "Probably just missed her between her office and the prep room."

"I don't think so Lily," Howard said, turning around and facing the young intern. "I think something's wrong. I think something's happened to her."

Howard saw Lily glance at the clock. Looking back over his shoulder, he read the time. Eleven forty-five. Fifteen minutes until the show was supposed to start.

"Maybe she's in the ladies' room," Lily said, turning to her right. "I'll go check. Then I'll check her office again."

"Yeah. Okay. Whatever," Howard said as he watched the young girl hurry away. He knew it would do no good.

His first clue something was wrong was never in her six years of broadcasting had she been this late. Save a few minutes here or there for traffic, she usually got to work at right about the same time every day. So when he did not see her sitting behind her large desk at the quarter to elevenish that he showed up, he immediately began to worry. Not only had her office been dark, it had that stale feeling of emptiness that all offices have first thing in the morning. It was obvious no one had entered that room yet, and that meant she had not yet arrived.

"What about her cell phone?" someone yelled from down the hallway.

"I tried it," an anonymous answerer shot back. "Keep getting her voice mail. It's probably full by now."

"Well, what about her satellite phone?" the first voice called again.

Howard moved quickly into the hallway. "Yeah," he yelled hurrying in the direction of the unknown voice. "Call the satellite phone. Hurry up. We gotta go on the air in twelve minutes. Do you have the number Ron?" he asked through broken breaths.

His production assistant grinned tightly and shook his head. "I'm calling it right now." He put the receiver up to his right ear and then lowered it so it was barely touching the top of his shoulder. "It's ringing," he whispered before raising it back up to his ear

Howard raised both hands in front of his chest and displayed two sets of crossed fingers. Ron nodded back at him.

"Yes…hello," Ron snapped excitedly into the receiver.

Howard let out a sigh of relief, slumping his shoulders and closing his eyes.

"Are you okay?" Ron said quickly. "We've been worried sick about you. Where the heck are you?"

Howard was smiling and suddenly craving a cup of coffee. He glanced at the break room. *I think I saw some donuts in their too.* Things were going to be okay.

His smile vanished when he heard Ron say, "Wait…what? Who is this? Lily? What the hell you doin' on the phone?"

Eyes squinting and mouth forming the word *what*, Howard stared at Ron. "Well hang up the damn phone, and don't ever answer it again!" He watched Ron slam the phone onto the receiver.

"Dumb bitch. Dumb...bitch." Ron looked up at Howard. "She heard Dr. Sue's phone ringing in her office and decided to answer it. Can you believe it?"

It was clear to Howard people were beginning to panic, and he knew he needed to calm everyone down. He had to hold the team together especially if this grew into a crisis. "Hey man, she was just trying to help. It's not her fault," He said, reaching out and touching Ron's elbow. "Give her a break, okay?"

Ron closed his eyes before shaking his head and letting out a sigh. He opened his eyes again and stared directly at Howard. "Something's happened. This isn't good."

Howard's hand fell from Ron's elbow. "Looks that way," he said, glancing up at the clock.

"Well boss. Show starts in seven minutes. What're we going to do?"

Howard rubbed his sweaty palms together in front of him. "Pull that last *Best Of* tape we played the last time she was on vacation. Tell her listeners she had a sudden *thing* she had to take care of. Emergency. Family death. Make something up. I don't know. We'll wait another hour, and if we don't hear anything, we'll call the police."

Howard saw Ron staring at him in disbelief. He nodded his head toward the booth. "Go ahead man. Go. Make the announcement. We gotta go on in a couple of minutes. Don't want any dead time. We still have a show to run, Dr. Sue or not."

Howard watched Ron turn and slowly walk toward the broadcasting booth. He took a deep breath. *Better call the Rick*, he thought. *Man I hope she's okay.*

Brett Nelson tried to concentrate by taking deep breaths, but every time he inhaled, his twirling world accelerated. He shook his head, attempting to clear the cobwebs. After a few moments, he began to sense an odd smell, and this odor, in conjunction with his spinning surroundings, nauseated him. He gagged and then dry-heaved. Nothing made sense.

Head throbbing, and mouth drier than it had ever been, Brett felt something hard resting against his forehead, but despite his best effort, he was unable to identify the object.

Things were not right. Up appeared to be down. He could barely make out the blurred brightness of daylight between his feet, and a tremendous amount of pressure was being exerted on the very tip of his throbbing head.

The dull and constant sound of a deeply humming car engine was the only sense that seemed to register in his mind. Gritting his teeth, he forced himself to concentrate.

He closed his eyes and counted to sixty before opening them again. The tearing in his eyes produced a blurry picture, but as the tears cleared, his world slowly came into focus. His head was killing him, and he could now feel pressure on his stomach as well.

He squeezed his eyes tightly and counted to sixty once more. This time when he opened them, the world immediately came into focus. Without moving his head, he scanned the area and instantly recognized his surroundings. He could clearly see the hard object pressing against his forehead was the top of the dash, and the tremendous pressure that was squeezing the top of his head was the actual weight of his own body. He saw he was upside down in his Hummer, pressed up against the dash and resting on the ceiling. Someone was leaning against him, and that body was causing tightness in his midsection.

Fear instantly gripped him, and his heart thudded against his chest. His breathing picked up, which caused his world to spin again.

"Dr. Sue," he said. "Dr. Sue. Wake up. Get off me." Nothing. "Dr. Sue. I can't feel my legs. I can't feel my arms. Dr. Sue."

He squeezed his eyes tightly, holding them closed for ninety seconds this time. After that, he blinked away the tears and surveyed the situation once more. Things became terrifyingly clear. His face grew hot, and his bottom lip quivered at the instant realization the pressure on his abdomen was not Dr. Sue but the force of his lower body folded over on top of him.

He desperately tried to move his fingers and toes, and he wanted more than anything to feel pain somewhere else besides his head, but after what seemed like an eternity, Brett understood that feeling in his extremities would never again exist. At that moment, he knew he had broken his neck, and for the first time in over a decade, he broke down and wept.

Howard didn't have to wait the full hour. In fact, about two minutes after Ron announced Dr. Sue would not be on the air today due to a sudden family tragedy (probably not the best reason to give), his private phone line rang. He knew who it was without even looking at the number.

"Hello," he said into the receiver.

"Howard. It's Rick Stein. Is everything all right?"

Howard let his balding head fall into the pudgy palm of his free hand. He sat motionless, his left elbow supporting his weight as it rested on the edge of his desk. *How could I have been so stupid*, he thought.

"Howard. You there?"

"Yeah. I'm here."

"What's wrong? What happened? I heard on the radio Suzie had an emergency. Let me talk to her."

Howard's mind raced, trying to decide what to say, what to do.

"Howard. What's going on?" He could detect alarm in Dr. Sue's husband's voice, but he didn't know what to do. *Think Howard! Think!* Nothing. "Uh, Rick. Well. We may have a problem."

"Oh no," Rick whispered.

"Now it may be nothing," Howard stammered. "We're not sure. We haven't even called the police."

"Police? Why? What's going on, Howard?"

"Le' me talk Rick. Just give me a second." Howard heard silence on the other end of the line. "She's late for work. Probably caught up in traffic or something. I'm sure everything's fine."

"Obviously you don't think so, or you wouldn't have mentioned the police Howard. Did you try calling her?"

"We tried her cell. We keep getting her voice mail."

"What about the SAT phone? Did you try that?"

"We tried that too, but she left it here at work, on her desk."

"Something's wrong Howard. I can feel it. Something's wrong. Call the police. She would have called if she was stuck in traffic. Brett would have called if the car broke down. Call the police now Howard. Something bad has happened."

"Okay. All right. I'll call. Maybe you should get down here."

"I'm grabbing little Rick, and we'll be down there ASAP. I just have a bad feeling right now, and I can tell you do too. We'll be down there in a few hours."

Howard shook his head in agreement. "Hopefully you're wrong Rick. I'll send a car to the airport to pick you up. Call me when you're air…"

"F--- the car! I want a helicopter," Rick yelled. Howard could clearly hear panic in his voice. "Call the mayor and arrange something. I'll call from the airplane. Bye."

Howard heard the click before he had a chance to respond. He gently set the receiver into the cradle, took a deep breath, and then picked it back up.

"Operator. Get me the police. I think something's happened to Dr. Sue."

Chapter 14

Riley found a parking spot directly in the middle of the hospital's lot. Out of his mind with excitement, he listened to the end of the news broadcast before killing the car's ignition and yanking the keys from the steering column. Hopping out of his vehicle, he slammed the door without even locking it and hurried across the large parking lot toward the hospital's glass doors. When he finally reached Patty's room, he was out of breath. "Hey. Did you hear? I need your..."

But before he could finish the sentence, he saw Patty wasn't there. "Who're you?" he heard himself ask.

"Who am I? Who the hell are you, come barging in here," an elderly man with saucer eyes and a tiny tube in his nose shot back. "What are you, some sort of madman?"

"Sorry," Riley said, ducking back into the hall to verify he had the right room. He saw the numbers were correct so he leaned back inside, holding onto the doorjamb. "Where's the woman that was in here before?"

"Hell if I know. Get the hell out of here!"

"Never mind. Sorry." Riley darted back down the hallway and grabbed the first person wearing a white coat he could see.

"Detective Marx. Where is she?" he asked the bitter face of a woman with short red hair.

The woman yanked her elbow from Riley's grasp. "She's gone. Discharged this morning. Who're you?"

"Sorry. I'm a friend. I was going to surprise her and pick her up."

"Well, she left about an hour ago. A girlfriend of hers picked her up."

"Short black hair?"

"Yes."

"Thanks," Riley said, turning and trotting back toward the hospital entrance. He hurried through the sliding glass doors and into the bright daylight. Once outside, he sprinted toward his car.

Exactly thirty-eight minutes later, he pulled into Patty Marx's driveway, behind a dark blue Volkswagen Beetle he knew belonged to her best friend. He looked at himself in the rearview mirror and decided although a little beaded and shiny on the forehead, he looked fine. He had calmed down a little since he left the hospital, but he was still pretty psyched about the potential story and about his inside connection to the LAPD.

He slammed the car door and followed a narrow cement walkway to a blue front door. Before he could knock, it opened.

"Oh, it's you," the face said.

"Nicole," Riley said with a nod. "Sorry to disappoint you."

Nicole stood in the doorway and stared at Riley. He stared back.

"Can I come in?" he finally said, breaking the silence.

"I suppose," she replied, stepping out of the way to let him by.

"Who'd you think I was?" he asked as he walked past her.

"Pizza man," she said from behind him. He heard the door close. "We ordered a pizza."

Riley walked the few steps into the family room where he saw Patty, left arm in a dark blue sling, sitting on a green leather couch, watching the news. "Hey kid," he said. "How ya feelin'?"

She looked up at him. "Fine. Thanks for the ride."

"I just came from the hospital," he said. "Seriously. You'd already left. I swear," He recognized her trademark *don't bullshit me* look, the one where she tilts her head down and stares from beneath arched eyebrows, over the tops of her gold-rimmed eyeglasses. "Seriously. I burst in on some ninety-year-old man. Call the hospital. I thought the old guy was going to hit me with that little green oxygen bottle."

"Would've served you right," Riley heard. He turned his head and watched Nicole stride into the room and then plop down onto the couch next to Patty, causing her to wince.

"Sorry," Nicole said, squinting tragically at her friend.

"You swear," Patty said to Riley, with puppy eyes.

Riley was taken aback by the sudden show of affection. "Well, yeah," he stuttered. "Of course." He saw her look away and blink before looking back up at him. His neck started to itch.

"Thanks for the balloons," she said. "Sorry I was such a bitch yesterday. I've been on an emotional roller coaster for a few days. Doctor says it's normal. Don't be surprised if I bite your head off again." She smiled and then shrugged her right shoulder. "I guess I can't help it."

Riley didn't know what to say so he did what he thought he should do. He plopped down onto a matching green Lazy-boy directly across from the green couch.

The tension in the room was stifling so he directed his attention toward the television set. "Can you believe this?" he said about the broadcast. "Been on the news for about the last hour and a half."

Patty's eyes widened. "I know," she said. "We've been watching for a while. I can't believe Dr. Sue's missing. I hope she's okay."

Riley contemplated the moment and decided now was not a good idea. Instead he said, "Yeah. Probably nothing. These things always work themselves out. Right?"

"But, what if it doesn't?" Nicole said, a statement that got Riley's heart pounding again. "I mean. What if she was kidnapped or killed or something? That would be awful."

"Come on," Patty said. "Who'd want to kidnap Dr. Sue?"

"I don't know. You tell me," Riley heard himself say. *Oh shit.* "What I meant was," he stammered, but he knew it was too late. The toothpaste was out of the tube, and all he could do was endure the ensuing heat. He cringed. Her upper lip bristled with beads of shiny sweat, and he could actually see a vein pulse between her left temple and eye.

"You son-of-a-bitch," Patty said, squinting. "You son-of-a-*bitch*."

"What?" Riley said. He could feel his face getting hot.

"That's why you came to the hospital."

"Now come on," he said, standing up. "I came to pick you up because I wanted to. What? This?" he said, shrugging and pointing at the news report. "No. Come on. Wait. You think I came to pump you for information on this? It's a coincidence. I wouldn't…"

"Just go," Patty said, using her good arm to point toward the door. "Get out before I get my gun and shoot you right here."

"I thought you had to turn in your gun."

"I've got a lot of guns."

"Come on. You're overreacting babe."

"Overreacting? You want to see overreacting? I'll show you overreacting." She reached down and snatched up an empty beer bottle from the floor next to the couch.

"Is this one of those *hot and cold* moments, or is this actually real?" Riley asked. The bottle crashing against the wall next to him answered his question.

"You better get out of here," Nicole said, flinching at the sound of broken glass. "She's had a few of them, and they're all down there next to her."

Riley saw Patty reaching for another bottle so he dashed out of the family room and toward the front door. "And stay out, you son-of-a-bitch. I never want to see you again," he heard from the room.

He paused at the front door, grasping the doorknob. "I'm sorry," he yelled over his shoulder.

"Go to hell," he heard back.

"Nice job," he said to himself as he opened the door and stepped outside.

He nearly bumped into a pimply-faced, teen-aged girl who had apparently emerged from a red mustang that was now parked along the curb in front of the house. She was carrying a pizza box above her head.

"Be careful," Riley said to the girl. "Some crazy woman lives there."

He saw the girl freeze and then slowly inch toward the front door. Reaching his car, he popped open the door and fell into the driver's seat. "Damn it," he said, squeezing his lips into a thin line. "What now?"

Chapter 15

As Riley approached Parker Center in downtown Los Angeles, he noticed the mob of reporters that gathered on the front steps of the police department headquarters. He glanced at his watch. Although the press conference wasn't scheduled to start for another twenty minutes, the place was already pretty crowded, and he could sense an eager buzz. *Good thing I got here early*, he thought.

Taking the last swig of mocha latte from the familiar green and white paper cup that he always seemed to find himself carrying, he tossed the carcass into a nearby metal trashcan and then took his place among the other couple dozen reporters that herded themselves into the press pool to find out what they could about the disappearance of Dr. Sue.

Riley really wanted to scoop everyone on this story. He looked around, unimpressed, at the group of lethargically eager faces, who he was sure, wanted to scoop him as well. He hated press pools. They seemed so junior varsity to him. He was spoiled, and he knew it. He used to have a leg up on everyone, but it looks like he screwed that one away.

He thought about Patty, who he really did like. He had not been trying to use her, no matter what she thought. Sure he would have appreciated it if she would have done some snooping for him, but that was not the *entire* reason he had gone to see her earlier.

Who am I kidding, he thought as he ran his right hand through his blond hair. He needed to figure a way to make her believe he had all the best intentions. If he could just find a way to regain her trust, then she could help him, and that help could give him the edge he knew he needed to break the story before anyone else. Then he could publish his story and give *her* all of the credit, and that would make everything okay, for everyone.

He fished his tiny green notebook from his back pocket and flipped the pages over until he found a blank one. The bitter taste of warm milk and dry chocolate coffee coated his tongue. He searched the pockets of his sport coat before remembering he left his pack of Dentine in the car, and there was no way he would make it out to the parking lot, through security, and then back before the press conference started. That meant everyone around him would have to suffer.

Clicking his pen while waiting, Riley's thoughts drifted once again to Patty. Had he just been a little more patient and maybe a little more caring…He pursed his lips and shook his head. He definitely punted this one into the stands. It was his last chance at reconciliation with the only woman, in a long time, who had given him the time of day, and he had let his stupid ego get in the way. Yup, he blew it. Completely his fault. No doubt about it. He coughed into his right fist and then inhaled through a quick, dry sniff. He definitely needed a piece of Dentine. He was so close to patching things up with her after his last debacle. So close. *Damn it!*

"Ladies and gentlemen." A metallic female voice sliced through the dry, still, dusk-colored air. Riley withdrew his silver ballpoint pen and clicked it, ready to write. "Chief Bruggeman will be out in five minutes. He's prepared a short statement, and then he will take some questions. Richard Stein, Dr. Sue's husband, and Howard Thorsen, her producer, will accompany him.

"Please be, well...realize Mr. Stein is pretty shaken up. I shouldn't have to remind you to please watch the tone of your questions. Thank you."

Riley watched the young woman leave the podium and then walk back into the building. *Nice butt*, he thought.

A little more than five minutes later, two men in suits and a man in the familiar midnight blue uniform of the Los Angeles Police Department appeared and walked toward the bank of microphones. Riley could barely make out their faces as the men were being relentlessly bombarded by a continuous stream of photoflashes.

After a short pause, Chief Bruggeman tilted his head forward toward the microphones and began to speak.

"Ladies and gentlemen. Today, at approximately 10 A.M., syndicated talk show host, Dr. Susan Stein, was apparently abducted from her vehicle just outside of her home in the hills overlooking the San Fernando Valley. Her bodyguard, Brett Nelson, of Redlands, California, was severely injured in the kidnapping. Right now, my police department is investigating the crime scene and are working many leads to solve this apparent crime."

Chief Bruggeman produced, from behind the podium, a two-foot by three-foot photograph of Dr. Sue and held it up for all to see. This effort was greeted by another volley of flashes from the group. He set the photograph on the step in front of the podium.

"Dr. Sue is a familiar face," he continued. "I'm sure most of you have seen this picture on the back of the buses here in town. If anyone has seen her since earlier today or has any information as to her whereabouts, please call the 1-800 number at the bottom of this photo. Upon completion of this press conference, my people will be distributing flyers with this photo and the number. Please feel free to take as many as you'd like."

Chief Bruggeman laid his notes onto the podium and looked out at the small crowd in front of him. "We suspect foul play, and my department will do everything in its power to apprehend the person or people who took Dr. Sue. She has been an exemplary citizen who has donated a lot of time and money to those in our society who have needed it. My department will not rest until whoever did this horrific act has been apprehended and brought to justice, within the full extent of the law." He paused for dramatic effect and then added, "I mean business on this one folks. I'm taking this case personally. Now, I'd be happy to answer a few questions."

Orley turned off the radio. *Fat chance*, he thought as he took a long drag from his menthol cigarette and then exhaled the biting fumes. The plan had been executed perfectly. He had transferred the doctor without a hitch, and then he had dumped the car a good two miles from the middle of nowhere. His trail was clean. *Besides*, he reasoned, *he only needed her for a few days*. Then, he'd let her go back to her high horse and loving city, but only after he'd knocked her down a few pegs and only after she gave him what he wanted.

Lounging in one of the two rear-facing easy chairs that sat directly behind the driver's and passenger's seats, he looked through the small hallway that led to the rear bedroom of the motorhome. He could see the edge of the queen-sized bed that took up a large portion of the tiny room in the back of the coach. He knew what lay beneath that bed, and he understood the implications of what he had done.

He took another drag on his cigarette and then reached down and grabbed the bottle of Jack Daniel's Whiskey that sat on the floor beside the chair. *Yeah*, he thought as he took a giant, bitter swig of warm whiskey, relishing in its buzz-inducing burn. *He'd get her to do what he needed.* She'd do it his way, or the hard way. Either way, she'd do what he said.

He set the bottle back onto the floor and stubbed the cigarette into the nearly full ashtray that sat on a small table to his left, next to the passenger's side bulkhead. He closed his heavy eyelids and thought about what he still needed to do.

He was not ready to reintroduce himself just yet. He'd spent some time in solitary confinement in prison. He knew what a day or two in complete blackness could do to a person's head. He also knew what depriving a person of food could do as well. Yeah, he'd take it slow with this one. She seemed pretty strong-willed. But even the strong fall eventually, and the higher they are, the harder they fall.

Riley scribbled into his notepad. After the chief had taken his last question, Riley watched the small group of men turn sullenly back toward the building and then disappear into its confines. He slid the notebook into his back pocket and then returned the pen to its small sheath in the inside of his jacket.

As he walked back to his car, he reflected about what the chief had just said. It was clear to Riley the police were banking on this being some sort of an extortion case which seemed logical since he and everyone else in the public sector knew Dr. Sue had both a lot of money and a lot of enemies. Riley deduced the authorities were content with sitting by and waiting for some sort of ransom note.

Reaching his car, he unlocked the door, opened it, and collapsed into the driver's seat. He yanked the door closed. There was something gnawing at the back of Riley's mind, but he couldn't figure out what it was. He sat there for a long moment and tried to dig the thought from its dark reaches. Realizing it was a futile effort, he jammed the keys into the ignition and started the car. He decided to give it some time before swallowing the whole ransom and extortion bit. Another angle always existed, and he was confident he could find it.

Craving another mocha latte, he led the car out of the crowded parking lot and toward the closest Starbucks. He wished Patty was with him so they could talk about the day's events, but since she had nearly killed him earlier in the day, he knew any future endeavors with her were but a fleeting dream.

So be it, he thought, as he pulled into the parking lot of the coffeehouse. *I don't need her help on this. I'll figure this out myself. She'll see. Everyone will see.*

Chapter 17

I get to meet someone special. Uncle Kent says we've struck gold. He shaved me close this time, really close. He keeps saying this one is going to be special. He tells me to act really young.
I'm kind of getting excited. Maybe this one will help me. Maybe I can finally run...

The sudden shock of bright light smacked Dr. Sue in the face. Squinting at its brightness, she had no idea how long she'd been in the dark. Her hands, bound behind her, were anchored to the wooden platform on which she lay. Her pinkies and ring fingers had gone numb an eternity ago, and since she had been tethered in one spot and forced to lie on her side, the entire right half of her body ached, especially her head. She had long ago quit trying to stop it from slamming into the floor. As terrified as she was, she welcomed the large wedge of light, though. It, along with the pain, confirmed she was alive.

Blinking her vision into focus, she realized she was not on a wooden floor after all, but in some sort of shallow, wooden crate. Although her surroundings were warm, fear made her shiver uncontrollably. She felt helplessly vulnerable despite her confined surroundings. Instinctively, she tucked her cold bare legs up to her chest, curling up as best as she could into a protective fetal-like position. A tear dropped onto her right cheek, and her jaw vibrated in the yellow silence. Had she not been gagged, the sound of her chattering teeth most certainly would have filled the warm tiny room. She sniffed wet mucus through her nose and then let out a slight whimper.

A shadowed figure appeared before her, paralyzing her with fear. Heart pounding wildly in her chest, her eyes began to well up, but she was too frightened to cry. She stared at the silhouette, afraid to move, afraid to breathe, grasping onto an irrational belief that if she held completely still, maybe it wouldn't see her. But it did see her.

"Well, well, well," she heard the figure say. "The good doctor has fallen off of her high horse I see. Shew. Smells like a prison cell in here. No-no now. No need to get up. I'll change that diaper, too."

Dr. Sue looked down at her bare knees. She seemed to recall wearing a pair of pantyhose when she had left for work on...what day was it? With her thumb behind her back, she reached out and felt the unmistakable texture of a diaper. Despite the fact she was not completely naked, she felt herself begin to blush.

"No need to be embarrassed," the voice said. "I seen 'em all. Young ones. Old wrinkled ones like yours. I prefer the young ones, I'll have to admit. Less hair." He pointed a crooked finger at her and made small circles with it in the air above her waist. "You really should do something about that forest down there."

The man's voice sounded familiar, but Dr. Sue could not place it. She wished she could see his face.

"Are you thirsty?" the voice asked.

Dr. Sue found herself shaking her head. She forced herself to stop.

"Oh it's okay. I'm not here to hurt you. Don't worry. If you're thirsty, I'll give you some water."

Her heart still hammered in her chest despite the calmness of the stranger's voice. She tried to say yes, but couldn't. A small tear dropped from her right eye. She nodded her head once more. Her mouth was terribly dry, and her throat burned considerably.

"Now," the voice said, "I'm going to remove the tape from your mouth. It might hurt a bit when I do this. It's been on there for a few days."

Through wide eyes, Dr. Sue watched as the shadow leaned toward her, and then she winced when she felt his right hand push her head firmly into the wooden floor. Intense pain engulfed her entire body.

"Don't try anything stupid," she heard him say.

After a few seconds, she could feel his fingernail scraping at her cheek as he attempted to free a corner of the tape.

"It's really sticky…when it's been on there…so long…there we go," the voice said.

Dr. Sue heard the tape rip from her skin, and then she felt the stinging burn that instantly followed. She wanted to rub at the pain but couldn't. She fought against the straps behind her back, but it was no use. Instead, she inhaled deeply and then let out an acidy burp, her stomach burning ferociously. She felt him lift his hand from her head, and then she watched him slowly back away.

"There. How's that?" the voice said.

Dr. Sue, for once in her life, had no idea what to say. Her mouth free from its confines, she instinctively began to scream.

"Help!" she yelled with a scratchy voice. "Somebody help me!"

The faceless figure stared at her, hands on his hips. After a few more bouts of useless yelling, Dr. Sue realized its futility and shut up.

"You through?" the man asked. "There's no one around to hear you. You can scream as loud as you want, but no one will hear you except for me. Now, do you want some water or not?"

After a short pause, and between deep breaths, Dr. Sue whispered her response. "Yes. Please. I need some water."

She licked her lips and forced herself not to cry. The calmness of the faceless man scared her to death.

"Okay," he said. "Now that wasn't so hard. Was it?"

Dr. Sue saw the man reach behind himself and produce a large plastic sports bottle with a long, skinny tube attached to its end. Holding the bottle up with his right hand, he guided the tube with his left so it dangled in front of her face. Taking her cue, Dr. Sue reached out with her teeth, took the end of the tube into her mouth, and then sucked in a small sample of liquid. It was horribly warm and plastic tasting, like water from an old garden hose that had been sitting in the sun all day, and it was fantastic. She took numerous long, hard sips, sighing loudly between swallows. The burning in her throat began to cool.

"Thank you," she said, her voice still scratchy despite the water.

"You're welcome," he replied. "Least I can do. Want some more?"

Dr. Sue shook her head. "No," she said. "Thanks."

She saw him shrug and then set the bottle onto a small shelf next to him. The tube stayed next to her face.

"If you want some more, the tube's right there."

She saw him turn to his right to leave.

"Wait," she said quickly. She didn't want to be alone again, even if it meant spending time with the shadow.

He looked down at her. She still could not make out his face.

"What?"

"Can I ask who you are? Where I am? Why I'm here?"

He remained where he was. She couldn't tell if he was looking at her or not.

"You're under the bed in my motorhome," he said. "Who I am doesn't really matter to you right now. You screwed me once. Now you're going to help me."

"I don't understand."

"And you wouldn't!" he yelled. "You wouldn't," he said again, this time in a calmer voice. "You're too high up to know what we *commoners* go through to try to live our lives. But you'll understand soon enough, after a few more weeks in the hole."

She watched him reach up and grab the lid of her crate, which she assumed was the mattress to the bed under which she understood herself to be.

"No, wait," she said desperately, eyes welling up. "Please don't close the lid again. Please don't put me in the dark…"

"You give bad advice," he said, and then he slammed the lid.

Dr. Sue heard a buckle being clasped and then the quieting thumps of footsteps as they walked away from her. She began to sob as she once again found herself covered in complete blackness.

Riley awoke feeling rejuvenated. Blinking at his digital clock, he realized he had not slept past nine in the morning in a long time. He slid out of bed and turned on his computer while making the short walk to his bathroom. After successfully transferring the previous night's two beers into the yawning toilet bowl, he flushed it and then made his way back into his room. He could smell the coffee that had automatically begun to brew downstairs.

Plopping down in front of his computer, he double-clicked the internet icon which brought up the home page for the *Los Angeles Times*. As he had expected, the disappearance of Dr. Sue took up most of the space. He quickly glanced through a few of the stories, taking notes on a small, spiral-bound notepad he kept next to his beloved machine.

Satisfied with what he had read so far, he stood and slowly made his way down the stairs, pondering the stories. Everything, so far at least, had pretty much made sense. The statements of Chief Bruggeman, the husband, and the producer were logical. The theory of a future ransom note made complete and obvious sense. Why then, Riley wondered, could he not help but think there was something amiss, some other possibility.

After what seemed like an eternity, his tall, creaky body finally reached his small kitchen. The warm smell of coffee filled the air. He snatched a maroon and gold mug that sported the Southern California logo of his alma mater from a cabinet above the coffeepot and quickly poured himself half a cup. He sipped at the hot liquid while simultaneously inhaling its rich aroma. There was something eating at him, and he couldn't quite put his finger on it yet.

After devouring two bowls of Grape Nuts, he refilled his mug and then splashed in a little bit of milk before heading back upstairs. Something in his mind, that little voice he had always trusted before but lately seemed to ignore, was screaming at him to look at the facts of the case and to go in the exact opposite direction of everyone else. His present situation showed *not* listening to that little voice had pretty much gotten him nowhere. So, he decided to listen up and see where that little voice would lead him.

Chapter 18

Riley jumped into his car at a little before eleven in the morning. After making the obligatory stop at Starbucks and ordering *the usual*, he sipped at the perfectly made mocha latte before making his way to Cedars-Sinai Hospital.

Listening to smooth jazz while negotiating the light freeway traffic, he mulled over his first few steps toward writing the perfect story. He absolutely needed to talk to either the bodyguard or someone close to him. The newspaper reported the bodyguard had been in and out of surgery yesterday for the better part of nine hours. Riley read the family was hopeful, but the prognosis was bleak. It looked as though his injuries would leave him paralyzed from the end of his toes to about his mid-abdomen. Although the article did state doctors were not ruling out some feeling a little lower in the body, Riley was pretty sure life from now on was going to be difficult for that guy.

As he drove, he continued to sip at his drink while pondering his options. If the police or the hospital would not let him talk to the patient (a long shot no doubt) he would then make his way to the radio station to try to talk to the show's producer. If that too was a no-go, then he really only had one other option. He would purchase a boxer's mouthpiece and an athletic cup and maybe some shin guards and then make the drive back to Patty's house where he would beg, plead, pay, grovel, do anything required to put himself into a position where he could pry from her at least a few ounces of something he could turn into a story.

After pulling into the hospital's parking lot, Riley parked the car and then made his way into the building's giant complex. He followed the signs until he found himself in the intensive care unit. The sight of a uniformed police officer sitting in a chair outside one of the rooms confirmed to Riley he was in the right place.

As Riley approached, the officer stood. "Can I help you?" he asked, resting his right hand on the pistol grip of his side arm.

"My name's Riley. *L. A. Times*. Any chance I can talk to Mr. Nelson?" Riley knew he was shooting for the moon.

"Mr. Nelson is not taking any visitors except for family."

Riley leaned to the right. Craning his neck so he was looking past the officer's head, he could see through the slightly opened door a small group of people sitting in chairs around an occupied hospital bed. The repetitious, slow beep of the heart monitor and the typical sanitary smell of the hospital's hallway dominated the area.

The police officer stepped to Riley's right, blocking his view. "You'll have to come back later or wait for the press conference."

"Right," Riley said. He shifted back to his left so he could barely peek into the room. Catching a glimpse of a young, blonde-headed woman, he willed her to look in his direction. "Is he able to talk or anything?"

"I don't know. Sounds like it. He's had his family in there pretty much all morning."

"Doctor say whether he is going to walk or anything?" Riley asked, trying to stall. He thought maybe if he caught the woman's attention, she'd let him in.

"I don't know. I'm no doctor. Look, Mr. Reiman…"

"Riley."

"Yeah, Riley. Whatever. Look Mr. Riley. You're not going to get anything from me. There'll be a press conference this afternoon. Just wait 'til then, and you'll get what you want."

Riley withdrew two business cards from his shirt pocket and thrust them at the officer. "Could you please give these to Mr. Nelson's family and ask them if they wouldn't mind…"

The police officer pushed Riley's outstretched hand away. "I don't think you understand. I'm not giving those to anyone. In fact, I am now asking you to leave. If you don't get out of here by the time I count to three, I'll have you hauled in. One…two…"

He saw the blonde-headed woman look in his direction. His heart leapt slightly when he caught her eye. "Okay. Okay. I'm out of here. Just trying to make a living you know."

"Me too," the officer said.

Riley turned and walked away from the room. *Maybe not a total loss*, he thought.

To say Riley had to go to the bathroom was an understatement. His bladder hurt so bad, it actually stung. He was doubled-over and squirming to control the pain. Although he had managed to stop by a men's room before leaving intensive care section, he also managed to grab another mocha latte at a little espresso cart in the hospital's lobby before making his way to his parked car. So now, having sat in the car for nearly two hours and forty-five minutes, that same mocha latte was not just begging for a release, it was demanding one.

He glanced to his right at the empty coffee cups that littered the floor beneath the passenger seat and briefly contemplated using one of those to recycle his spent drink. Putting the thought on hold, he looked up at the red digital numbers that were displayed on the tiny clock that sat atop his dashboard and decided to give it another ten minutes before he would duck back into the hospital to use the facilities. He looked up at the building's entrance, forcing himself to ignore the discomfort in his bladder.

Finally, he thought when he spotted the blonde-headed woman from Brett Nelson's hospital room as she emerged from the sliding glass doors. Leaping from his parked car, he trotted toward the hospital's entrance.

"Excuse me. Excuse me miss," he said as he approached the woman. The girl stopped and looked up at Riley as he came to a halt in front of her.

"Yes," she said from behind a large pair of black sunglasses.

"Hi," Riley said, trying to catch his breath. He could see black streaks below the low-riding lenses. "Sorry. I ran over here when I saw you come out. Guess I need to get in shape." Riley smiled hard, but he saw the woman was not amused. "Anyway, I saw you in Brett Nelson's room, right?"

"Yeah. Who're you?"

"Greg Riley. Friends just call me Riley." The pain in Riley's bladder forced him to bend slightly at the waist. He saw her take a step back. He hoped she wouldn't get scared and run.

Instead, she said, "Are you okay? You don't look so good."

"Yeah, I'm fine," Riley said. Itchy sweat dotted his forehead. "Too much coffee."

"How'd you know Brett? He never mentioned no Riley," the woman said, crossing her arms in front of her stomach and slouching onto her right leg. From what he could tell, she was very beautiful behind the big glasses.

"Actually," Riley said, coughing into his left fist, "I didn't really know him. I'm a reporter. *L. A. Times.*"

The woman dropped her arms to her sides and started to walk away.

"Wait," Riley said, grabbing her arm. "Please. Just a moment of your time." He let her lithe arm go, and it fell back to her side.

She stopped and looked up at him. He smiled. She didn't smile back.

"One minute," she said. "Then I gotta go." She pushed the bridge of her glasses up onto her tiny nose and then slouched back onto her right leg.

"Okay," Riley said, fishing his notebook from his back pocket. "Look. There's something telling me the cops are way off on this one. I'm not looking for anything to write just yet. I'm just trying to get some facts. Nothing you say'll be quoted. I promise."

"Swear?"

Riley put his right hand over his heart. "I swear."

"Thank you," she said, sighing. "I'll tell you what I know, I guess."

Riley thought he detected a hint of a smile. He took a deep breath. He really needed to pee.

"Umm...did he, I mean...can he talk?"

"He's in and out. Still pretty medicated."

"Has he been saying much?"

"Every now and then. Keeps talking about a dark blue Jaguar. Brand new. Still had paper plates."

"Did he say which dealer they were from?"

"No. I don't think I've heard him mention that."

"What do you think happened?" Riley asked. He saw her bring a tiny fist up to her mouth, and then she started to sob. He noticed a huge tear dangle from her cheek. He watched it drop to the ground mere seconds before her swiping hand failed to prevent its fall. Her fist dropped back to her side.

"I don't know." She sniffed, cleared her throat, and then swallowed. "From what he keeps saying, he got out to help the man push his car. He was nicely dressed. Blond hair. New car. Brett was helping him push the car, and then the next thing he knew he was upside down in

Dr. Sue's truck, and he couldn't feel his legs. That's all I know." She sniffed again.

"That's it, huh?"

"That's it."

"Didn't recognize the guy?"

"Nope."

"Did he say anything else?"

"Nothing."

"Thanks," Riley said after a short pause. "Thanks a lot. You've been a big help." He withdrew one of the two business cards from his left front pocket and handed it to the young girl. She took it. "If there's anything else you can remember, or anything he says you may think I would like to know, please, call me."

"Whatever," she said. "I gotta go."

"Hang in there."

Riley watched her acknowledge his comment with a nod before she turned and walked away. He counted to ten, so as to not be rude, and then he sprinted toward the hospital and toward the relief he desperately needed.

Chapter 19

I tried to run away once. Someone found me and brought me back to Uncle Kent. He burned me with a cigar in my armpit and told me if I ever do that again, he'd burn me down there. Next time, I'll run faster...

Orley lowered the radio's volume. There it was again. He strained hard trying to detect the origin of the sound. Nothing. *Must've been something in the road*, he thought.

He took a drag from a cigarette and then rested it on the edge of a crowded ashtray just below the radio's controls. As soon as his hand reached forward to turn the volume back up, he heard the noise again, a thumping from the back of the rig. He looked back over his right shoulder toward the bedroom, from where the sound appeared to be coming. After a few seconds, he turned his attention back to the dark road.

"Oh shit," he said as he jerked the oversized steering wheel to the left. He heard the tires squeal as the large coach slowly leaned to the right before steadying back up in the center of the highway's right-most lane. His heart pounded in his chest. *That was close.*

He reached for his cigarette, but it was gone. Glancing down at the gray carpet, he spotted it smoldering on the floor between the two seats. He quickly snatched it up and returned it to the ashtray before reaching back down and tamping out the smoking ash with an empty silver soda can. Amid quick glances between the carpet and the road, he swept away the small pile of ash with the back of his right hand until he noticed a perfect tiny black circle scorched into the floor. "Terrific," he said.

He heard the thumps again. They were growing in both frequency and volume, and they were really pissing him off. Looking ahead, he saw the outline of a sign as it rapidly approached from the darkness. As the green square grew in size, he read the next exit was a mile ahead.

One minute later, Orley veered the motorhome to the right and onto the off ramp that led to an extremely dark road. The road ran perpendicular to the highway so he followed it for a few minutes to give himself a buffer. Stopping the rig on the dirt shoulder, he lowered the driver's window, killed the engine, and listened to his dark surroundings. The silence and the complete blackness of the surrounding area reassured him he was alone. *This will do.*

Orley plucked the still smoldering cigarette from the ashtray and took an extra-long drag before flicking it out of the driver's window. Climbing out of the driver's seat, he felt his way through the darkness, toward the rear bedroom.

Once inside the tiny room, he closed the small wooden door behind him and then clicked on the light, squinting at its sudden brightness. He stared at the unmade bed for a few moments and then kicked its wooden frame.

"Let me out of here, you bastard," the muffled voice said from beneath the mattress.

"Go to hell," Orley said kicking the bed's frame again. "You almost made me wreck."

"I gotta use the restroom. It's an emergency."

"You got a diaper on. Just go."

"I gotta go number two really badly."

"Then go number two. I don't care. I already changed one of your K-Mart burritos. What makes you think it would bother me to do it again?"

"What do you want from me?" the muffled voice asked after a rather long pause. "I've got money, if that's what you want. Call my husband. Call Howard. They'll give you whatever you want. I'm having hot flashes. Just please, let me out of here."

Orley chuckled and shook his head. "I don't want your stinking money, Doctor. I already got plenty of money…"

"Then what the hell *do* you want?" the voice shrieked.

"I'll let you know when I let you know. For now, consider this my version of the *Fairness Doctrine*. You're done giving bad advice, okay? So why don't you just lay there, in your piss and shit, with your hot flashes, and think about all of the bad advice you've given in the past. Lay there in the dark and think about it all, and in a few days, I'll let you know how you're going to help me. For now, stop that fucking pounding, or I'll stop it for you. It's driving me crazy. Do you understand me? I'm not kidding around. Stop the fucking pounding or else."

He turned, clicked off the light, and felt his way back to the driver's seat, ignoring the muffled scream from beneath the bed. Climbing back into the seat, he started the engine, cranked the music up, executed a three-point turn, and then headed back to the highway, the one that would take him to Monterey.

Dr. Sue kicked her heel into the wood one last time and then collapsed with a sigh onto her numb right side. She had tried her best to rest her bumping head on the wooden floor, but the constant rattling was unnerving.

She could feel a tear run down her cheek and tickle her nose. Anxiety overwhelmed her as she desperately needed to wipe its tickle away, but with her hands still bound behind her back, she was unable. She forced herself to deal with the situation. Squeezing her eyes tightly, Dr. Sue sniffed the dripping mucus from the tip of her nose and then gagged at the stench.

She had tried her best to hold in her feces, but after a while she accepted her only option. So, humiliated, she went, thankful for the darkness, lying on her right side, into the itchy diaper that had not been changed in God only knew how long. She had felt helpless, like an infant, and embarrassed despite her isolation. Then, almost immediately after that, as if on cue, her body exploded into a demoralizing hot flash that was exasperated by her cramped and blackened surroundings. The itching and the stench and the debilitating heat were unbearable.

Oh no, she thought when she heard the motorhome's engine crank. Not again. She broke into a body jerking sob. Her body lifted and then fell, and before she could tighten her neck muscles, her head once again slammed into the floor. *Lift, slam, rattle. Lift, slam, rattle.*

She had no sense of time. Urine and feces and sweat dominated the blackness, and her inability to stop her head from banging into the floor below her was slowly driving her insane. Although she wanted to die, she knew she wouldn't.

Chapter 20

"Mr. Thorsen," Riley asked as he approached the radio station's parking lot. He hoped he had the right guy.

"Yes," Howard replied, squinting at the taller man.

"I'm sorry to bother you, but I was wondering if I could ask you a few questions?" Riley said, suddenly self-conscious at the high pitch his voice seemed to carry.

"Do I know you?"

Riley was used to the question. "No. I'm Greg Riley. *L. A. Times.*"

"Oh," Howard said, walking past Riley. He shook his head and waved his hand next to his right ear. "I've already given my statement to the press. I have no additional comments."

Riley walked next to Howard. "Please Mr. Thorsen. Just a few questions. It'll only take a second. I swear."

Howard continued walking. "Make it quick Mr. Rigley. I'm in a hurry."

"Okay. I will. And it's Riley."

"What?"

"You said *Rigley*. It's Riley."

Howard stopped as he reached his black BMW and then glanced at his watch. "Time's ticking Mr. *Riley.*"

"Right," Riley said. He noticed the shorter man arch his eyebrows and purse his lips. "Okay. I'm not writing a story. Everything that has needed to be said has been written already."

"So then, why are you bugging me?"

"Just collecting facts. In case something breaks."

Howard opened his car door and lowered himself into the driver's seat. "I don't have time for this. I gotta go."

"Just one minute, please. I'll never bug you again. I promise."

Howard looked at his watch. "All right, you got a minute."

Riley fired off a series of questions beginning with, "Aside from the fringe elements out there who didn't like what Dr. Sue stood for, can you think of anyone else who would want to do something like this?"

"I suppose some glory seeker who is looking to get his name in the paper."

"Wouldn't there be a ransom note then?"

"Who says there isn't?"

"Is there?"

Howard stared at Riley. For some reason he trusted the goofy-looking reporter. "Let's just say although I am not at liberty to say, and this is totally off the record, the cops are sitting on their asses like a bunch of dumb buffoons."

Riley smiled.

"Don't quote me on that."

"Right," Riley said, scribbling the word *buffoons* into his little notebook. "Has she had any personal threats recently? Any confrontations?"

Howard shook his head. "No. Nothing I can remember. She would have told me if…wait," he said straightening up and looking up at Riley.

"Yeah. What? Did something happen?"

Howard paused a moment and then shook his head. "Naw. It was nothing."

"What. I can tell something happened. Maybe something minor?"

"Well. Saturday at Disneyland, she got freaked out by some guy. He tried to get an autograph or something. I don't know. I'd gone to the bathroom, and then when I got back, he was there. Nothing really happened, but she was pretty freaked out at the time."

"An autograph?"

"Yeah. He handed her a piece of paper. He wanted her to sign it. He was kind of creepy. Lots of tattoos on his forearms. Normal looking other than that."

"Why was she freaked out?"

Howard shook his head. "I don't know. She didn't want to talk about it. It happened in front of the kids and all. Some of them were afraid. I could tell. He must have freaked them out, too."

"Did you tell this to the cops?"

Howard looked up at Riley. "You know. I don't think I did. I guess I should, don't you?"

Riley suddenly grew hot, and his heart began to thud in his chest. This was the moment of truth. Do the right thing, or get the story. He could feel the sweat beading on his forehead, and his face was beginning to feel numb. The butterflies were racing in his stomach. He made a snap decision.

"Naw," he heard himself say. "Probably just some whacko. Don't sweat it."

Howard sighed. "Yeah. You're probably right." He started the car's ignition and then looked at his watch. "More than a minute. Sorry. Gotta run."

"Wait," Riley said holding the door open with his left hand. He could hear a continual ding that announced to the two men the keys were in the ignition, but the door was still open. "You said some girls were freaked out. What girls?"

"DSCF."

Riley stared at Howard. The dinging continued.

"Dr. Sue's Children Fund," Howard said, blinking. "Her fund for underprivileged children. Now if you'll excuse me, I really gotta run." Howard yanked the door from Riley's hand.

Riley moved out of the way as Howard closed the door, which finally silenced the annoying sound. He watched the black car back out of the parking spot and drive into the darkening night air.

"No problem," Riley said. "And thank you very much."

Chapter 21

A loud thump startled Dr. Sue out of her murky haze. The right side of her body hurt beyond all belief, and the chafing of the thin plastic straps burned her wrists. Her heart thumped in her chest as she felt herself begin to cry again.

A wedge of light slowly inched its way across her body. She looked up, squinting. Slowly, the dark shape of a human began to form.

"Shew," the man said. "I guess your shit does stink. Don't it."

"Can I have some more water please?" Dr. Sue managed to ask through a hoarse voice.

"Looks like your tank's a little empty," Orley said, nodding at the nearly drained water bottle before reaching out and grabbing it. "I'll be right back." He turned to his right and exited the bedroom. "Don't go anywhere," he said, giggling.

A few minutes later, he reentered the room and placed the bottle back into position on the shelf above the bed. Dr. Sue grabbed the thin plastic tube with her teeth and pulled it into her mouth. She took a sip of warm water. It was colder this time.

"You look like a horse trying to eat an apple through a fence," Orley said. "I should charge admission for this. Tape it. Put in on YouTube. Probably get a few million hits."

"An apple sure sounds nice," Dr. Sue said. Although her stomach had stopped growling some time ago, she was terribly hungry.

"No way," Orley said, shaking his head. "No more food for you. You should be all shitted out by now. You haven't eaten in nearly a week. This is probably your last shitty diaper. Thank God for that. I'll keep giving you water, though. Piss, I don't mind. But, shit. This is getting old. You can go a long time without eating."

When Dr. Sue saw him turn to leave again, she realized she had no sense of time. Had it really been that long? Had she been lying in her little hell-hole for almost a week? The way she ached, it could very well have been a…

She startled as the man walked back into the room, totally naked. She screamed with every ounce of force she could muster. "Please, no! Stay away from me, you bastard," she yelled. "Somebody help me, please!"

Orley stood there and stared, hands on his hips. After a few moments, she stopped screaming.

"You through yellin'?" he asked. He could see she was shaking, and that nearly aroused him. "I'm standing here like this to make a point."

Dr. Sue attempted to blink the tears from her eyes. Fear made her shake uncontrollably.

"Look," Orley said as he rested his limp penis on the fingers of his right hand. "Totally flaccid." He let it fall back into place and then put his hand on his hip again. "You *do not* turn me on. I am not going to rape you; so don't worry."

Dr. Sue took a deep breath. She sniffed loudly and then swallowed. "What do you want?"

"What do I want?" Orley said. "Let's see. What do I want? I want the demon to go away, Doctor. Can you make it go away? Can you? No. No one can."

The sight of the naked man disgusted her. She stared at his face. "Wh…What demon?" she managed to say, forcing herself to calm down.

"What demon you ask? I'll tell you what demon. The one that makes me do bad things."

"We all have demons," she said.

Orley stared down at her. "Yeah. I guess you're right, good doctor. I guess we do. Then I have no need for you now. Do I?"

"Wait," she said quickly, as it looked like he was about to shut her in the dark again. "Wait."

He took his hand off of the mattress. "What?" he said calmly. "Oh yeah," he shook his head and then thumped his forehead with the heel of his palm. "I'm an idiot. Where are my manners? You really stink. I need to get you out of those nasty pants, don't I?"

Dr. Sue cringed when she recognized he was going to change her diaper. Embarrassment and disgust overrode panic as the nude stranger's shaking hands slowly reached toward her aching body. She squeezed her eyes tightly and began to sob again.

"It's okay, Doctor," she heard the voice say. "I've seen it before, and look. Still limp as it gets. In fact, it even seems a little smaller." She heard him giggle.

Continuing to squeeze her eyes and grit her teeth, her body twitched when she felt his warm hands touch the outside of her upper left thigh, and she felt herself become nauseous. Her shaking continued as the knuckles of one of his fists slid underneath the elastic waistband and ripped it apart with a jerk.

After that, she felt him reach underneath her and do the same thing with her numb right side, the side she had been lying on for apparently about a week.

"Look. Corn off the cob," she heard the man say. He chuckled. "Heard that in a movie I saw once. Thought it was funny. Can't remember which one." She heard him giggle again.

The heat of embarrassment chased a chill from her face down her neck, and into her torso. She felt herself give off a shiver as her lip quivered in fright; again she wanted to die. "Just hurry up damn it," she snapped between sobs.

"Well well. Feisty. That's good. I like that. You can't rush something like this, though. This is a very delicate matter. Gotta make sure I get it out of all that hair. Plus, it doesn't really smell that good either."

Eyes still closed, Dr. Sue caught a hint of the unmistakable odor of a baby wipe only moments before she felt the cold damp cloth penetrate the cheeks of her buttocks. "Oh God," she heard herself whisper. She continued to sob.

"Almost done," the voice said.

She felt him wipe around her bottom a few more times, wincing as she felt his finger glide over her anus.

"Much better, and not too bad for an old ass," he said before slapping it firmly.

Only after she felt a new warm cotton diaper slide up over her hips did she finally open her eyes.

"There now. That wasn't so bad, was it?" Orley said, admiring his work. "Nothing to get all worked up over."

Dr. Sue took a deep breath and then a big sip of water. She had never felt so humiliated. "Who are you?" she said, sniffing noisily through a wet nose. "When are you going to tell me what you want from me?"

Orley walked out of the room and after a few moments returned, this time wearing a pair of gray sweatpants and a plain white tank top. He held, in his right hand, a folded-up piece of notebook paper.

Dr. Sue watched him unfold it and then hold it in front of her face. A sudden flash of fear heated her body as she immediately recognized the tattoos on his right forearm.

"Remember this?" Orley said as he held the note up to her face. "All you had to do was sign this damn piece of paper. But no, you were too good for that." He snatched back the paper and refolded it into a neat, white rectangle.

"Well, now you're going to help me the good old-fashioned way."

"What? I don't...I don't understand."

"Of course you don't understand," Orley thundered. "That's because you don't really listen when people talk to you. You just feed 'em that hefty-do bullshit and get paid millions of dollars. I needed your help, and you blew me off. You gave bad advice, and now you're going to undo it."

Before Dr. Sue had a chance to reply, Orley slammed the lid. "About another week in there, and you'll be doing whatever I tell you," he said to the mattress. "Another week in the hole. And don't be shitting no more. That was as bad for me, believe me, as it was for you."

Chapter 22

Jason Frank looked at his interrogator and wondered why the man did not believe him. This was not the way he had ever imagined the police treating a man of his wealth and stature.

"Come on Frank," the detective said. "Just tell us where she is, and we'll convince the D. A. to go easy on you."

Jason rubbed his ebony face with his large hand and sighed. "Look," he said from behind tired eyes, staring at the detective who sat across from him. "I don't know why you're questioning *me*. It was *my* frigging car that was stolen." He looked over at the mirror to his left and knew faces were staring at him from its other side. He had seen this very scene take place every week on television, but he could not believe it was actually happening to him. He gestured toward the mirror. "Ask them. I told them, too. Why doesn't anybody believe me?"

"Well," the detective said, opening a manila folder in front of him and glancing down at a handwritten piece of notebook paper. "Let's see. A shoe, her shoe, found in *your* trunk. The smell of chloroform all over *your* trunk." The detective looked up at Jason's face. "Homosexual. You are a homosexual, right?"

"What's that got to do with it?" Jason said. He could feel himself blushing.

"How can I be sure you didn't *lend*," the detective traced invisible quotes with both index and middle fingers while saying the word *lend*, "someone, an accomplice, a friend, a lover, your car in order to commit the act and then report a *stolen*," more quotes, "car? Hmm? Why should we believe you?"

Both men stared at each other, but neither said a word. After a few seconds, the detective stood and put his left foot onto the seat of the metal chair.

"Look, we know how you guys feel about Dr. Sue. We do. It makes sense. You guys hate her 'cause she lets everyone, you know, realize your behavior is…not exactly…normal. Not saying I agree with her, but she does tell it how it is, and I know it drives your people crazy."

"My people," Jason repeated under arched eyebrows. He could not believe what he had just heard. He forced himself to calm down.

The detective glanced down at the notebook paper again and said, "And in addition to the shoe and the chloroform, we found tire tracks from *your* car at the scene of the abduction. So, it looks to me we have motive, evidence, and a weak alibi on your part, not to mention the marijuana in your system…"

"But I didn't do it."

"Put yourself in my shoes Frank. What would you see?"

Jason swallowed. "An innocent man," he said. "I swear."

The two men looked quickly at the door when it suddenly swung inward. Another man wearing a gray suit entered the room.

"Let him go," the suited man said as he walked in. "His alibi checks, and we got a ransom note." He looked at Jason and then said, "Mr. Frank. Looks like today's your lucky day. You're free to go. Sorry for any inconvenience we may have caused you."

Jason was fuming. "That's it? Sorry for any inconvenience? This is unbelievable. I'm gonna get a lawyer and sue the department for harassment."

"Good luck with that Mr. Frank. We're just doing our job. Protecting and serving. Whatever it takes. Do you need an escort out?"

Jason slowly stood. He wanted to rip their heads off, but instead he took a deep breath and composed himself.

"What about my car?" he said. "When can I get my car back?"

"Yeah. That's a little tricky," the second man said. "We're going to need to keep it for a while. It was involved in a major crime, and right now we're still looking for evidence. Then there will be a trial...not sure how long it will take. The city will provide you with an adequate rental until we can get your vehicle back to you. Until then, you're just going to have to be patient. Sorry."

Jason rubbed his face with both hands. "Whatever," he said, shaking his head. "I don't think I even want the damn thing anymore." He walked past the officers and let out an over-exaggerated sigh.

"The clerk up front will help you with the paperwork," the second officer said, following him out of the room. "Again, we're sorry for any inconvenience we may have caused you."

Jason ignored the cop and walked toward the front of the building so he could fill out the paperwork.

"A ransom note, huh?" the first detective asked, tossing his empty coffee cup into the wastebasket.

"Yeah. He may not be involved, but it does look like a gay thing."

Riley knocked on the thin door of the dilapidated apartment building. *Not exactly the nicest neighborhood*, he thought. He nervously glanced at the name on the printout. It was the ninth and last name on his list. The others had all been a wash. He hoped this was quick. This place gave him the creeps.

Just before knocking again, Riley saw the door slowly crack open. Looking down through the narrow space between the door and the jamb, he saw a single blue eye staring up at him. "Nikka. Nikka Rubertski?" he asked. He noticed a slight nod in reply. "Is your mommy home honey?"

"No," the voice that went with the eye whispered.

Riley heard the muted sounds of sirens over the constant buzz of a struggling fluorescent light bulb. The stench of dried urine, cracked linoleum, and chipped lead paint permeated the dimly lit hallway. Fending off a nervous panic that suddenly invaded his body, he said, "Can I come in?" He knew the answer before he even asked the question.

"Uh-uh," the little girl said. "Mommy says I can't let strangers in. I'm not supposed to be talking to you right now either."

"Where is your mommy?"

"She's at work. She cleans rich people's houses. She doesn't come home until late."

Riley looked at his watch. Five forty. He wondered what late meant. He decided to take a chance.

"Look honey," he said, bending way over so his eyes were even with those of the little girl. "Do you mind if I ask you a few questions? I'm not here to hurt you or anything. I'm your friend. I write stories that are printed in the newspaper."

"Like the man on TV," Nikka replied.

"Right. Only better," Riley answered, still stooping over. "I'm just going to sit on the floor right here, okay?"

"Okay," Nikka said through the cracked door.

Riley glanced around the hallway and then eased himself onto the hard floor. He sat cross-legged, facing the tiny opening. It suddenly occurred to him the door was probably being secured by both a flimsy chain and the weight of an eight-year-old girl. He was quite certain if he wanted to, he could get into the apartment. Thrusting the thought aside, he made a mental note to warn the little girl before he left she really should not stand with the door slightly ajar and talk to strangers. First things first though.

"Did you hear what happened to Dr. Sue?" Riley asked.

"Yes."

"Are you one of Dr. Sue's children?"

"Yes. Well, not a real child, just a pretend one. She does stuff with us."

Riley grinned as hard as he could at the little girl. "Did you go to Disneyland with her on Saturday?"

"Uh-huh," the girl replied.

"Now, I want you to think really hard and try to remember your best," Riley said, tilting his head slightly forward and looking at her from beneath a wrinkled forehead.

"Okay," she said.

"Did anything happen there that made you feel scared? Not a scary ride or anything, but a person. Did you see a person who maybe frightened you?"

The girl stared at Riley. He could see she was blinking away some tears. *Bingo*, he thought. "It's okay. You can tell me."

The girl nodded her head up and down.

"How did he scare you?"

"He grabbed Dr. Sue's arm and said mean things to her."

"Do you know what he said?"

"Na-uh," the girl said, wiping a tear from her high cheekbone. She sniffed loudly.

Riley stared at the little girl. "Did you tell anyone about that?" he asked.

"No. Mr. Howard said everything was going to be okay."

"What did the mean man do?"

"He picked up a piece of paper and walked away," she said.

"Did you ever see him again that day?"

"No."

"Did he have yellow hair?" Riley asked, smiling.

"No," she said. "It was black, like mine. But short."

Riley dropped his smile. He sat back in disappointment. "Are you sure?" he begged. "Black hair? Was it dark out?"

"No. It was daytime. He had black hair."

"Do you know what a mustache is?" Riley asked.

"Yeah."

"Did he have a mustache?"

"Yeah. And a chin one, too."

"A chin one?" Riley said. "You mean a beard?"

"No. Not a beard," Nikka said touching her chin with her small index finger. "Just on his chin, and the side of his mouth."

Riley nodded and scribbled the word *goatee* into his little notebook. "Was there anything else about him you remember?"

"His arms had pictures on them," she said.

"Pictures," Riley asked staring at his notebook. He looked up at the girl. "Tattoos. He had tattoos on his arms."

"Yeah. Tattoos. Like in mommy's movies."

"Can you think of anything else?" Riley said, reviewing the notes in his little book.

Nikka shook her head. Riley grabbed the doorknob and pulled himself up.

"Well little Nikka. Thank you for your help. You be good, okay. And study hard."

"Okay. Bye," she said, closing the door.

Riley turned and walked down the musty hallway. He reached the elevator just as the bell rang and the doors parted. Before he knew it, Riley found himself standing face to face with a grown-up version of the little girl with whom he had just spoken.

"Excuse me," he said as he slid past her into the elevator. He watched the woman make her way down the hallway, and then the doors to the elevator slammed shut in front of him. Poor little girl, he thought as he pushed the button for the first floor.

During the bouncy elevator ride, Riley considered his next move. Although he had some new information, his theory had pretty much been blown out of the water by the little girl's revelation. *Crap!*

He reached the ground floor and glanced around before walking out of the building. The rhythmic beat of a base drum could be heard in the distance. His white car remained parked underneath the only working streetlight. All appeared clear.

Taking a deep breath, he hurried outside and trotted to his awaiting car, unlocking it along the way using the tiny remote control on his key chain. Once he reached the car, he yanked open the door, plopped into the seat, and slammed the door shut, locking it as quickly as he could. He jammed the key into the ignition, gunned the engine, and then pulled out of the dark lot without haste.

"Black hair and a goatee?" he said out loud. "That's not right."

Chapter 23

Orley clicked off the radio and swallowed the last burning sip of whiskey from a red plastic cup. Although it had already been four days since he had snatched Dr. Sue, he was somewhat surprised the LAPD had allowed the press to report his ransom note on the same day he left it. He figured they would sit on it for a few days before making it public knowledge. *Oh well*, he thought. *It'll be too late for them when they realize what really happened.* He stared at the back bedroom.

Having just finished off the better part of a fifth of Jack Daniel's Whiskey, he was feeling pretty good. He stood up from his recliner, steadying himself on the arm of the gray leather chair, and then made his way to the back bedroom. "Time da have a little fun," he said to himself as he stumbled into the dark room.

He flicked on the light and kicked the wooden base of the bed. Grabbing the bottom side of the wooden platform that held the bed's mattress, he lifted it up to the stops where it remained, despite the fact he was no longer holding onto it.

"Wake up Doctor," he yelled, blinking the tiny woman into view. "Your day of reckoning is almos' here."

Through saucer eyes, Dr. Sue looked up at the slightly swaying man. Panic seized control of her as she could see he was drunk. "What do you want from me now?" she managed to say, unable to hide the fear in her quaky voice.

"You made her go away. Now you're going da get her back," he said.

"Disneyland," Dr. Sue suddenly blurted out. "You're the guy from Disneyland."

"Happiess' place on earth," he said, slurring his s's together so the sentence came out like one long word. Staggering backward into the mirrored wardrobe behind him, he steadied himself with his hand and then stepped back forward to stare at Dr. Sue.

"I'm sorry for whatever you think I did to you," Dr. Sue said.

"Sorry? 's too late for sorry," he said.

"Please," Dr. Sue said. "I'll help you do whatever you want. Just let me *help* you."

Orley stood staring at her, mouth slightly open. "You can't help me. No one can help me. But you're gonna help me get 'em back. Then, you won't be giving any more bad advice."

"What do you mean?" Dr. Sue said, suddenly cold.

"What do I mean?" Orley said loudly. He bent over a little more, holding onto the wall for balance. "I mean…I don't know what I mean." He stood back up, this time using his left hand to steady himself against the back wall. "You made her go away right when I was beginning da win the battle."

Dr. Sue saw a tear drop onto the man's cheek. Gaining strength from his sudden vulnerability, she cleared her throat and asked, "Do you have a name?"

Orley stared at her.

"Okay. Do you have a nickname, something I can call you? Anything?"

"Orley. Everyone calls me Orley," he said softly, swaying slightly.

"Okay, Orley," Dr. Sue said, fighting off the wave of hunger that suddenly washed over her body. "How can I help you?"

Orley jolted out of his trance. He scowled at Dr. Sue. "Don' give me that radio voice bullshit. I'll tell you what you're going da do da help me."

"I'm sorry Orley," Dr. Sue said, cringing at his sudden shift in attitude. She could tell he was unstable. "Do you want me to sign that note for you? You'll have to untie my hands for me so I can sign it, if that's what you want."

"Fuck the note," he yelled. "'s too late for the note. You already had a chance da sign the note." He sniffed and then wiped his left cheek with the back of his right hand.

Dr. Sue recognized she had to change the subject. She needed to get back to the softer man with whom she had been speaking. "What battle were you talking about before, Orley?"

"Wha'," Orley slurred, looking down at Dr. Sue. His world was twirling. "Wha' you talking about?" he said quickly.

"You were talking about winning a battle. What battle?"

"Time da go back da sleep Dr. Sue," Orley said, reaching for the lid. He needed to lie down. His world began to twirl, and he felt like he was going to throw up.

"No Orley. Wait. Please. It's lonely in here."

"I know," Orley smirked. "When I was in Folsom, I had da spend two weeks in the hole once for something I didn't do. It's lonely in the dark. It makes you think. It makes you insane." He stared at Dr. Sue for a few moments.

Folsom? Folsom? Dr. Sue racked her brain. *Nothing.* "What were you in prison for, Orley?" she asked.

"I can't help myself, and no one can help me either," he said.

"Maybe I can help, Orley."

"No one can help me," he said again. "She was beginning da help, but you told her da leave me."

"Who left you, Orley? I've never met your…is it your wife?"

"She called you, and you told her da leave. You gave her bad advice, and now you're going da help me."

Dr. Sue stared at Orley. She continued to rack her brain, trying to figure out what the heck he was talking about. "Does she have a name?" she asked.

"Amy. Her name's Amy, and you told her da leave me."

"Why did I tell her to leave you, Orley? I don't remember an Amy ever calling." She reached deep into her memory. So many calls. So many problems. So many names. There was no way she could remember them all.

"I have a problem," Orley stammered.

"So you've said. What is it? How can I help you?"

"You can't help me. You're too ol' da help me," he slurred.

The name suddenly hit Dr. Sue and she blurted out, "You met Amy in prison, and you knocked her up. You were in there for drunk driving or manslaughter or something like that, and she thinks you're molesting young girls," she said quickly.

"Yes," Orley said softly. "Now you're going da help me get her back." He slammed the lid to the bed, snapped the light off, and staggered out of the tiny room.

Riley sat in front of his computer, sipping at a cup of hot coffee. He wasn't buying the news accounts of a ransom note. Although he had not been privy to the note's exact contents, he was quite certain it probably said something about paying a couple million dollars or she'd be killed. The police were all over it, though. So was the media. He had heard the chief was getting pressure from the governor who was a good friend of Rick Stein. So, it didn't surprise Riley at all they would jump onto the first lead they could find.

Looking at the small clock at the bottom right of his computer screen, he forced his attention back to his current task. For the past six hours he had been reliving the various problems Dr. Sue's callers were pouring out for the world to hear on her radio show. He was searching the show's archives, listening to calls and advice, trying to catch anything, any clue. In his gut, he knew this was neither a random nor a ransom event.

He double-clicked the icon that would allow him to download the previous Wednesday's show. Having already gone through five days' worth of replays, he wanted to get at least a month of them under his belt before moving in another direction. He had an itch that needed to be scratched, but he just wasn't quite sure what that itch was, exactly.

The small window appeared on his monitor advising him the download would be complete in about thirteen minutes. He really needed to get a faster computer. But hey, that was just enough time for him to take a bathroom break, pop downstairs for a snack, and then make his way back up for a few more hours of archived shows.

After ten minutes, he was back in his room. Returning to the chair in front of his computer with a relieved bladder and a plateful of steaming pizza pocket bites, he noticed the download was nearly complete.

He awakened earlier that day feeling a little better than he had when he went to sleep the night before. It was conceivable, he rationalized, the blond-haired man changed his appearance before going to Disneyland or vice versa. Hair color was the easiest thing in the world to alter.

It was the tattoos that worried Riley. The sister of the bodyguard hadn't mentioned tattoos when she talked to him. Surely, that would have been the first thing her brother would have noticed when he went to help the guy.

Of course, he thought. The woman said her brother remembered the man being nicely dressed. It was conceivable the tattoos had probably been covered up if the guy was dressed in a suit. That must have been why Brett was quick to help the guy. He probably looked harmless. A trained bodyguard wouldn't have just stopped for anyone. *Sneaky*, Riley thought.

A tone from the computer announced the download was complete so Riley set the plate onto the desk next to the keyboard, and lining up the cursor arrow with the appropriate icon, he clicked the play button to listen to the show.

Dr. Sue lay in the cramped darkness. Wide awake now, the few minutes she had just spent with the drunk man allowed her to concentrate on something besides the numbing of her hands and the constant ache in her body. Hunger came now in waves, but those waves subsided quickly. She hadn't had a hot flash in some time, and that wasn't exactly disappointing.

Orley, she thought. *His name was Orley.* She made a note to remember to call him by his name whenever she talked to him, to personalize their relationship. A defensive maneuver on her part, she hoped even a small bond might dissuade him from hurting her. She needed to build trust between the two of them. She knew it was a long shot, but she had nothing to lose. It was either try to do something or rot in her little hell-hole.

Dr. Sue had long ago quit struggling against the bindings that drew her wrists together. It had become painfully obvious, early on, that struggling against them only made the straps tighten even more. At first, the panic was maddening when she lost feeling in her hands. But she soon learned when she calmed down and forced herself to relax, blood was allowed to flow back into her fingers as evidenced by the tingling that usually indicated a waking limb.

After fiddling with the straps behind her back, she had determined they were anchored to a hard object that felt to be screwed into the floor. She had initially attempted to unscrew the bolt but discovered, once again, that even slightly rotating her arms caused the straps to cinch tightly. If only she could get her hands out in front of her, she could figure something out that might help her make an escape.

She heard the motorhome's engine kick over. *No*, her mind pleaded, preparing herself the head bouncing that was sure to follow. *Plus, he's drunk!* Tears flooded her eyes uncontrollably.

No! No! No! She heard and then felt the motorhome lurch forward and bounce as it hit something in the road. Feeling her body lift slightly, she floated for a millisecond before slamming into the floor. Once again, she tried to tighten her neck muscles in anticipation, but she was too slow, and the right side of her face slammed onto the wooden surface. *Lift, float, slam. Lift, float, slam.* Her head throbbed in pain, and, despite the pure blackness in which she now lay, she could see little white spots floating in front of her face. She was afraid she was going to die and worried she wasn't going to die at the same time.

"You bastard," she yelled at the top of her lungs. She was sobbing now, her head bouncing off of the hard wooden floor. "You son-of-a-bitch!"

Anger engulfed her. The gnawing feeling of loneliness and the guilty feeling that came from wishing for death vanished. Instead, they were replaced by a seething rage. She decided, right then, she must escape.

Her mind raced, searching for a way out of her misery. Struggling furiously against the straps behind her, she knew it was useless so she forced herself to stop and think. The last thing she needed to do was create an even worse situation by giving herself nerve damage in her hands. Taking a deep breath through her mouth as it still stunk profusely, even though the odors were her own, she forced herself to concentrate. An idea suddenly hit her.

Tucking her knees into her chest, she scooted her rear end up as high as she could toward her face. Her surroundings were tight, but thankfully, she was small. Once she was scrunched up as tightly as she could make herself, she eased her rear end back down between her arms. As soon as her butt passed through the tight opening, she brought her knees up to her chin and then shoved her feet down behind her back through the gap between her arms. Following with her knees, she allowed herself a smile in victory as she found herself lying with her hands now bound in front of her body. A sobbing joy overwhelmed her as she rested her head atop her hands, which had formed into a perfect tiny pillow that helped to soften the blows of each miserable, noisy bump.

"Thank you," she sighed as she was finally able to stop the incessant pounding. "Thank you, thank you, thank you."

After a few minutes, she stopped crying. She wiped her cheeks on the backs of her hands and then used her index fingers to wipe her nose. It was wonderful to be able to wipe the tickle away and finally scratch her cheek.

Thinking about her predicament, she quickly realized the first thing she had to do was practice getting back into the *hands bound behind the back* position. She shuddered to think of what Orley would do if he found her different from the way he had positioned her.

Three sets of ten repositioning exercises, she decided, would help her in both stretching her aching body and also passing time. It would also allow her to get used to quickly slipping back into position once she felt the motorhome come to a stop and shut down.

So, as the huge house on wheels rumbled down some unknown highway, Dr. Sue practiced her repositioning. Finishing her exercises, she lay resting, covered in sweat, but proud of herself for her first small victory.

She took the last sip of water from her drinking tube and then rested her head on her small fleshy pillow. For now she was content with her one victory, but she told herself not to rest on her laurels. She was pretty sure Orley's allusion to her not giving any more *bad advice* was not his way of telling her she should learn from her mistakes. She was certain he planned to silence her tongue, but there was no way she was just going to lie around and let that happen without a fight.

Riley yawned and then looked at his watch. Drawing toward the end of Wednesday's show, he had been able to filter out all of the commercials and fast forward through most of the jabbering Dr. Sue managed to spew throughout the course of her program. When all was said and done, Riley determined Dr. Sue really only dedicated about an hour and twenty-nine minutes of the allotted three hours to taking calls. So, going through each show was not taking him as long as he had originally thought it would.

He picked up his nearly empty coffee mug, and took the last sip of cold coffee. *One more caller*, he thought, and then he'd sneak back down for another cup and something to munch on.

He listened to the last call for that day and then bolted straight up in his chair. Clicking the cursor arrow on the small, backward facing triangle that brought him back to the beginning of the call, he listened again. He scribbled furiously into his notebook. Rewinding the call once more, he looked at his notes as he listened to the caller's metallic voice. His heart started pounding in his chest.

"Relax," he said out loud. "It's probably nothing." He listened to the call one more time, and then exited from the archive folder. "This is it. I know it," he said out loud. "This has got to be it."

He grabbed his notepad, threw on a pair of jeans and a maroon sweatshirt, slipped on some brown Docksider shoes, and bounded down the stairs, holding onto the rail with his left hand while taking the steps two at a time. Once outside, he dashed down the small hill in front of his townhouse to his car that was parked alongside the curb and jumped in. Speeding toward his office, he didn't even notice it was already dark outside. "This is it," he kept saying. "Oh God, please let this be it."

Chapter 24

I must've started men-stating because Uncle Kent is really mad at me. There's blood, but not a lot. There's been blood before, but he was never this mad. He keeps telling me he can't believe I had to start now and we were so close to the big payoff. He slapped me with the front of his hand which still hurt but didn't leave a bruise and then said he didn't care. He wasn't going to miss my special date. And then he hit me again. I'll run away after the special date...

Orley pulled his large rig into the parking lot of a convenience store. He needed a quick shower before driving the short distance to pick up his wife and son. It had been a few days since he'd snatched Dr. Sue, and he hadn't showered since that morning, at his apartment. Hung over and smelling like ass, he definitely needed something to help him snap out of his present funk.

Supplies were getting low too, and he needed gas and fresh water. So he decided he'd jump in the shower before popping into the store to grab some groceries. Then he'd fill the motorhome's tanks. He was going to need a robust supply of food and gas since he didn't know how long he and his family would need to exist in an isolated area while they "worked things out."

Orley had no idea what he was going to do with Dr. Sue once he no longer needed her. After all, she knew his name and enough about his past that it would not be too difficult for the authorities to figure out who he was. She had seen him with dark and blond hair, shaven and bearded, naked and clothed... He knew he'd hosed things up bit. *First things first*, he thought. *I'll deal with her later.*

Parking the motorhome at an isolated corner of the lot, Orley closed the curtains that covered the huge front window. He quickly stripped and then jumped into the small shower that formed the left side of the narrow hallway that led to the back bedroom. Not wanting to use too much of his water supply, he took a quick *Navy* shower, only turning on the water to wet down and then again to rinse the soap from his body.

After the hasty but refreshing wash, he dried himself, pulled on a pair of clean blue jeans and then struggled into a gray sweatshirt. He grabbed his lucky Detroit Tigers baseball cap from atop the cluttered table and cinched it down onto his blond head, glancing approvingly at the image in the small mirror that hung on the wall opposite the shower.

Orley, realizing he had not actually been outside in a few days, opened the door and stepped out into the cool dry air. He took a few deep breaths and was charged by its crispness. The fresh air contrasted greatly with the smell of sewage that wafted through the closed confines of the motorhome.

As he walked toward the convenience store's entrance, he noticed the store doubled as a welcome center for a nearby campground. He made a mental note of the place's location as it looked like something he could use in the future.

"Morning," an elderly woman said from behind a small wooden counter as soon as Orley stepped into the wood-paneled room.

"It's afternoon," Orley replied, walking toward the food section near the back of the store.

"Oops! Staying with us for the night?"

"Naw. Just getting some supplies. Heading up north for the spring and summer."

"Well that sounds wonderful," the woman said with a smile. "If you need anything, just ask."

"Okay," Orley replied. He saw the woman reach for and then answer a phone that had started to ring next to her. As he filled a small red basket with a mix of Spaghetti-Os and Ramen noodles, he listened to the one end of the conversation.

"Okay, yeah we have room tonight," the woman was saying into the phone. "I'll need a credit card number to hold a space for you."

Orley stopped what he was doing and listened.

"Okay, I'm ready," the woman said.

He glanced over at her and noticed she was writing the information onto a slip of paper. "Come on," he whispered. "Come on you old hag. Let's hear it." She didn't let him down.

"All right dear," the old lady said into the receiver. "I got it. Let me read it back to you to make sure I got it right."

Orley heard her read the entire credit card number as well as the expiration date. He wrote the whole thing down onto the back of a receipt that he had dug from his pocket. She even told him the code on the back of the card. He waited for the name.

"Okay, Susan Sage. That's S-A-G-E, right? Okay, I got it. What's that? The card's name is under a Michael Sage. Okay. I got that, too. We'll see you next week. Good-bye dear."

No. Thank you! Orley thrust the receipt into his pocket and walked up to the counter.

"That it?" the woman asked.

"That's it," Orley replied. He paid the woman the required amount of cash and received his change.

"Have a nice day sir," she said, smiling.

"Thank you," Orley said, smiling back. "Thank you very much. I'll need some gas too. Do you have pay at the pump?"

"Sure do."

"Great," he said, grabbing his bag. "Thanks again."

"You're welcome."

Orley quickly made his way back to the motorhome and climbed in. Starting its engine, he pulled the large rig over to the gas pumps. His was the only vehicle present which was fine with him since he had decided not to gag the doctor for the fuel stop.

Ten minutes after jumping from the motorhome to fill the large gas tank, he climbed back inside, started the engine, and then maneuvered his way back toward the highway.

Things were going pretty well, he decided. He glanced at the map and noted the distance he needed to travel. Although he was only about forty minutes from getting his family back, he decided he should wait an extra couple of hours until it was dark before he actually confronted his wife, just in case things got ugly. Plus, he needed to gag the doctor again so she would not make any noise when they arrived at his destination.

The fax machine finally began to purr next to Riley. He took his last warm sip of mocha latte and then tossed the empty green and white paper cup into the tiny wastebasket next to someone's vacant desk. The fax machine beeped indicating it was done printing. Riley snatched the single sheet of paper that sported the California Department of Corrections logo on the top left corner and read the list of twelve names that were displayed about halfway down the computer-generated page.

Taking the sheet back to his glassed-in office, he plopped into his huge leather chair and quickly ran a *Yahoo!* people search on his computer, starting with the first name on the list. The name came up, but it did not fit the bill so he continued down the list until, right before his eyes, the information for which he was searching suddenly appeared.

"Yes," he yelled, raising his arms in a victorious triumph.

He took a huge breath. His heart was pounding with excitement. Snatching up and shaking an empty Starbucks cup that had been setting on his desk from God knows when, he tossed it into his own empty wastebasket and then looked around. *Nothing.*

He needed to do something. He had just cracked the case, but there was nothing for him to do and no one for him to tell...so he just sat there and...did nothing. *What a buzz kill,* he thought.

After a few smiling moments, he told himself to get a grip and come up with a plan. First he had to run home and take a shower. He felt greasy, and he was sure he stunk. He looked at his watch. 7:30. He rubbed his stubbly chin. *A shave,* he thought. *I definitely need a shave.*

Okay, he would go home, stopping by Starbucks on the way, of course. He would grab a shower and a shave, throw on something respectable, and then head back to Parker Center to lay his theory out for the chief.

His eyes snapped to his watch. "Holy crap," he said out loud. *Seven thirty?* By the time he did everything, it would be near midnight. There was no way the chief would still be there at midnight, but he couldn't go now, looking the way he did, like a total slob.

"Crap," he said again. It would have to wait until tomorrow.

Not all bad, he thought. That would allow him time to gather his notes, arrange his thoughts, and make a half-eloquent pitch of his theory. Hopefully, the chief would buy it.

Snatching the faxed memo, he grabbed his car keys and hurried out of his office.

***

Dr. Sue felt the motorhome stop, and then she heard the engine cut off. Heart pounding in her chest, she curled her body up, as she had practiced, and began to squeeze herself back into the uncomfortable position of having her hands behind her back.

She heard the familiar heavy thumping as the footsteps rapidly approached. They seemed to be moving quicker than before. Panic overwhelmed her as she was having trouble getting her feet up through her bound arms. She could hear her heart thundering in her ears as the thumps hurried toward her. Pulling as hard as she could, she finally pushed her feet through the opening between her arms, and her body slid back into position just as the lid popped open. Feeling the sweat beading on her forehead, she blinked the lighted room into focus.

"What's the matter?" Orley asked through squinted eyes. He could tell something wasn't right.

"Where should I start?" Dr. Sue replied, hoping he would not see through her tough-girl façade. She hated to think what he would do to her if he found out she could move around in her cramped little world.

He stared at her for a long moment, and she could feel the sweat dripping off of her forehead.

"You shit again?" he asked.

"No," she said, suddenly feeling flushed. "I had a hot flash. I'm post-menopausal. It passed. I'm also starving. I need something to eat. And I'm out of water."

Orley shook his head. "Naw. You're done eating. I can't change one more of those things."

"How long have I been in here?" she asked.

"'bout two weeks."

Dr. Sue was surprised at the remark. She wondered if he was telling the truth. She had read some books about brainwashing when she was in medical school and knew that disorientation was one of the first goals.

"I'm really hungry. You need to give me food, or I'll die."

Orley shrugged his shoulders. "Not my problem," he said, glancing at the empty water bottle. "You can still have water. You can go a long time with just water. Trust me. I know."

"How? How do you know Orley?" Dr. Sue asked.

"Doesn't matter how I know, does it Doctor?" he snapped back. "I just know. Life in prison isn't very easy. Let's just leave it at that."

"Sorry," Dr. Sue said. She swallowed hard. "What are you going to do with me Orley?" she asked.

"Depends on what you do for me," he said blandly.

"I'll help you Orley. Let me out of here, and I swear I'll help you. I've learned my lesson. I really have."

Orley stared at her for a long time. She appeared small and fragile, lying in a red sport coat and a diaper. She was definitely a looker though, and there was no doubt she was a knockout when she was young. He felt a twinge in his crotch, but it didn't last.

Reaching behind him, he grabbed a role of duct tape from a small desk beneath a covered window and ripped a six-inch strip from the roll.

"What're you going to do with that?" Dr. Sue said, awash in panic.

"Right now, we're eight miles from the middle of nowhere. You can scream all you want, and nobody would hear you. In about an hour, we'll be back in civilization. I can't afford to have you screaming and alerting someone of your presence. So, I have this." He held up the strip of duct tape. "To give me that warm fuzzy. This will ensure you'll keep your big mouth shut."

"Please, no," she said through blurry eyes. The claustrophobic fear of drowning returned, thrusting her into an uncontrollable panic. "I won't yell. I promise." She was serious.

"I wish I could believe you Doctor," Orley said. "I really do. But, it really was your big mouth that got you into this mess."

Orley slowly leaned forward lining the tape up with her thin, pursed lips. Dr. Sue shook her head, rolling it from side to side. Seeing him move toward her, she began to hyperventilate. *I'm going to drown again! I'm going to drown again!*

"Hold still bitch," Orley said, holding the tape a few inches from her rolling head. Letting go of the tape with his left hand, he reached forward to grab her head so he could hold it still, but instead, he cried out in pain.

Dr. Sue felt her teeth sink into the meaty part of his hand, the part between his thumb and his forefinger. She bit down as hard as she could and then held on for dear life as he attempted to jerk his hand from her clinched jaw. Tasting the unmistakable saltiness of blood, she fought back the urge to gag and instead clamped down even harder.

Orley felt the pinching tear in his left hand as he tried to rip it from its snare. The look in Dr. Sue's eyes indicated she had no intention of letting go.

"Let go bitch," Orley said, before reaching up with his right hand and then driving his right elbow as hard as he could into her right temple. He heard a *thump* as her head slammed into the wood, and she immediately unclamped her jaw.

Tiny black spots danced in front of Dr. Sue's face. Confused, her head was suddenly engulfed in a tidal wave of pain that over road every other pain in her body. Trying her best to blink the black spots away, she felt her mouth suddenly close, and then she smelled the gluey plastic odor of the duct tape as it was slapped onto her dizzy cheeks.

Not wanting to vomit, she forced herself to focus on something else. She tried to stare at her captor, but no matter how many times she blinked, she could see no less than three fuzzy figures in her field of view.

Orley ripped another piece of tape from the roll and slapped it onto Dr. Sue's face as well. Satisfied, he jammed his left hand into his right armpit and stared down at the obviously dazed doctor.

"You stupid bitch," he said through deep breaths. "Couldn't leave well enough alone." He took some more deep breaths and then said, "Let's see how thirsty you get now." He reached up with his right hand and threw the lid closed.

Dr. Sue floated in the darkness, the taste of blood dominating her senses. Tiny spinning spots turned from black to white and then slowly disappeared. The smell of the new tape, the dull odor of feces, and the spinning of her world were unbearable. Her head throbbed. She fought the urge to throw up and instead forced herself to relax, recognizing that panic was not going to help the situation at all.

She was a dead woman, and she knew it. But despite her present pain, she recognized the fight had been worth it. It had given her that momentary sense of control she desperately needed. Ignoring the stench and the pain in her head, she inhaled deeply through her nose and forced herself to calm down. She was committed to the fight and vowed not to go down without swinging. She needed to rest and save her strength, though, if she was going to make it out of her predicament alive.

Orley shoved his shaking hand, palm down, underneath the faucet in the motorhome's tiny bathroom and watched the blood drop into the sink from the stinging gash. Her teeth had punctured the skin and tiny pieces of fleshy meat were peeking out of each bite mark. With a shaking right index finger, he painfully pushed those pieces of meat back under the skin where they belonged.

Dizzy, he shut off the water and grabbed a huge wad of toilet paper from the roll that hung near his right leg. He covered the gash with the toilet paper and then applied direct pressure to the wound by squeezing his hand with his other shaking fist. He stood in the bathroom for a few minutes fighting against a slowly growing nausea. It was no use. He yanked open the lid to the toilet and dry heaved into the gaping commode.

"You stupid bitch," he yelled after wiping the drool from his chin with the shoulder of his shirt. He dry heaved once again.

Closing the lid, Orley plopped onto the toilet seat and took a few deep breaths. He ripped another handful of toilet paper from the wall and replaced the blood-soaked wad. The new paper immediately turned red so he squeezed the wound with all of his might.

After a few minutes, he hefted himself up and walked back into the bedroom. Grabbing the roll of duct tape, he used his teeth to get a strip going and then wrapped a long piece around the palm of his hand so it held the red toilet paper in place. After tracing three complete laps around his palm, he ripped the strip from the roll and then tossed the remaining tape onto the bed.

Staggering up to the cab, he jumped into the seat, and started the engine. "We're going to get my family, you stupid bitch," he yelled. "And then I'm going to fucking kill you!"

Chapter 25

"All right Edward, you sure you got it?"

"Yeah Uncle Mickey. I got it."

Eddy stood behind the wooden counter and shooed his uncle away with a thin arm and a flopping hand. "Go," he said. "Don't worry."

Mickey stared at his nephew. Although he knew he was taking a chance, so far Edward had not let him down. But this was the first time he would actually leave him alone to watch the store. Having promised his sister he would make a man out of the youngster, Mickey had no choice but to give him an ounce or two of responsibility. He didn't want to disappoint his little sister, but he was a little uneasy about leaving Edward alone. He hesitated for a few seconds before turning to leave.

"Don't take any more beer," Mickey said as he walked out. "I counted it all. I'll know."

Edward watched his uncle walk out of the store. After counting to sixty, he walked over to a set of glass doors that contained a mix of soft drinks and juices. He scanned the shelves until he saw the beer. *There we go*, he thought, opening the door and snatching a cold, silver can. Popping the top, he sipped at the bitter foam that immediately escaped with a fizz. He squinted at the bitterness and then walked back to the counter where he dropped three dollars into the register. *That ought to cover it.*

He checked out his surroundings. A plethora of merchandise sat all around him, and he planned to take advantage of as much as possible. His uncle had instructed him to "close up at ten," a mere three hours from now. *It shouldn't be too hard to maintain a nice even buzz for three hours*, he thought, relying on the fact not a single soul would enter the store between now and then. He had no idea how his uncle had managed to stay in business for so long. Nobody ever came into the store. Ever. *Oh well*, he thought. *Not my problem.*

He opened the cash register again, and dropped in a twenty-dollar bill. Might as well pay in advance, he thought. That way, he can't blame me for any of the "missing" beer.

Finishing the first can with one last giant swig, he shook away the cold-induced headache, let out a huge burp, and then walked back to the refrigerator, dropping the empty can into the trash bin along the way. *This was going to be a good night.*

As he returned to the counter with a second beer, something outside the store caught his attention. Glancing through the window that took up most of the upper portion of the front door, he watched as a pair of headlights pierced the darkness.

Instinctively, he placed the cold, sweating can onto the small shelf below the cash register and continued to look outside. He saw the headlights proceed through the blackness and into the massive dirt parking lot that dominated the large area behind the small store. Judging the speed of the vehicle, he decided it was not going to stop.

He walked the few steps to the front door and watched as the red taillights disappeared up the narrow dirt trail that led out of the back of the lot and over the low hill directly across from the store.

Edward ran his right hand through his shoulder-length hair and then walked back to the counter. Picking up the can, he took another drink of warming beer. His face was getting numb. He was finally beginning to think clearly.

His uncle had told him about the young lady and her kid that had moved into the cabin last week, right before his arrival. Although he had only seen her once, the quick glance he had gotten had told him she was someone with whom he would like to know intimately, at least once or twice before he had to go back to college. *She obviously puts out. How else do you explain the kid?*

After finishing the second beer, Edward made his way back to the glass doors, once again dropping the dead can into the trash along the way. He fished out a third beer. *Yeah, things were becoming very clear indeed.*

Returning to the counter, he looked at his watch. He could stay in the store until ten o'clock, absolutely sure no customers would stop by, and then close up like he was supposed to. Or, he could pound a couple more beers and then maybe check to see if the young lady up the road needed any neighborly assistance. The right answer became apparent to Edward after he finished his third beer.

The road to Orley's destination was surprisingly dark. He had only been here once, and that had been during the daytime. He had no idea it was so sparse. He did see more than a handful of lights sporadically twinkling around him though, and he was grateful he had decided to gag the doctor before making his way up here.

Orley recognized the long, dirt driveway. He decided to park perpendicular to it so the main door was facing the tiny home. That way, if things got ugly, he could still get his wife and son into the coach without much notice from someone who may happen to pass by at an inopportune time. He pulled the motorhome up so it blocked the end of the driveway and then brought the large rig to a halt.

Looking down at his throbbing left hand, he cursed the little bitch for having done this to him. He climbed from the driver's seat and walked back to the washroom so he could change the dressing one more time.

After painfully unpeeling the tape, he separated the sticking toilet paper from the wound. Although the bleeding had stopped, a horseshoe-shaped mound of torn, purple flesh had formed between his thumb and forefinger.

Fighting overwhelming nausea, he forced himself to look away from the gruesome gash. Although he had never really gotten sick looking at other people's misery, for some reason, he could not stand to see himself hurt. *Relax*, he thought. *It'll be covered up soon.*

Orley quickly dressed the wound, and once again wrapped a long piece of duct tape around his palm to keep the toilet paper in place. When finished, he clicked off the small bathroom light and walked back into the coach.

He grabbed the nearly empty fifth of Jack Daniel's Whiskey from the small kitchen sink and unscrewed the cap. A long pull from the bottle and the warm burning liquid chased the nausea away, and Orley felt a little better. He wiped his mouth with the back of his good hand, replaced the cap, and then set the glass bottle back onto the small cluttered table.

"Here we go," he said.

He pushed the door open and stepped down into the cool night air. Taking a deep breath, he zipped his jacket and propped the collar up to protect his neck from the cold breeze. Tugging on the brim of his dark blue baseball cap, he walked up the long, dark, dirt drive.

By the time he reached the front door, he was out of breath and craving another drink of whiskey. Heart pounding in his chest, he wondered why he was nervous. He took a deep breath, going over what he had rehearsed in his head during the day's long drive. Satisfied, he withdrew his right hand from his coat pocket and knocked on the thick wooden door.

***

Amy Price broke from her trance when she heard the knock. She jumped from the couch, eyes darting around the tiny cabin. Looking at her watch, she saw it was eight fifteen. She must have dozed off after the long drive to the bank and back. Panic engulfed her as she wasn't expecting anyone. She shook the drowsiness from her head.

"Who's that Mom?" Joel asked as he emerged from the bedroom.

Amy looked at him through wide scared eyes. "I don't know honey. Go hide under the bed. Don't come out until I tell you."

She watched her small son dart back into the room. A second series of knocks froze her in place. She could barely see through the throbbing tears in her narrowing eyes. *How could he know I was here?* she thought. She heard herself sniff and wondered if the sound carried through the wooden door that hung a mere five feet away.

The next knock, this time harder, forced her into action. Dashing into the small kitchen, she withdrew a large knife from one of the drawers. Holding it in her right hand behind her back, she made her way to the door. He heart was pounding in her chest. With her shaking left hand, she grasped the small, brass handle, took a big breath, and then exhaled. "Who is it?"

Orley knocked one last time. He was about to turn and walk back down the hill when the door suddenly opened.

"Oh my God," Amy's mom said when she saw the clean-shaven man standing on her porch.

"Hi Ma," he said, smiling. "Is Amy here?"

Amy's mother tried her hardest not to cry. Through a large lump in her throat and tearing eyes she managed to say, "She's not here Orlando. She came by last week and then left."

"Where'd she go?"

"I don't know. She didn't say."

Orley stared at his wife's mother. Although not a spitting image, the two were definitely related. Her mother had the same tiny nose and cheeks that made them both look much younger than their actual ages.

"Can I come in Ma?" he said. "I'm not leaving until you tell me where she is. I know you know. I'm not going to hurt her. I just want to talk to her. I want her back. Monterey is not exactly close, you know. I've driven a long way to at least talk to her."

Linda Nicholes stared at her son-in-law for an extended moment. She wanted to scream for the police, but she knew it would do no good. She wished she had not opened the door.

"Okay. Come in," she said. "Do you want something to drink?"

Orley stepped into the warm house and closed the door behind him. "No thanks," he said. "Smells like you started smoking again. So much for New Year's resolutions."

"No one's perfect," Linda said.

"Look Ma, I just want to know where she is, so we can talk this out."

"You swear you're not going to hurt her?" Linda asked.

Orley withdrew his hands from his coat pockets and put them out in front of his body.

"I swear. I just wanna talk," he said and then quickly lowered his duct-taped left hand.

"What happened?"

"Nothing," he said, jamming his left hand back into its pocket. "Cut it changing a tire on the motorhome on the way up here. Didn't have a bandage."

"You know," Linda said, "when she said she left you, I wasn't exactly angry."

Orley could feel his blood begin to boil. "I don't really like you either," he said, forcing himself to calm down.

Linda walked to the phone and picked it up. "If I tell you where she went, will you leave?" she asked.

"Yep," Orley said, nodding his head.

"She told me not to tell you."

"She told me she loved me."

"If you don't leave, I'll call the police."

"Just tell me where she is. I swear. I'm not going to hurt her. I want my son back. I want my wife back. They're all I have left."

Linda felt a tear drop onto her cheek. She wanted to believe him. She really did. "She went to Utah to see a friend from high school."

"Where in Utah?"

Linda stared at Orley. She flinched when he shouted the question again.

"Green River," she said quickly.

"Who's she seeing?"

"I don't know," Linda said.

"Who's she staying with?" Orley yelled.

Linda dialed the operator with a shaky finger. Orley lunged for her, yanking the phone from her hand. He slammed it down onto the receiver and grabbed his mother-in-law by both arms.

"Just tell me," he yelled, shaking her. "I don't want to hurt anyone, but you know how I get when I'm mad."

"I don't know," Linda cried. "I swear. She didn't tell me."

Orley stared into his mother-in-law's startled eyes. He squeezed her tiny arms as hard as he could until she cried out in pain. Letting her go, he walked back to the front door.

"Green River, Utah," he said, looking over his left shoulder. "Okay. But if she's not there, I'm coming back here to get you." He yanked open the front door and stormed out into the dark air.

Linda watched him slam the door. Bringing a shaking hand up to her mouth, she sobbed uncontrollably. After a few minutes, she took two deep breaths to compose herself. Arms crossed in front of her heaving chest, she rubbed at the pain in her upper arms and then walked toward the phone in the kitchen.

Outside, Orley took a few angry steps down the driveway and into the darkness before darting back up from where he came. Grateful she did not have a dog, he made his way in the darkness around to the side of the house.

When he was inside his mother-in-law's home, he had noticed a small window in the kitchen that was slightly ajar. He followed the side of the house until he stood next to that open window. He could hear his mother-in-law sobbing as well as the unmistakable sound of a Bic lighter attempting to light. The clicking sound stopped, and then he smelled the familiar odor of tobacco smoke as it drifted out through the opening next to his head. He suddenly craved a cigarette.

"Yes, information," he heard his mother-in-law say. "I need the number for Mickey's Mart in Green Valley, California. Thanks. Yes, could you please dial that for me? Thank you." Orley heard his mother-in-law sniff and then cough. He really needed a cigarette and a shot of whiskey.

"Shoot," he heard his mother-in-law say. He was confused until he realized she had probably gotten an answering machine. He heard her say rather quickly, "Mickey. It's Linda Nicholes, Amy's mom. I need you to get a message to her, quickly. Tell her Orley was here, and I told him she was in Green River, Utah. He has the motorhome. He hurt me, but I'm okay. Just scared. Call me here if you want me to come down." She passed him the number. "Thanks, Mickey. Watch over my girl and grandson for me. Talk to you later. Bye."

Seething, he heard her hang up the phone. *That bitch*, he thought. *She'll pay for this.* He was about to go knock on the window when he heard her suddenly say, "Operator. Get me the police. I want to file a complaint against my son-in-law..."

Not needing to hear anything more, he quickly ran down the long driveway to his motorhome. He was well outside of the boundaries of his probation. The last thing he needed was to be stopped by a cop and arrested for something as minor as that.

"Bitch," he whispered. He would deal with his mother-in-law soon enough.

After sprinting to the motorhome, he yanked open the door and then jumped into the seat. Gunning the engine, he tore off as quickly as the large motorhome would take him into the dark night. He wasn't sure if the cops would actually look for him, but he didn't want to risk it. *Looks like more back roads to Green Valley, wherever the hell that is.*

After a few moments, he began to calm down. Everything was still okay. *Just a little bump in the road*, he thought.

He decided to head south for a few hours before finding somewhere to stop for the night. Plus, he needed to grab some cash from an ATM. He was getting a little low. Then he would find out where the hell Green Valley was located and revise his plan. He was still in control. Everything would be fine.

Edward staggered back down the dirt road toward the market. Things had not gone very well. As he had expected, the woman with the kid was a hammer, and he was surprised to find out she was actually twenty-six years old. She looked seventeen. He'd never bagged an older woman before. That thought alone made him excited.

Before leaving the cabin, he managed to invite her to his bonfire party at the South Portal Campground, just up the road. He promised her it would be fun. A little booze. A little dope. A little bonfire. She had not exactly said *no*, and he still had a few days to try to schmooze her into going with him. He was convinced he could seal the deal. *How can anyone resist a stud like me?*

When he got back to Mickey's, he opened the door and then realized he had forgotten to lock it when he left. He made a quick, dizzy survey. Nothing seemed to be missing. Checking the register, he verified the correct amount of money was still there. Things appeared to be okay. There's no way his uncle would know he had been gone.

A blinking red light on the phone's answering machine caught his attention.

"Crap," he said. Some dude was supposed to call about a delivery for the next day. He had totally forgotten about it. Edward stared at the blinking light. His uncle was going to be pissed. He had specifically instructed Edward not to miss that specific call.

Wait, he thought as an idea popped into his head. *Plausible deniability.*

He saw the light stop blinking after he hit the delete button. There we go. No message. No call. No evidence of a call. *I'll just deny anyone called.* No evidence, no conviction. *Not bad for a pre-law undergrad.*

Satisfied, Edward glanced at his watch. Nine forty-two. He walked over and grabbed a six-pack from the glass doors. His uncle wouldn't mind if he closed a little early. No one had come all night, and no one was going to come. He'd just tell his uncle he had stayed until ten like he had promised. Nobody would know the difference. Plus, he was starting to lose his buzz.

He grabbed the six-pack and walked back outside, turning off the light switch and locking the front door behind him. Pulling a can of beer from the pack, he popped open the top and sipped at it as he walked to his uncle's car. He pondered how he was going to convince the hottie at the end of the road she needed to go with him to the bonfire on Friday night. He needed to bag her, at least once, before he went back to Yale.

Chapter 26

Dr. Sue's spinning world finally slowed into a painful reality. She had hoped to be waking from a nightmare, but instead she realized the utterly horrific events of the previous night had all been hideously real. Although it was pitch black in her confined area, she could tell she was unable to open her right eye. Her head was throbbing, and she could smell the unmistakable odors of urine and blood through her unobstructed left nostril.

Disturbing images appeared in her mind. She tried to shake them away, but they would not leave. Her groin hurt, and her anus burned. She realized her diaper was missing. As the horrible visions flashed in her head, she forced herself to not cry. She didn't want to suffocate again, but it was impossible to block the images as the nightmare flashed into her head once more.

She recalled being ripped from her darkness when the lid to her world suddenly rose. She could see Orley standing over her, yelling at her, but she couldn't for the life of her understand what the heck he was saying. It was obvious he'd been drinking, and he was yelling loudly. All she could decipher was, "the bitch took all my money. The bitch took all my money."

Then he began to slap her repeatedly, his hand, wrapped in duct tape, holding her own duct-taped head. He slapped her over and over, until her world went numb.

When she felt like she was going to pass out, she suddenly felt his full weight move on top of her. She struggled against him at first, but she was weak, confused, small. He managed to bend her legs up so that her knees were next to her ears, and her arms, still tethered to the floor, were crushed beneath the weight of their two bodies. He sat, his back toward her, on her hamstrings, and at that point, she teetered on the verge of suffocation, her one tiny, unclogged nostril barely providing enough air. Had she actually died then and there, she would not have had to endure the next string of horrifying events, but unfortunately, she had not been so lucky.

Heart in her throat and tears in her eyes she could still vividly feel the cold, hard, glass bottle that he jammed into her vagina. Over and over, he drove it into her, and she screamed, her voice muffled by the duct tape, a scream that, had it been loosed, would have gurgled with bitter bile.

The visions came in patches. Black and gray. His broad tattooed back in front of her. Her one good eye unable to provide depth, making it seem like he was a million miles away. But the reality had been he sat on top of her and used the whiskey bottle to do what he could not do with his own penis. He violated her repeatedly, and then when the pain became unbearable, he removed it from her vagina and stuffed it into her anus. He rammed it in so deep she was sure he had drawn blood. After he finished, he climbed off of her, and then he urinated on her.

At some point, she had become disassociated with her body. A self-defense mechanism perhaps, it was as if she had been sitting there, outside of herself, watching the gruesome scene unfold before her one good eye. Improbably, she could still hear and feel the gnarled, terribly hard bottle as it entered and exited her body, and the pain was unlike anything she had ever experienced in her life. But, for some reason, she couldn't look away. She sat, forced to watch it all play out, simultaneously, in that detached state, and that made it even more unbearable and utterly horrifying. She watched herself scream in muffled agony while her mind's voice pleaded for him to stop, and after an eternity, he finally did.

Now, thankfully, she found herself lying in darkness. She knew it was futile to try to stop herself from crying so she allowed herself to break down and sob, a nonstop pool of mucus pouring from her one unclogged nostril.

Dr. Sue had never been raped, but she was a doctor, and she had provided help to many women who had. She thought she had a good grasp of what they had endured, but she now realized she didn't have a clue.

Before now, she could only attempt to feel their frightened pain, their unceasing anxiety, their pure horror of having endured such a horrific event. Now, she realized none of the terrible scenarios she attempted to simulate in her mind were even close to what she had just experienced. She felt dirty, lying naked, covered in urine and sweat and blood. She felt weak, insignificant, and disgustingly small. It was far worse than anything she could have ever imagined, and she knew it would haunt her for the rest of her life.

It's not my fault, she kept repeating to herself. *I was just doing my job... I was helping people... I didn't ask for this. He's the evil one, not me*, but she found herself doubting the thoughts, and she couldn't understand why.

A series of questions stormed her cloudy mind. *Why am I here?* she asked herself. *Why couldn't I have been just a normal person, with a normal life and a normal job? Why did I need to be on the cutting edge? Did I really ever help anyone? If anything, it made me feel good when I proved someone wrong, and that was not how it was supposed to be. Why should I feel good knowing other people were miserable?*

But then she caught herself. *No. I was helping people*, she thought. She forced herself to concentrate on the positive. *I never told people what to do unless they asked...I offered advice...They called because they had gotten themselves into a mess and needed help getting out...It wasn't my fault...I didn't put them there...I didn't tell them to call...I provided them with options, but it was ultimately up to them to extricate themselves...It was up to them...It wasn't up to me.*

And that's when it hit her. *It's up to me!* She needed to get *herself* out. She needed to escape. No one else was going to help her. She could either give-up, wither away, and die, or she could fight back and at least try to escape. It was painfully obvious to her unless she found a way to get out on her own, she was not leaving the motorhome alive, not after what he had just done to her.

She swallowed as best she could and then squeezed her eyes together. She would not go down without a fight. She was determined to live, and if she was going to die, it would not be in a shit-stinking box.

Orley felt bad. He had been out of control, and he definitely crossed the line. There had been no physical pleasure at all. None. He hadn't even been able to get himself off when he was done. Glancing over at the empty whiskey bottle that sat on the small shelf next to the bed, he reached over and knocked it to the ground, and then he sat up slowly, the hangover making his head throb.

Throwing his feet over the side of the bed, he leaned forward and rested his head in his hands. The room smelled of urine and blood. He could hear a muted sobbing coming from beneath him. He plucked the whiskey bottle from the floor and then set it onto the tiny desk that sat opposite the end of the bed.

Standing up and bracing himself against the wall, he lifted the bed and then winced at the sight before him.

"I'm sorry Doctor," he said, relieved to see she was actually alive. "I was out of control last night. I'm sorry."

Dr. Sue blinked her one eye into focus. Her mouth was still taped shut so she couldn't talk. She sniffed loudly instead, flinching at the stinging pain in her right nostril.

"I'm going to take that tape off Dr. Sue," Orley said. "If you bite me, it's going right back on though. Understand?"

Dr. Sue nodded, thrown by his sudden tenderness.

Orley reached forward and grabbed a corner of the tape. "This may hurt a bit," he said as he quickly ripped the tape from her skin.

Dr. Sue took a deep breath through her mouth and let out a tiny whimper. She grasped the drinking tube with her teeth and took a long sip of warm water before sniffing loudly again. She tasted warm coppery blood as an intense pain dominated her right nostril.

"You *raped* me," she said softly.

"I said I was sorry."

"You raped me!" she yelled.

"Technically, Jack Daniels raped you," Orley said. "I just introduced you two."

Dr. Sue stared at him.

"Don't look at me like that. I said I was sorry, okay? I can't turn back time. If I could, it wouldn't be to fix this. I have other things I'd like to undo. All I can say now is sorry."

"I wish I could forgive you," Dr. Sue said. She saw Orley staring at her naked waist, and she suddenly felt embarrassed. "I'm cold. Could you put a diaper on me, please?"

Orley grabbed one of the jumbo-sized slip-on diapers from a pack that sat on the floor next to the bed and slid it onto Dr. Sue. "I barely remember last night," he said, smirking. "Did I piss on you?"

"You did more than that, you bastard. I'm glad you think this is funny."

Orley shook his head. "I guess it wasn't that funny for you, was it?" he said. "Once again. Sorry." He paused a few moments before saying, "But, you'll be happy to know we're headed back down south. Back to good old L.A."

"Can I ask where we are now?"

"Sure," Orley said after pondering the question. "We're a few hours south of Monterey. We're going to a place called Green Valley, near Magic Mountain. That's where Amy and Joel are. I'm not sure exactly where their place is though so we'll have to find it. But that shouldn't be too tough."

"What are you going to do with me?"

Without pausing, Orley said, "After you help me, I'm going to kill you and dump you in a hole in the desert. I can't have you talking to the cops. They'll send me back for sure now."

The intense fear of death and the matter-of-factness of Orley's statement turned her ice cold. Through a giant lump in her throat, Dr. Sue managed to ask, "Did you take pleasure in raping me last night?"

"No. I already told you. I like little girls. I can't help it. Not too young though. Just so they're old enough to have no hair down there. You know," he said, pointing toward Dr. Sue's diaper.

"You're married," she said. "You have a son."

"Yeah, I know," Orley said. "It's weird. It used to work with her. She looks really young. I had her shave her snatch and everything. Bald as a porn star. Worked for a while, then nothing. So then I went elsewhere."

"Elsewhere?"

Orley stared at her. "Don't look so surprised, Doctor. We're everywhere. We know where to get it. We know how to get it. We know who has it. It's easy. The internet makes it real easy. It's out there. You wouldn't *believe* how it's out there. I never hurt any of them though. They all volunteer their services. Plus," Orley said, raising his left duct-taped index finger, "I always use a condom."

Dr. Sue wondered if she was in a dream, no, a nightmare. How could someone be so nonchalant about what happened last night or about molesting little girls?

"There is help for you," Dr. Sue said. "You can get help. *I* can help you."

"You *are* going to help me, Dr. Sue."

"I mean real help."

"Yeah. Real help. You're going to *really* help me." Orley stood and grabbed the duct-tape roll. "Okay, now listen," he said. "I'm going to put this back on you. If you bite me, you're getting old Jack Daniels again."

Dr. Sue glanced at the whiskey bottle that was resting on the desk behind him. She thought she saw a tint of blood around the rim. "Okay," she said. "I won't bite."

"If you're good, I'll take the tape off tomorrow for the last time. I need some relief tonight though, if you know what I mean. I can't have you jaw-jacking back here while I'm doing my thing."

Dr. Sue began to panic. "What do you mean?"

"You're old, Doc. You just don't do it for me." He reached forward and slapped two pieces of duct tape onto her protesting mouth. As if reading her mind, he looked into her sad left eye and said, "They like it Doc. Trust me." With that, he slammed the lid.

"Chief Bruggeman?" the metallic voice said from a small box next to his telephone. "Howard Thorsen from the radio station is here with a reporter from the *L. A. Times.*"

"Reporter?" the chief said into the box.

"Yes, sir. A Mr. Riley."

"Great," Chief Bruggeman mumbled. "Send 'em in." He sat back in his chair and sighed.

"Chief," Howard said, nodding toward the sitting police officer. Riley followed him, smiling brightly. "I couldn't convince Rick Stein to join us. He wanted to stay home with his son. He's not taking this whole thing too well. What do you expect, I guess."

Chief Bruggeman didn't stand. He offered the two men seats by motioning toward two empty chairs in front of his desk with a sweeping right hand. Taking their cue, Howard and Riley each sat down.

Riley noticed a perceptible awkwardness in the atmosphere of the rather large office. He cleared his throat and then sniffed loudly. It seemed like an appropriate thing to do. As tiny prickles of sweat formed on his forehead, he wondered if this was a good idea.

Chief Bruggeman leaned forward and stared back and forth at the men seated in front of him. "The only reason I am doing this is out of a favor for Mr. Stein," he said, fixing his attention on Howard.

"Okay," Howard said, withering beneath the chief's intense stare. "Mr. Riley here has some interesting information about the case sir." Swallowing, he looked over his right shoulder at Riley and nodded. "Go ahead."

Riley glanced at Howard and then at the chief. He could feel his legs shivering in spite of his sweating, and he could think of a thousand other places he would rather be than in the office in which he now found himself. Suddenly doubting his own theory despite his rock solid information, he told himself to get a grip.

"Well Chief," Riley said, "I heard about the ransom note and the homosexual community activist angle, but to me it just doesn't add up. I mean, they've always been vocal in the past, but this…well, I mean, they've never really resorted to kidnapping or extortion."

"This is your expert opinion Mr. Riley," the chief said sarcastically.

"Well, yeah Chief. I guess." He cleared his throat again and then said, "Chief, I've been doing some investigating on my own you know. Things just didn't add up. And, well, I have a different angle on it."

"This should be good," the chief said with raised eyebrows and pursed lips.

"Okay," Riley said. "Just follow me here for a minute. Dr. Sue gives advice to people for a living. I mean they call in and ask her for her advice, and she gives it to them. Well, what if she gave someone some advice that…you know…wasn't so good. What if she told someone to do something, and someone else didn't like that advice, and that other person is out for revenge to get the first person so that second person kidnapped Dr. Sue…"

Riley was really beginning to sweat now. As he rambled, he heard how ridiculous he sounded, and he wanted to dash out of the office as fast as he could. He saw the chief staring at him and noticed one eyebrow had actually, during the explanation, risen slightly higher than the other. Nothing else on the chief's face had changed. Just the eyebrow. So he focused on that eyebrow, praying for someone or something to make him stop babbling.

Thank God Howard came to his rescue. "Chief, I think what Mr. Riley is getting at is…"

Chief Bruggeman leaned forward and interrupted Howard. "Mr. Thorsen, let me fill you in a little bit on our friend Mr. Riley here, if I may."

"Go right ahead sir," Howard said quickly. Who was he to tell the chief what he could and couldn't do?

"Okay. You see Mr. Thorsen, old Mr. Riley here wanted to be a cop a long time ago. He wanted to be a part of the long blue line. Only, he couldn't make it through the academy. Couldn't handle the pressure, I guess. For whatever reason, he washed out. A lot of 'em do.

"Well, good ol' Mr. Riley here decided instead to become a reporter, I guess, like he was when he was in the Army, writing for the old *Stars and Stripes*; isn't that right, Mr. Riley? Didn't think I knew that, did you?"

Riley nodded his head.

"Well I do," the chief continued. "Mr. Riley here decided to serve the community in a different manner. He decided to report the news. Let the people decide. You know, put it all out there. Only, Mr. Riley wasn't happy just reporting the news. He felt he needed controversy. Muddy the waters a little. Couldn't rely on his writing skills so he needed to create little messes, to draw from his inadequacies, I guess.

"We have a fine detective on our force. A detective Patricia Marx. Investigates child kidnappings and child rapes. In fact, she was involved in a shooting 'bout a week ago with a suspected kidnapper. Killed him right after he shot her in the shoulder, I believe.

"Well it seems Mr. Riley here had a thing for Detective Marx. They were in the same academy class. He got in her good graces. Got pretty serious, so she thought. One day, good ol' Mr. Riley here decided to do an exposé on women in the police force. Show how they impact the community. Did a pretty intimate interview with Detective Marx. Asked some real personal questions and received some pretty candid answers. She trusted him, you know. They were a thing.

"Well Mr. Riley here decided to muddy the waters a little bit. Build some controversy, since I guess his writing ability, well, sucks. He put a huge spin on the story. Maybe you read it a few months back about quotas in the LAPD and how women had actually brought down the quality of police officers in our community. Went over like a fart in church, huh, Mr. Riley?"

"More like a turd in a punch bowl," Riley said squeamishly.

The chief continued without smiling. "Now, I heard the only reason Mr. Riley here was not fired was because of that story he broke about the AIDS vaccine a couple of years ago. National story. Won a big award and all. Made him, I guess, untouchable."

"I thought I recognized your name," Howard said, looking at Riley.

Riley shrugged back.

"So you see, Mr. Thorsen. Good old Mr. Riley is not too welcome around here and neither is his opinion, or did he forget to mention that to you? Why do you think he asked you to come along? For the company? I think he's using you like he's used a bunch of other people to, you know, make a name for himself.

"Now. If you two will excuse me. I have an investigation to oversee. For your information, Mr. Riley, we got another ransom note and a key to a hotel room up near San Jose. The FBI sent some agents to take a look, and they went into the room and found a red skirt belonging to Dr. Sue and another note asking for three million dollars to be sent to an account. The person who left the note paid for the room with a visa card. We tracked the number to someone in the L. A. area. The FBI's hostage rescue team and the LAPD SWAT team are en route as we speak. So you see, we have solid leads and are on the verge of solving this crime. We do *not* need your help Mr. Riley. Good-bye."

Howard stood quickly and so did Riley.

"Sorry to bother you sir," Howard said, embarrassed at having just wasted the chief's time.

"Just telling you the facts Mr. Thorsen," the chief said smiling. "Just telling you the facts."

Howard followed Riley out of the office. He heard the door close behind them. The two men nodded at the pretty blonde-headed secretary who sat with a smug look from behind a rather large desk just outside of the chief's office. The next thing Howard knew, he was outside of the small office and standing in a linoleum-tiled hallway.

"Thanks for the heads-up," Howard said, rubbing his sweating head. "That was a complete waste of time."

Riley spun around and looked down at the man. "Look, Howard. I know I'm right. You've got to believe me. These buffoons are not going to get your boss back. They're chasing shadows here."

Howard looked up at Riley, and Riley could see the man was confused and upset.

"Why didn't you give me a heads-up about you and the chief? Would've been nice to know the odds going in."

"You're right," Riley said. "I should have told you. I'm sorry. I'm sorry for a lot of things I've done. Unfortunately, they're *all* coming to roost right now."

"I wish I could feel sorry for you," Howard said.

"Don't feel sorry for me Howard. I've done this to myself. But if you stick with me on this one, I *know* we'll find Dr. Sue. I just know it. What I have is solid, and you know it too. Or you wouldn't be here."

Howard rubbed his cooling face with his pudgy left hand and then shook his jowly head. "Ah, I don't know what to think. Even if you're right, what're we going to do?"

Riley took a deep breath and put a hand on each of Howard's shoulders. "Look Howard. I know you don't know me from Adam. Hell, for all you know, I could be a total nut. For all *I* know at that. But the same as with that vaccine story, my gut is telling me I'm right. You've *got* to believe me." Riley let his arms fall from Howard's shoulders. He ran his fingers through his own blond hair and said, "I know what I have to do. I should have done this a while ago. Howard, I need you to trust me, despite what the chief just said."

Howard looked up at the reporter. For some reason he believed the gangly man whom he had only met for the second time this morning. "You're certain," he said, staring into Riley's face.

"Completely," Riley replied, smiling.

Howard sighed. He had no other choice. Just by his being with Riley, he knew he had lost any graces he had previously held with the chief. He took a deep breath and then nodded his head. "Okay," he said. "What now?"

"What now? Well, how's a mocha latte sound for starters?"

"Sounds okay I guess."

Riley smiled and nodded toward the end of the long hallway. "Come on. I'll buy. There's a place just down the road."

The two men walked down the hallway and then hurried into an awaiting elevator just before its doors closed behind them. Riley heard Howard sigh. He looked down at the shorter man.

"Trust me. It'll be all right. I swear."

Chapter 27

Uncle Kent made me wear the scratchy dress again. He shaved me. I needed to be extra smooth. This was the big payday, he told me. We were finally in the big league. I walked from the back of the car to a huge motorhome and knocked on the door. It was really big and really nice, until the man opened the door. It smelled really bad. I could tell by the way he looked at me I was in trouble...

A casual observer would not have thought to look twice at the UPS truck as it stopped in front of one of the many beige stucco houses. It was, after all, a typical suburban neighborhood. Why should there not be a UPS truck there in the middle of the morning? The "driver" looked the part too. Brown shirt, brown shorts, brown socks pulled up to his knees, and a nice pair of brown shoes. The only thing the casual observer might have noticed, if he or she had really cared to look closely, would have been the tiny, clear wire that spiraled its way from the driver's dark sunglasses and into his right ear.

The driver stepped from the truck and grabbed a long, cardboard box from the seat next to him. Glancing around the neighborhood, he noticed a large amount of cars parked parallel to the curb up and down the street. Satisfied, he made his way quickly toward the house.

Upon reaching the door, he found himself suddenly flanked on both sides, by two pair of dark figures wearing black jumpsuits and gas masks. All four had matching submachine guns, and had the driver been able to see through their dark goggles, he imagined he would have seen the same eager look of relaxed anxiety he knew was being blocked by his own sunglasses.

He rang the bell once and waited. The door had a line of four small windows at about eye level, high enough for him to see into the foyer. He reached down and gave the pair of figures who were crouched to his right a thumbs-up as he saw a tired-looking man walk slowly toward the door. The FBI agent smiled at the man as he approached, but the man did not smile back.

As soon as the front door opened, the four dark-clad figures burst into the house, guns at the ready.

"Freeze! FBI!" the driver shouted as he followed the four men into the house. He grabbed the startled man by the collar of his light blue robe and pulled him to the floor, placing his knee on the man's neck.

"What's going on?" the guy managed to wheeze. "What do you want?"

"Where is she Mr. Sage?" the driver shouted. "Where's Dr. Sue?"

The last thing Patty Marx thought she would see when she opened her door was Riley and a chubby bald man standing on her front porch. "What the hell do *you* want, and who the hell are *you*?" she said, squinting in the noon sunlight.

"Hi Patty. This is Howard Thorsen, Dr. Sue's producer. Can we come in and chat?" Riley wore his most sincere smile. He hoped she would buy it.

"Why?" she said, still squinting.

"I need your help babe."

The two men flinched as the door slammed shut in front of them.

Riley banged on the door. "Come on Patty. Just hear us out. Look, I'm sorry okay? I'm printing another story in the paper, and then I'm resigning. I shouldn't have done that to you. You trusted me, and I used you. I let you down, and I understand why you hate me. Please. Open the door. I think I know who kidnapped Dr. Sue. Chief Bruggeman…"

The door slowly opened in front of the two men. Riley smiled at Patty again. "Look, the chief wouldn't hear us out. He tossed us from his office. They're on a wild goose chase. I've got evidence…well, I mean, I've got an idea. It makes sense, though. Just give us ten minutes. Please. Just ten minutes."

After an uncomfortably long pause, Patty stepped aside and motioned for the two to enter by sweeping her arm much the same way the chief had done earlier that morning.

"You look good," Riley said as he walked by.

"Cut the shit Riley. I'm still pissed at you. I'm only doing this because…hell, I don't know why I'm doing this. How do you do, Howard is it? I'm Patricia Marx. Everyone calls me Patty." She slowly raised her left arm to adjust her glasses, wincing slightly. "Sorry. Shoulder's still kind of sore I guess."

"Nice to meet you Detective. It *is* Howard. Howard Thorsen. Like Riley said, I'm Dr. Sue's producer." Howard took Patty's hand and noted the firmness of her grip as well as the calluses on her palms at the base of each of her fingers.

"Why don't you guys have a seat? I made a pot of coffee. I've also got some juice, water, Diet Pepsi. Beer's all gone."

"No thanks," Howard said.

"I'm fine," Riley chimed in. For some reason, he felt like a dork.

Patty led the two men into the small family room where she fell into the overstuffed recliner. Riley and Howard each took their places on the matching sofa that sat directly across from her. The three stared at each other until Riley finally broke the silence.

"I'm serious what I said out there. I'm quitting. The chief pretty much laid it all out today. He was right-on. I'm an idiot. I shouldn't have done what I did. I really am sorry Patty. I truly am."

Patty stared at Riley. She wanted to believe him, but she knew better. "Whatever," she said. "It's in the past. Let's talk about now. What evidence do you have, and why do you need *me* to help *you*?"

Dr. Sue was exhausted. She could feel herself growing weaker, which she attributed to a lack of food and the loss of blood. The waves of hunger had ceased who knows how long ago, and the hot flashes seemed to have ceased as well, making her existence bearable.

But emotionally, she was drained. She could feel her inner will beginning to wane. Death suddenly did not seem so bad. At least the pain and the wretched odor and the overwhelming bouts of claustrophobic anxiety would leave her as the nightmare would finally end.

But images of her son and her husband held back the temptation to quit. Like nourishment for her will, these visions provided her with that little bit of resolve to go on, to battle until the end, and she used this as fuel to sustain her determination to fight and to live.

She slowly pushed her sore rear end back through her arms and scooted down so her hands were in front of her face. Searching through the dark with her index finger, she found the bottom corner of the duct tape and dug her fingernail into its edge. Working a good portion of that edge away from her skin, she grasped the small end of tape between her thumb and forefinger, tugging at the tape slightly and then wincing in pain. She could tell her face was chafed where the tape had been previously removed. Ignoring the stench, she took a deep, noisy breath through her one nostril, closed her eyes tightly, and ripped the rest of the tape completely off. Her eyes began to tear as the burning pain waited the obligatory second and a half before rushing into the skin that surrounded her mouth. She breathed through her mouth, gulping the putrid, stale, humid air. Wanting desperately to ball up the tape and throw it as far away from her body as she could, she resisted the temptation, knowing she would need it when Orley came back. As before, she didn't want to give away her little secret. God only knew what he would do to her.

She reached forward with her face, searching in the blackness for the drinking tube. Initially frustrated, she continued to probe the dark air with her chin until she finally felt it hit her nose. Grasping the tube with her teeth, she sucked on it and was rewarded with a giant gulp of warm water, careful not to drink too much since she was supposed to be gagged and not able to drink from the bottle. Far from satisfied but feeling better nonetheless, she rested her left cheek on her pillow of hands. It didn't take a genius to know she needed to find a way out.

Dr. Sue once again pulled against the ties that bound her hands. She tugged a few times and then pulled as hard as she could against their anchor, but the harder she pulled, the deeper the straps dug into her wrists. As her fingers were beginning to grow numb, she again understood pulling away was not an option. She relaxed her arms and allowed the blood to flow back into her hands, using the time to ponder other options.

Still holding the tape in her left hand she straightened the fingers of her right hand to feel what was keeping her tied to the floor, but her small fingers were not long enough, and it was too dark to see. She couldn't even see her hands, and they were only a few inches from her face.

Wait! She reached out with her tongue until she felt it touch her left wrist. Leading with her tongue, she traced it along her skin toward her hands until she felt the junction of straps that tied her wrists together. To her untrained tongue, it felt like plastic draw ties, like the white ones she had seen at Home Depot or the kind the police used to bind prisoners when there are not enough handcuffs to go around. *No wonder I couldn't break them*, she thought.

She continued with her tongue, searching to determine what was anchoring her to the deck. Her tongue hit a metal ring that felt like it was protruding from the wooden floor, and it felt as if a separate tie connected the straps that bound her wrists to the metal ring. She dug her tongue into the dark tangle of straps and discovered she could actually bore her way into the small gap between the straps and her skin.

She rested her cheek on her hands again and thought about what she could do with the information she had just discovered. Leaning forward, she found the drinking tube again and took another small sip of water. Another idea popped into her head.

Using her tongue to guide her back toward the junction of ties, she found the strap that was tied to the metal loop and began to nibble at it with her pointy teeth, the ones near the corner of the left side of her mouth. The entire right side of her face was incredibly sore, but she fought through the pain. After only a few minutes, she felt the plastic begin to separate as she gnawed at the strap. *Almost there*, she thought.

Heart pounding in her chest, she continued to gnaw, adrenaline driving her to a frenzied pace. Each time her teeth fell from their target, she quickly shot her tongue out to find the mark again so she could immediately resume tearing into the straps. She pictured herself resembling a starving rat with a rotten piece of cheese, but she didn't care. She chewed and chewed and gnawed and gnawed.

Feeling the plastic coming apart beneath the relentless sawing of her incessant teeth, she could feel she was almost through. Her saliva gushed onto her fists as she chewed and pulled. Sweat dripped from her forehead; she heard herself moan. Confident the binding would give, she was just about to pull one last time when her heart suddenly dropped into her stomach.

She froze when she heard the door to the motorhome open. Her hands began to shake, and she almost dropped the pieces of tape. She knew she was close to breaking free, but she dare not try. Without thinking, she slapped the tape over her mouth and maneuvered herself so her arms were once again behind her back. She lay still and strained to hear as best she could over the beating of her own heart what was happening outside of her black world.

Confusion, comprehension, and then a horrible sense of despair simultaneously overwhelmed her. The sound was unmistakable. No one, no matter how talented, could perfectly imitate the sound of a giggling child. Tears streamed down her right cheek. *No*, she thought. *No, no, no.*

She heard the muffled sound of music in the distance, and then she heard the giggling stop. There was a pause and then a stifled scream, the desperate cry of a little girl, a cacophony of indecipherable sounds, the hollow thumping of an object against a wall, the breaking of glass, and then finally the eternal rhythmic squeaking from the lid to her black world that could only mean one thing.

Dr. Sue quickly threw her body back through her arms so her hands were in front of her. Grasping the edge of the tape with her finger, she ripped it from her face and then opened her mouth to scream for him to stop, but she froze.

Mouth agape, she lay in blackness and did nothing. She knew if she screamed, he would continue to do what he was doing, and then he would come back, open the lid to her box, see she was not as he had placed her, and then beat her again. She could not take another beating. Her body ached, and she was weak. She just could not endure it again.

Impotent, she sobbed violently. She could not even help *herself*, let alone that poor thing who she knew was being violated the same way she herself had been the night before. The bottle, his evil eyes, and that chilling smirk dominated her being. Dr. Sue knew what he was doing to that child, and it crushed the last bit of defiance out of her. Quaking and sobbing, she replaced the tape and slowly slid herself back into position where she was forced to endure hearing the rape that was occurring mere inches from her aching face. After a loud grunt, the squeaking thankfully stopped. A sudden deluge of guilt drenched Dr. Sue's body. She cried uncontrollably. She should have done something, *anything* to help. She was worthless, an utter failure.

The lid to her world opened and something warm hit her on her left cheek. She couldn't see what it was as the lid closed soon after it opened, but whatever it was, it stuck to her cheek, and no matter how hard she shook her head, it would not go away.

The mystery object slowly began to grow. It expanded from her cheek inching its way down her neck. Her good eye shot open, and she shook her head violently. *No*, she cried in her head. *Get it off. Get it off.* The vision of him raising his finger and proclaiming he always used a condom played in her mind. She felt like she was going to vomit. She dare not squirm back into position to actually peel it from her cheek for fear he would suddenly lift the lid and discover her little secret. She forced herself to think about something else; her home, her family, anything besides the little latex package of horror that dripped its innocence-stealing liquid all over her quivering neck. She did not stop crying until she felt the motorhome rumble to life and then proceed away from its present place of horror.

***

"You guys are shitting me, right?" Patty said, looking back and forth between the two men who were sitting across from her.

"Serious as a heart attack," Riley said.

Patty sat back and laughed hysterically. She laughed for a long time and then removed the glasses from her face to rub her eyes.

Howard could feel himself getting hot. He was sure his face was the same color as the half-eaten apple he could not stop staring at as it rested atop the glass coffee table between them.

"Don't give me that goofy stare only you could pull off Riley," Patty said between laughs. "No wonder the chief threw you guys out." She replaced her glasses and took a deep breath. "I'm sorry guys." She took another deep breath. "I'm really sorry. I said I'd hear you out, but this is ridiculous."

Howard began to stand, but Riley put a firm hand on his left knee forcing him to sit back down.

"Patty," Riley said. "You know I'm not like other guys. I see things differently. I figure them out. This is no different. I know this is right, and I need your help. Dr. Sue needs your help."

"Let me get this straight. You want me, a detective on convalescent leave, to get you access to a man's apartment who you believe kidnapped Dr. Sue because she gave his wife some sort of bad advice?"

"In a nutshell, yes," Riley said, smiling.

"Did you say *nut*-shell?"

"Come on babe. Look at the evidence. Here's a transcript from the call." Riley handed Patty a piece of typewritten paper. "She said her name was Amy. She's twenty-six. She has a son from a man who knocked her up when he was in prison. Folsom. The man who knocked her up was released less than a year ago. These things narrowed a search to about ten guys who fit the bill. This one name, Orlando Price, manslaughter, married a woman, a girl, named Amy Nicholes who he impregnated during a conjugal visit about seven years before he got out. Here's his mug shot." He handed her a black and white prison photo. "Howard *swears* this is a younger version of a man who verbally assaulted Dr. Sue at Disneyland last week. Here's a statement from the Disneyland security about the incident. Here's a statement from a little girl who witnessed the exchange. Here's a..."

"All right Riley. All right," Patty said, handing him back the stack of papers. "Say you got something here. So? What can I do? I'm on leave."

"Just come with us to the apartment. If he's home, you can laugh at me and buy me dinner. He hasn't shown up for work in more than a week, so I'll bet I'm right. If he's not home, you can help me convince the super to let us in to take a look."

"Without a warrant," Patty said.

"We're just taking a look. Not looking for evidence, unless you want to ask the chief to ask a judge to get us a warrant."

"What? So he can think I'm an idiot too?" Patty said.

"Detective Marx, please," Howard said. "The police are pursuing this ransom note thing. If they're right, they'll get their man. But, if they're not, who knows what will happen to Dr. Sue?"

He paused and stared at Patty. "Please. Let's just take a look. If it's nothing, and it could very well be nothing, we'll leave you alone and let the cops handle it. But if it's not, we may be the ones to save Dr. Sue."

Silence dominated the room as all three stared at each other. Howard once again broke the silence.

"Look, she has done a lot for societal consciousness during a time of indulgence and self-greed. It's about time someone stepped forward and helped *her*."

Patty glanced at Howard and then at Riley. She shook her head and sighed.

"Damn you Riley. Damn you."

"Does that mean you're in?" he asked.

"I don't even like Dr. Sue," she said before leaning back in the big chair. "I know I'm going to regret this. It's totally crazy. You're totally crazy…I don't know what it is about you Riley. You have this ability to…shit!"

"Does this mean you're in?" Riley asked again from beneath arched eyebrows.

"I hate you Riley. I really, really hate you," she said, closing her eyes and shaking her head. "Yes damn it. I'm in."

Riley and Howard stood, and for some strange reason, they all shook hands.

"I knew I could count on you to do the right thing," Riley said, grinning. Man he felt like a dork.

"Yeah well, I'm just gonna go throw something on and freshen up a bit. I'll be right back."

"Go ahead girl," Riley said. "Take as long as you need."

She stopped about halfway down the long hallway that led to one of the house's two bedrooms and turned around to face the two men. "By the way," she said, "it's because of what he said and not you." She pointed at Howard and then at Riley. "I still don't know if I'm ever going to speak to you when this is over. And please, stop with the babe and girl crap. Okay? It's fricking annoying."

Chapter 28

"It's time for you to go," Amy said, hoping to sound as annoyed as she was feeling.

"What's the hurry?" Edward said, stepping closer to her. "Joel's still asleep, right? Don't you like this song?" He looked down next to him at the small radio that sat on the kitchen table.

Although Amy took another backward step, Edward countered with his own forward step. Her rear end bumped into the kitchen counter, and then she felt the toe of his shoe crash into her big toe, bending her red painted nail painfully backward.

"Ouch," she said, flinching at the pain. Edward immediately jumped backward a couple of feet. Amy could smell beer on his breath.

"Sorry," he said. "Guess I got a little too close."

Amy brought her right foot up behind her left bun and squeezed her big toe between her left thumb and forefinger. "Yeah. Too close," she said.

"So, you coming tonight?" Edward asked. "Big party. Gonna be a lot a fun. Lots of people going to be there, including yours truly." He smiled as hard as he could. His buzz was just beginning to kick in. He knew it was now or never.

"I don't think so kiddo," Amy said. "Unlike you, I grew up a while ago. I don't have time for stupid bonfires and smoking dope."

"Hey. You're never too old to grow up. Maybe this is what you need, you know, to help you escape from what you are escaping from."

"No. What I need, *Eddie*, is for you to please leave. I've already asked you once."

Edward took a deep breath and shook his head. He refused to accept *no* for an answer, and he was not going to quit.

He exhaled loudly and then said, "Look. I know this is difficult for you. Really I do. One time I had to break up with this girl I was seeing for a long time. You know like almost a little more than a year."

"Oh yeah," Amy said, sliding past his approaching body and making her way around the couch and toward the front door. He followed her like she hoped he would.

"Uh huh," Edward said, nodding his head. "I was really bummed out. I mean really. Thought about killing myself. I was that bummed."

"Should have done us all a favor."

"But I didn't. All I did was let loose, you know. Partied it up. Got high. Got drunk. Soon enough, actually that night, I met someone else who took all my cares away." He closed his eyes and wagged his head gently back and forth.

"Wish she'd come and take you away right now," Amy said, grasping the front door and pulling it open. She jumped when she saw Mickey standing on her porch. "Mickey," she said between gasps. "You scared the crap out of me." She put her right hand on her chest.

"There you are," Mickey said, reaching up and grabbing his taller nephew by the collar. He yanked the younger man out of the door. "I told you to leave her alone."

"I's just checking on her, Uncle Mickey," Edward said, stumbling out of the door.

"Been in the beer again, haven't you, you little shit," Mickey said, yanking him forward once more. He let go of Edward's shirt, letting the gangly youngster fall onto the dirt in front of the porch. "Sorry about him Amy," Mickey said. "I think there's no hope for him after all. I'll keep my thumb on him now. I promise. He won't bug you again."

"Oh, I'm sure he's harmless," Amy said. "I think he's pretty drunk, though."

"Yeah well, he won't bother you again today. I'll make sure of that."

"Thanks Mickey," Amy said, shutting the door. She could hear Mickey's muffled curses as she imagined the older man dragging his young nephew down the hill.

"Who was that, Mom?"

Amy turned around and saw Joel standing in the doorway to the small bedroom. "No one honey. It's okay."

"He's the guy from the store, huh?" Joel said, yawning and rubbing his left eye. "Why does he keep coming here to talk to you?"

"I don't know, honey. I think he's lonely."

"I'm lonely. I wish we had a TV like at home."

Amy pursed her lips so the corners of her mouth turned down slightly in a mock frown. "I know, Joel. It's not so bad though." She moved the radio from the small kitchen table to the even smaller coffee table that sat in front of the brown sofa and turned the dial until a happy song from Radio Disney came into tune.

"Come on, hun. Let's dance," she said reaching down and grasping her son's tiny hands.

Joel giggled and started gyrating his body wildly. Amy laughed out loud as she watched her son's tiny limbs move about aimlessly in no step, whatsoever, to the rhythm of the tune. She twirled a circle, and he copied her, giggling. She twirled again, and so did he.

He tried to stop moving when the song ended, but he lost his balance and fell to the floor. Amy could tell he was dizzy by the wandering look in his small round eyes. Joel attempted to stand but immediately fell onto his right knee. Reaching up with his right arm, he grabbed hold of the coffee table and used it to pull himself up, but as he did, the table tilted toward him, and the small radio tumbled onto the wooden floor. The music stopped after a loud pop emitted from within the small gray box.

Joel's frightened eyes stared up at his mom, searching for forgiveness. She patted him on his brown head and then reached down and picked up the radio.

"Sorry Mom."

"It's okay," she said flicking the switch from AM, to FM, and then back to AM again. "Think it's broke, though."

Joel crossed his arms in front of his chest and pouted. "Now we don't have a TV or a radio."

Amy gave him another mock frown, this time accenting it with tragic eyes. She smiled. "I'm sure Mickey has one we can borrow. Hey," she said, walking to the window that faced the rear of the cabin. She pushed the heavy lime green curtain aside and looked through its wooden panes. "Looks like a nice day today. Why don't we pack a picnic and walk to the top of that hill there? I remember the view was so awesome when I was a kid."

Joel walked to the window, and standing on his tiptoes, looked out too. He glanced up at his mom. "That big hill over there?" he asked with big eyes.

"Yep."

He lowered himself back to his flat feet and scratched his neck. "Well. Okay. But can I have a PB and J this time and not another bologna sandwich?"

"Sure," Amy said, rubbing his head. "You can have whatever you want."

Orley took a long drag from his cigarette. He had a growing buzz, and he was feeling pretty good. There was something about a good stiff drink early in the day that put him in a really good mood. Plus, he had just gotten laid not too long ago…

Stubbing the cigarette butt into the overflowing ashtray next to him, he reached across the table and picked up the road map he had grabbed at the truck stop right after he dumped his *date* a couple hundred miles up the road. He was getting near the Grapevine, and he needed to pick a route up the mountain and over the two passes to Green Valley, wherever the hell that was.

Lifting the front panel of the long, folded map, he ran his index finger along the list of city names until it stopped on the town for which he was searching. He read the alphanumeric number that was printed next to the words and then found the corresponding location on the map.

"Bingo," he said. He traced his finger south along the 5 Freeway until it reached Magic Mountain Boulevard. From there he noted he would be able to jump onto San Fransiquito Canyon Road, and that, he saw would lead him east into the hills, toward Palmdale, and right to Green Valley. *Easy enough*, he thought throwing the map back onto the table.

He grabbed his nearly empty plastic cup of whiskey and took the last sip. He was feeling pretty good. *Wonder what the good old doctor is up to?* he thought, hoisting himself from his seat and making his way to the rear of the motorhome.

Unlatching the lock on the bed frame, he lifted the wooden plank that held the mattress and flicked on the bedroom light. "You been crying again?" he asked, staring down at her. He reached into the box, and after peeling the dried condom from her cheek, ripped the tape from her mouth. She cried out in pain even though it didn't really hurt that much.

"How could you do that to that girl?" she yelled, holding back the sobs that were attempting to overcome her.

"Hey," Orley said, raising his hands up in front of his body. "She was good with it. She wanted it, too."

"How can you say that? I heard her screams, you *monster*, and she sounded like a *little girl!*" She heard herself scream the words "little girl," and then she finally broke down into a fit of painful sobs.

"Now now Doctor. You obviously don't know the ways of the world. There's those who want it, those who can give it, and those who can connect those who want it with those who can give it."

Dr. Sue sniffed and then cleared her throat. She wanted desperately to wipe the tear from her right cheek and the filthy stickiness from her left.

"What do mean?" she said. "You're saying she wanted it?"

"Yeah," Orley said, half-leaning and half-sitting on the tiny desk behind him. "You don't think NAMBLA is the only society out there, do ya? Come on Doctor. Don't be so naïve."

Dr. Sue didn't know whether she was confused or whether she just didn't want to believe what the monster standing over her was insinuating. "That was a boy?" she said.

Orley burst out in laughter. "No," he said, shaking his head. "Although I heard that can be pretty good too." He sniffed and then rubbed his nose with the back of his left hand. "Naw. I may have problems, but I'm not gay."

"You've got problems all right."

The whiskey induced buzz was making Orley feel unusually euphoric, so he decided to have a little fun with her. "Hey Doc, what'd you think about the old bottle in the keyster, huh? I mean you brought up the whole gay thing." He arched his eyebrows, waiting for her response.

"I think you're sick. I think you're going to hell."

Orley chuckled. "Yeah. Might as well enjoy the ride down though. Hey, I heard you didn't like fags none. Tell you the truth. I don't like them none either. That's why I sent the cops your skirt and blamed this on them."

"What?"

"Yeah. Don't worry. We're on the same team there. I mean regarding the queers. I think they're deviant, too.

You know. Not normal. I mean sex belongs between a man and a female, not two guys butt plugging each other. I'm normal in that regard. Even you have da admit that." The whiskey was really kicking in.

"You are normal in *no* regard," Dr. Sue said. "*You* are a sick, deviant bastard. An animal who preys on innocent little girls. You need to be locked up forever."

"Deviant huh?" he said. "You ever take it in the keyster before last night? Huh? Did ya?"

Dr. Sue stared silently at him.

"I never have," Orley said sniffing and rubbing his nose with the back of his hand again. "Naw. Never got popped. Wasn't my thing. But, I did a few sometimes. Sometimes you just need a release you know. Sometimes you gotta do what needs da be done. There was always someone willing in the joint da take care of you, and sometimes you had da just go take care of business even if they didn't want da. You know what I mean, Doc?"

"No, Orley. I don't know what you mean."

"Right. How would you unless you were me and have been through what I have? Prison. Like that's something so bad. You know what prison is, Doc? Prison is grad school for people like me. Networking. Refining techniques. Finding out where the good stuff is.

"You sit on your high horse and give bad advice and think you're all special and that. You think your way is the only way. You think I'm sick. I may be sick da you, but there's a lot of us out there and we like da share. We always share, and we'll never, ever, go away."

"What do you mean *share?*"

"Come on, Doc. How many missing little girls are out there on milk bottles and signs, huh? Where do you think they go? Like I said, don't be so naïve. This is the real world *I* live in. Not the fake little insulated castle you used da call home." He was really buzzing.

"Go to hell, you bastard," Dr. Sue said, closing her eyes, trying to keep the tears from leaking out.

"Come on Doctor. Don't you want da talk some more? You probably never shut up when you're getting paid da talk. I'll bet you love da run that pretty little suck of yours all day if someone is waving a few greenbacks in your face. Come on, Doc. Talk da me. Come on."

Dr. Sue lay in silence, eyes closed.

"Whatever," Orley said.

Standing and staring at her for a few moments, he realized he had done what he had set out to do; he had finally broken her spirit. She would do whatever he demanded. He owned her.

He had starved her, disoriented her, humiliated her, and plain old beaten her. She was small and weak. He felt strong and alive. Her thin skin sagged, and her unbeaten eye stared hollowly from its sunken socket. There was little color left in her lips and her cheeks, except for the permanent streaks of black that ran down from her black ringed eyes, were hollow and gray, except where the bruising was starting to show. Yep, she was his now, and he was fairly certain she would do whatever he wanted.

"I guess we're done talking then."

No reply.

"Okay," he said as he reached forward and replaced the tape on her mouth and then closed the bed and locked the latch. "We'll chat again later."

"Mom? Can we stay up here forever?" Joel asked, looking down the hill at the many valleys.

"We can stay up here as long as you want, Joel. It's neat, huh?"

"Yeah."

Sitting behind her tiny son, Amy put her hands on his small shoulders. "I love you Joel. I'll do anything for you."

"I love you too Mom," he said. After a long pause, he asked, "Why did we have to leave dad? Are we ever going to see him again?"

Amy fought back tears. "Your daddy is a bad man, hun. He did bad things to little girls. I should have never visited him in that jail."

Joel turned around and faced his mother. He saw she was crying. "What did he do to them? Did he hit them?"

Amy wiped tears from both cheeks with the back of her right hand while leaning on her left palm. "No honey, he didn't hit them." She had hoped Joel would be a lot older than he was now before she had to explain the birds and the bees to him, but she knew it was now or never. "You see honey. When a man and a woman love each other, they get married and then they lay down naked together and touch their private parts together." She could feel her face getting flushed, but she decided to continue. "He puts his penis into her vagina, and that's how babies are made."

Joel sat back and arched his eyebrows.

"Is that how I was made?" he said.

"Yes honey. That's how we all were made."

"Is that why Dad had to go to jail?"

Amy smiled. "No honey. Your daddy went to jail, because he accidentally killed someone in a car accident. When he got out, and maybe even before he went in, he started putting his penis into little girls' vaginas, and that is a really very, very bad thing to do. Only grown-ups should do that, ones who love each other and are married to each other." She reached forward and put her hands on Joel's shoulders again.

"Joel honey. I'm going to ask you a question, and I want you to tell me the truth. Okay?"

"'kay."

"Did daddy ever put his penis on you?"

Joel shook his head no.

"Are you sure? Mommy won't be mad at you if he did. I just need to know."

Joel shook his head again. A tear popped out of Amy's left eye and ran down her cheek. She pulled her son to her chest and hugged him tightly. *Thank you*, she thought. *Thank you, thank you, thank you.*

When she finally let go, Joel looked at her. "Mommy," he said slowly.

Amy's heart leaped into her throat.

"Yes?" she said, fearing what would come next.

"Can I have my sandwich now?"

Amy's shoulders collapsed into her chest. "Of course dear," she said, reaching into the brown bag and pulling out two sandwiches. She handed one to her smiling son. "One PB and J with the crust cut off, just like you like it."

Chapter 29

Dr. Sue was actually relieved to hear the motorhome's engine roar to life. She guessed Orley had taken a nap, and that was the reason for the long delay. She knew her time was getting short so as soon as she felt the rig begin to move, she pushed her body through the opening in her arms and once again started working on the plastic tie with her teeth.

It was difficult for her to chew at the strap while the motorhome was moving. Every little bump was transferred through the tires and into the confines of her small wooden box. More than once she could have sworn she had chipped a tooth on the metal loop to which she was tethered, but she would not be deterred. Pushing the pain aside, she did her best to tense her neck muscles in order to stabilize her head during the agonizingly bumpy ride.

Once more, she could feel the strap begin to give, so she anxiously chewed at the slimy, saliva-drenched bonds, using every ounce of pent-up, frustration-fueled energy she could muster. Finally, with one great pull of both arms and a loud grunt, she broke the thin plastic strap. Her wrists slammed against the wooden ceiling with a loud thud. Heart pounding, drenched in stinky sweat, Dr. Sue lay, still surrounded by her familiar putrid darkness, but almost free.

Wasting no time, she immediately went to work on separating the straps that secured her wrists to each other.

Since she could lie on her back, it wasn't so bad. Despite a seemingly unquenchable thirst, she gnawed at the plastic straps until she could feel them also begin to give. She chewed and chewed and gnawed and gnawed. Freedom was so close; she could literally taste it.

She paused briefly to take a few breaths and to steal a quick sip of water from the tube. Although she pulled against her bonds with all of her might, the strap stretched, but it did not give. She pulled harder, using the sharp pain of the plastic digging into her skin to motivate her. Finally, suddenly, it snapped, and her arms ripped apart from each other. A tear popped from her good eye and ran down her cheek.

She lay in the darkness, and sobbed, happy to be completely loose from her bonds. She thought of her husband and her son and how much she missed them and how much she desperately wanted to see them again. She was almost there. She was almost free.

Dr. Sue rubbed her wrists, doing her best to smear the pain away. After that, she wiped at both of her cheeks and then remembered the disgusting, dry, smattering of crusty semen that stuck to the left side of her face and neck. Licking her hands, she wiped the area with all of her might and then lifted the collar of her silk shirt so she could use it to scrub at the area as well.

A wave of regret washed over her. Try as she may, she could not push away the horrifying sounds she'd been forced to endure, the screams from the child and the grunts from the monster who stole the poor girl's innocence. Dr. Sue once again felt dirty and insignificant for having done nothing to help. She wretched acid and then swallowed it back down. The smell of her own feces and urine, mixed with the distinct stench of dried semen and thin rubber, made her heave and gag again. Thankfully, nothing came up.

She forced herself to drink more water, using the plastic liquid to calm her stomach. *There's nothing you could have done. He would have hurt you too.*

Forcefully, she drove her thoughts away from the girl and toward her family, convincing herself to keep fighting and to stay alive. She was almost there. She was almost free.

After a few moments, she was able to push her guilt aside and focus on her escape. She wondered if the lid was locked. Lying on her back, she reached out into the darkness and then immediately regretted her decision. *Oh dear God*, she thought. *It's too close. It's too small. There's no air!* The blackness closed-in around her. Anxiety and claustrophobia suddenly squeezed the air from her lungs, causing her to panic and hyperventilate. She pushed as hard as she could against the ceiling, but it would not budge, and this made the darkness feel even tighter.

She forced her mind to move from, *I'm gonna die! I can't breathe*, to *Relax! Breathe!* Compelling herself to calm down, she took more deep breaths, gagging at the stench. *Nothing has changed...It's still the same...It's not smaller...You're okay...Relax...Breathe.*

"There's enough air. There's enough air. There's enough air..."

She repeated these words until her heart rate slowed and her breaths came more easily. She dared once more to reach out to touch the ceiling, this time prepared to deal with the fact it was inches from her nose. She pushed against the wooden plank, trying to lift the bed by giving it a little nudge, but it would not move. She tried again, pushing a little harder. Still nothing. Not even a crack. She pushed once more, this time with all of her might, but once again, nothing. Panic reemerged, and she vainly fought the urge to cry.

"There's enough air. There's enough air. There's enough air..."

She struggled to remain calm as the crushing tightness of her black surroundings slowly squeezed her. Tears dripped from her eye. *It's useless*, she thought. *He is going to kill me and bury me in the desert.* She let the tears fall, even though she could finally wipe them away. No one would ever find her. *Ever.* People would search for a while. Then they would give up. Then they would mourn. Then they would move on with their lives, and all that would be left of her would be a pile of bones, a bra, and a dirty white silk shirt.

No! She shook the thought from her head and wiped the streams from her cheek. *I'm stronger than this.* She would *not* quit. She would fight until the end or find a way to escape. There had to be something here, in her black world, she could use to help her. She was hungry and weak and tired, but she was not going to fold. She would not end up a pile of bones in the desert.

"Howard," Patty said, sitting in the passenger seat of Riley's car. "Why don't you wait here? I'll call you on your cell if it's okay for you to come up. If we're not back, or you don't hear from me in fifteen minutes, call *911*. Tell them there's an officer who needs assistance."

Howard's eyes widened.

"Probably won't need to do that," Riley said, staring sidelong at Patty. "She can get a little melodramatic." He nodded at Patty who had already opened and was exiting the passenger door. Smiling at the obviously nervous man in the backseat, he said, "Sit tight. Give us a few minutes. I'm sure everything will be all right."

"Right," Howard said, leaning back and nervously fingering his cell phone.

Riley climbed out of the low car and slammed the door. He hurried after Patty who had already begun to ascend the stairs in front of them.

"Slow down," he said, grabbing her left elbow.

"Hurry up," she said, twitching it from his grasp and then wincing at the pain.

The stairs made a one hundred eighty degree turn as they led up to the second story of the apartment complex. Riley, still slightly lagging Patty, grabbed her elbow again when they reached the top of the steps, this time holding on as she tried to pull away.

"Let go of my arm," she said, yanking it harder and then wincing at the pain again.

"Wait," Riley said, pulling back. "Would you just hold on a minute?"

Patty stopped and faced him. "What?" she said, unsuccessful in her attempt to fight back a tear.

Riley looked at her, his back to the light of the hazy afternoon. A lump formed in his throat when he saw the tear run down her cheek. "Now that I've got you alone, I just want to say I'm sorry," he said. "For everything. The article. The jokes. The way I've treated you. I've been a real shit. I see now I've hurt you, and I'm sorry."

Patty looked up at the tall man. Once again, she could not understand why it was impossible for her to resist his huge, dumb, blue eyes. The man was an idiot. He was clumsy and not too bright, but she found herself drawn to him like a child to a puppy dog. She swallowed. "You really hurt me," she said.

"I know."

Riley drew her into him and wrapped his arms around her, kissing her wiry hair.

"I hate you," she said.

"I hate me too."

He felt her body twitch in his arms and wondered if it was a sob or a chuckle. He decided to take a chance. He relaxed his embrace and looked down at her shiny cheeks before lowering his own shadowed face so he could kiss her on her lips.

Patty's first instinct was to pull away, but before she knew it, his lips were on hers and she felt his mouth open slightly. Without thinking, she followed suit and accepted his darting tongue as she brushed it lightly with her own. It felt natural to her, and her head started to spin causing her to lose her bearing. After an eternity, a honking horn from the nearby freeway snapped her from her trance, and she slowly withdrew her lips from their warm, moist bed.

Riley looked down at Patty. She looked so cute. Her tiny nose held her small black-framed glasses in place. He could see a streak of mascara on her cheek so he reached with the back of his right hand to wipe it away.

She grabbed his hand and kissed it after it gently brushed her cheek. "We had better get going," Patty said, clearing her throat. "Don't want Howard calling in the cavalry down there."

"Right," Riley said, mimicking Howard.

"Thanks," Patty said, looking up at him.

Riley nodded in reply.

"What number are we looking for?"

"Ten twenty-three," Patty said, leading him down the pathway. Her heart was still fluttering. She wondered if his was, too. "Here we go," she said after following the walkway around a corner.

Riley looked at her. "What do we do?" he asked.

Reaching into her jacket, she withdrew her service pistol and held it down next to her body. "Stand over there," she whispered, pointing to a small area between the front door and a corner of the building.

"Where'd you get that? What do I do?" Riley asked as he backed up a few steps.

"Don't worry about that. Just stay calm and stay quiet. I know what I'm doing."

"Right."

Patty raised the pistol so it was a few inches in front of her belly and then pounded forcefully on the door with her other fist. She stepped back and then raised the pistol so it was level with her chin.

Riley noticed a nervous but determined look on her face, a side of Patty he realized he had never seen. He squeezed his body back as far as he could into the corner. He was scared shitless, and there was no doubt she knew this side of him.

Patty reached forward and pounded again before instantly assuming the same ready-to-fire stance. Once more, there was no answer. She heard Riley exhale so she looked over her left shoulder at him.

He shrugged at her.

She shrugged back and then lowered her pistol.

"What now?" he whispered.

"I'm going to go get the super," she said. "You wait here."

"Right," Riley said again. "What do I do if he comes out?"

"Run," Patty said as she disappeared around the corner.

"Run?" Riley said to himself. *Run where?* He stepped forward and stared at the door. He listened, but could hear no sound emanating from behind it. Looking at the base of the doorway, he saw nothing that would indicate the presence of someone inside so he was semi-confident the apartment was empty. He stole a quick glance at his watch, and determined it was too early for someone to be sleeping. *It was probably empty for sure.*

Just in case, Riley stepped back into the corner and leaned against the wall. He could hear tiny pieces of stucco crumble under his weight.

Closing his eyes, he relived the kiss that had just taken place, replaying the scene over and over in his mind. *Did that really just happen?* He reached up and touched his lips to verify the moment had been real. *Yup. It really happened.* He was in love, and he was ready to take it to the next level.

The sound of approaching footsteps startled Riley back into reality. *Crap! What do I do?*

Cornered, Riley glanced around the tiny landing. He leaned forward and looked over the black rail that protected the second floor. There was no way he could jump and then run away. He'd break a bone for sure. No. His only option was to duck down the steps from which he had come, but the sound of footsteps was coming from that direction. His heart was hammering away in his chest, and he didn't know where to go. He started to step forward just as Patty and a silver-haired gentleman rounded the corner.

"Jesus," he whispered between deep breaths. "You scared the crap out of me." He brought his right hand up to cover his heart.

"Not Jesus. Just me," Patty said.

Riley could tell she wasn't happy with his idiocy.

"Mr. Safrit, this is my *partner*, Greg Riley." She gave Riley the not so surreptitious wide-eyed nod as she said the word *partner*, and Riley quickly caught on.

"Nice to meet you, Mr. Safrit," Riley said, composing himself, trying to act *officerly*.

"Mr. Safrit here is kind enough to let us in to check if our parolee has, in fact, broken his parole, isn't that right, Mr. Safrit?"

"Uh, yeah," the older man said from stooped shoulders.

Riley watched the man fumble through a set of keys. After a few agonizing seconds, Mr. Safrit found what seemed to be the right one and slipped it into the keyhole. He turned the key to the right and the door clicked open.

Patty immediately withdrew her pistol, and placing her left hand on Mr. Safrit's right arm, pulled her way past the man, ignoring the stabbing pain in her shoulder. Pistol leading the way, she darted into the apartment, disappearing from Riley's view.

Riley held his breath for what seemed like an hour. Mr. Safrit blinked in confusion. Both men exhaled simultaneously as Patty emerged and slipped her pistol back into the holster that rested slightly below her left breast. Riley wished he was the holster, and then quickly dismissed the thought. *Later*, he told himself. *Later.*

"All clear," Patty said. "Thank you Mr. Safrit. We can take it from here. We're going to need some time to get some photos of his place for proof he's skipped town."

The super shook his head. "Well, okay," he said. "Don't want to argue with the law. Especially when they have guns. Please lock the door when you leave." He turned and disappeared around the corner.

"That was easy," Riley said, a slight look of confusion still residing on his face.

"Yeah. I'd better call Howard."

Patty pulled a small black cell phone from her coat pocket and quickly tapped in a number. "We're in," she said after a short pause. "Come on up. It's clear." She clicked a button and slipped the phone back into her pocket. "He's coming up," she said, looking up at Riley. "My shoulder's killing me."

Riley nodded. He still could not believe what he was doing.

Edward knocked on the cabin's door, and again there was no answer. *Crap*, he thought. *It was tonight or never.* His plane was leaving in the morning, and he had to score with her tonight or at least set something up for the next visit.

He trotted back down the path to the store and snatched a pen and a pad of paper from the counter. Quickly scratching out a note, he grabbed a thumbtack from the corkboard next to the restroom and then hurried back up the path and pinned the note to the door.

That ought to do it, he thought, taking a deep breath before turning around. He nearly plowed into Amy who had suddenly appeared from behind the cabin.

"Edward," she said, startled and stepping backward.

"Hi Amy," Edward said, smiling. "And it's Eddie, not Edward. Edward sounds so grown-up."

"Well, maybe it's time you grew into your name," Amy said.

Edward rolled his eyes.

"What does *he* want?" Joel said from behind his mom.

"I don't know. Edward, what *do* you want?"

Eager to impress, Edward exaggerated a hard smile. "Just wanted to remind you of the big bonfire we're having tonight up at the campground. Gonna be fun. I'm sure Uncle Mickey would watch the little one if you wanna come."

"I don't think so, Edward. I'm sure I've got something else to do."

"Aw, come on. There's going to be plenty of adult refreshments," he winked at Amy and nodded at Joel. "Liquid, and well, other forms, too." He nodded at Joel again.

"Well, Edward. That sounds so tempting, but," she winked and nodded at her smiling son, "like I said earlier, a night of booze and pot just doesn't have the same tempting feeling to me as I suppose it does to you."

"Why are you such a stick-in-the-mud?" Edward asked, dropping the smile and stepping forward. He reached out and put his right hand on her left shoulder. "I mean come on. You only live once. Let go. Live a little. You still look pretty young. I'll bet you could show me a thing or two about a good time."

Amy jerked her shoulder away, watching his hand fall.

"Joel. Cover your ears."

Joel's tiny hands snapped to his head.

Amy stepped forward and poked her finger hard into Edward's chest. "Look, you little shit," she said. "Leave me and my son alone. I'm not going to your party, and I'm not showing you any kind of time. Now, if you don't get out of here, I'm going to kick you in the nuts so hard, your kids, if you are ever lucky enough to find a women to have them with you, will be born dizzy." She pulled her finger away and then jabbed it into his chest once more. "Got it?"

Edward backed up, stumbling off of the tiny wooden deck. "Bitch," he said. He turned and walked down the path. Once he was a few safe yards away, he looked over his shoulder and said, "Probably a dyke anyway. Your little boy there's probably queer. Better off not knowing ya. You're uninvited to the party."

Amy watched him disappear, and then she looked down at her son.

"Can I uncover my ears now?" he asked.

Amy nodded, so Joel dropped his hands.

"Mommy?"

"Yes, dear," Amy said, opening the door.

"What's a dyke?"

Amy shook her head. "Never mind, hun. How about some hot chocolate?"

"'kay."

Amy ripped the note from the door, crinkled it into a ball, and then tossed it into the trashcan next to the cabin before gently closing the door behind her.

Orley could definitely see the difference in terrain as the high desert to his left climbed into the rising mountains to his right. Once he was through the Grapevine, he had decided to jump over to the 14 Freeway, which ran parallel to the 5 Freeway, but inland of the busier road. He was traveling during the day now, so he wanted to be safely away from the prying eyes of the many motorists who traveled California's most notorious Interstate.

In addition to wanting to keep a low profile, he had another reason for taking this back route. To his left, as far as the eye could see, was nothing but an expansive scene of empty desert. Save an abandoned trailer or a decrepit shack, there was mostly empty space, and he needed that empty space to dump one, if not three, unwanted pieces of baggage, if things did not go as planned.

He was pretty much set on dumping the good doctor at least. Right now, he knew the police, and hopefully the FBI as well, were on a wild goose chase up near San Francisco and down south of Los Angeles. That would put a spread of more than five hundred miles between him and them, enough distance to find and snatch his wife and son, dump the doctor, and be on his way to Mexico by tomorrow evening at the latest. Or maybe he should dump the doctor in Mexico? Oh well. He'd figure it out.

He took a sip of Diet Coke and saw the sign indicating his off-ramp was in two and a half miles. He finished the last bit of soda and set the empty can into the cup holder between his seat and the empty passenger's chair.

It would be good to get his son back. He had enjoyed camping with him. He knew he and his son had that special bond that a boy and his father should. He had never had inappropriate thoughts about him, but he had to admit the boy was good bait for helping him satisfy his demon.

He pushed the thought aside as he maneuvered the giant rig off of the 14 Freeway and onto Highway 138. After about ten minutes, he turned left onto San Francisquito Canyon Road near a city called Quartz Hill, and from his map study, that meant he was at the right spot. Heading west, Green Valley should be the next town.

He was not expecting much. Maybe a small town with a diner, a gas station, and a post office. Maybe a school. He'd know it when he saw it though, or he'd keep looking.

He planned to spend the night at a primitive campground just west of the city. From his map, he saw the campground was at the end of a dirt road called South Portal. It seemed like the perfect place to bed down for a few hours until dark. The campground was, he had seen, about three miles from the dot on the map that indicated the city of Green Valley. He planned to reconnoiter on foot once it was dark. It would be easier and less conspicuous than maneuvering the RV. Plus, the exercise would do him good. The cool, crisp, early spring mountain air would allow him to clear his mind.

After what seemed like an ungodly amount of time winding down a narrow two-lane road, he came upon a tiny gas station and mini-market. The small green sign let Orley know that he had just passed *Mickey's Mart, The Best Little Store in Green Valley.*

Startled by its sudden appearance, Orley fought the urge to slam on the brakes. He didn't want to draw attention to himself. He'd wait to see what else Green Valley had in the way of amenities before he decided what to do. But, before he could react, he passed another sign that informed him he was now leaving Green Valley.

That's it, he thought. *No fucking way.* Had he blinked, had he sneezed, had he reached down to pick up his can of Diet Coke, he would have missed the whole freakin' town. The road was too narrow to make a safe one-eighty so he elected to take the next road he saw and attempt to swing back around for another look.

After a couple of frustrating minutes, he saw a dirt road approaching from his right. He slowed the rig and read a small, brown, weathered sign that was nailed to the trunk of a large oak tree. South Portal Road. *Beautiful*, he thought as he eased onto the dirt road.

He slowly made his way up the dusty winding trail, passing a United Methodist Camp that sat on a small hill to his right. *Camp Cisquito.* It looked vacant. That was good.

Continuing gradually, he carefully maneuvered the motorhome counter clockwise around a large tree that split the road near the end of the drive. On the back side of the tree, he saw about a dozen flattened rectangles of hard dirt and decided this must be the campground. Thankful he had filled his water tanks earlier in the day, he nosed the rig into one of the spots and killed the engine.

Tired, he made his way to the back of the coach, tossing the empty soda can into the sink on the way. He kicked the wooden base of the bed.

"Good night, Dr. Sue. Sleep well. This will be your last night with us," he said, and then he plopped down onto the soft mattress. Tired from a long few days, he finally felt he was nearing closure. He set the small digital alarm clock next to his bed to wake him up in three hours. It should be after dark by then and the perfect conditions for getting his family back. With those thoughts in his head, he was asleep within minutes.

Chapter 30

Edward felt his head move before he eventually realized he was looking at a small clock. Blinking it into focus, he read it was almost five. That explained why everything outside was turning gray. He took a deep breath. *Maybe a little too early to have been hitting the bottle*, he thought.

His plan had him leaving the store no later than five so he could get to the campground by five thirty. That was the time everyone else would start showing up, and he wanted to be sporting a nice buzz when the party kicked off.

Reaching under the counter and grabbing a plastic cup, he took another sip of Jack and Coke and then shivered as the whiskey burned a trail into his stomach. *Needs more Coke*, he thought, feeling way too buzzed. He definitely needed to slow down.

As if watching a choppy movie, he saw the door to the shop open, and then he watched his short, bearded uncle walk in. He balanced himself by leaning forward against the wooden counter.

"Edward," Mickey said. "You got the shop tonight. I'm going into town. I gotta unwind a little."

"Tonight?"

"Yeah. Tonight. I told you about this Wednesday. I told you I'd be going to town Friday, and you were going to need to watch the store. Don't tell me you forgot."

"But it's Friday," Edward said, careful not to slur his words. "It's my last night. Some of the guys from down in the Valley and me were going to have a fire at the campground and stuff."

Mickey stared at Edward. He shook his head and rubbed his wrinkled, leathery forehead with the thumb-side of his right index finger.

"Edward. You're watching the shop. No argument. I'm expecting some important calls, and you have to take them. We talked about this on Wednesday. Remember? You said I wasn't giving you enough responsibility, so here you go. You need to take the calls and set up Monday's deliveries."

"Well, why can't *you* stay?" Edward whined. "It's my last night."

"That's right Edward. It's your last night. And it's my last night too. Look around. There's no one here but me. When you leave, I'm the one who opens and closes this place. I'm asking you for a favor. You can do me this one favor tonight."

Eddie needed another drink. It wasn't that he was losing his buzz. He just didn't want to give in to the little bit of guilt that was beginning to penetrate his inebriatic shield.

"Can I close early?"

"You can close after the calls come in. They should be in by no later than six thirty or seven. That should leave you plenty of time to get together with your new friends and tie one on if you want."

Eddie took a deep breath. "Okay," he shook his head. "Fine. Go. I'll stay."

Mickey smiled. "Thanks Edward. I knew you'd come through." He spun on his heel and without looking back said, "Lock up when you're done."

"No problem," he said as he watched his uncle disappear into the dusk. He reached down under the counter and then took another giant swallow. "No problem at all."

"Smells like no one's been here in a few days," Riley said, looking around the apartment. "You know. Kind of stale and stuff."

Patty nodded. She ducked down a small hallway that led to the master bedroom. Riley followed her.

"Shower's dry. Soap's dry too," Patty said, rubbing her thumb and forefinger together after touching the green bar of soap that was resting on the ledge of the white, plastic tub.

"Check this out," Riley said suddenly from inside the bedroom across the hallway.

Patty walked into the small room that was dominated by a queen-sized bed and a dresser of drawers. "What?" she said with narrow eyebrows as she looked around the room. "Looks like a bedroom."

"Notice anything weird about it?"

Patty, still confused, looked around. She shook her head.

"Closet's full of clothes," Riley said. "So's the dresser." He was smiling.

"So what, Riley? It's a damn bedroom."

"They're all men's clothes. No bras. No panties. No blouses. Nothing. Just a bunch of men's clothes."

"Hold on a second," Patty said. "Hey, Howard," she yelled down the hall. "Check the other room. See if there're any kids' clothes in there."

"Okay," Patty and Riley heard. "Give me a minute." The two looked at each other for a few dramatic seconds before Howard's voice broke the silence. "Nope. Totally empty, except for a few toys and some pictures."

"Looks like she left him," Riley said, smiling.

"Doesn't mean he kidnapped Dr. Sue," Patty replied. She walked out of the bedroom and back into the small family room.

Riley followed her out. "Well," he said, "he hasn't been to work since the Thursday before she disappeared, and then she disappeared on the next Tuesday. Timing's right."

"Yeah, but how can we know for sure? I can't go to the chief without proof. I'm not even supposed to be on the case. Hell, I'm not even supposed to be at work for another few weeks."

"Well, here's his picture," Howard said, walking toward Patty and Riley with a five by seven picture in a wooden frame. "That's the guy from Disneyland, all right. I'd recognize him anywhere. Those eyes and those tattoos." Howard shivered.

Patty took the picture and studied it closely. "Hold on a second," she said.

"Hey, what's this?" Riley said. He stooped over and picked up a pad of paper from below the table that sat between the tiny kitchen and the even smaller family room.

"There's something about this guy..." Patty squinted at the picture. She shook her head.

"What?" Riley said, walking toward the group, still holding the pad of paper in his hand.

"I don't know," Patty replied. "I...I can't place it. He just looks familiar."

"Well, check this out," Riley said. He held up the notepad.

"Yeah. So? It's blank," Howard said.

"That's right, but watch this." Riley withdrew a pencil from an inside pocket of his jacket and made his way back to the kitchen table.

"Don't tell me. Hardy Boys," Patty said, following him.

Riley smiled. "Nope. Encyclopedia Brown."

"What the hell are you two talking about?" Howard asked.

"Watch," Riley replied as he began to scribble lightly on the notepad.

Howard's eyes widened as he was able to make out the words on the piece of paper. "Holy cow," he said softly.

Patty read the letter out loud. "Orley. I called Dr. Sue, and she said I should leave you. You are a bad man for lying to me. Don't try to follow me, or I will call the police. I'm not going to my mom's so leave her alone, too. I have made a terrible mistake, and I will not let you raise my son. Good-bye — Amy."

"Wow," Riley said. "That's pretty brutal."

"Wait! That's it," Howard said, shaking his head. "That's why he had the note."

"What note?" Patty asked.

"He had a note at Disneyland. Said he wanted Dr. Sue to sign it. I'll bet it was a note he wrote for her to sign saying she said it was okay for her to come back."

"Did she sign it?" Riley asked.

"No. And then he got really mad. That's when I had one of the girls call security."

Riley looked at the picture. "She's cute," he said. "Doesn't look twenty-six. Maybe nineteen at the most. Cute kid, too."

"I wonder if that's their motorhome," Patty said as she stared at the picture. "Can't quite make out the license plate."

"How the hell could they afford something like that and live in a place like this?" Howard asked.

"He comes from money," Riley said. He took Patty's accusatory stare in stride. "I did some research. He has money from a trust fund. It's almost gone. He had to settle with some victims out of court."

Patty continued to study the picture. Something just wasn't right about what she saw.

"She mentioned her mom," Riley said. "Maybe we should try calling her. Maybe Orlando, Orley, I guess she calls him, has been to see her or called her or something."

"Worth a try," Patty said, still staring at the picture.

Riley withdrew his notepad from the breast pocket of his shirt and flipped through the pages. "Here we go. Amy Nicholes. Born in Monterey. Father died when she was a little girl. What do you think the chances are her mom never remarried and is still living not only in Monterey but at the same address?"

Howard shrugged. "Worth a try, I guess," he said.

Riley whipped his cell phone from its clip on his belt and dialed information. "Yes. I am looking for the number of a residence at the following address." He recited the address he had printed on his notebook. "Last name is Nicholes." He paused and extended two crossed fingers toward Howard. "Great," he suddenly said. "Okay, go. I am ready to copy." He scribbled the phone number into his pad with the same pencil he had just used to decipher the note. Closing his phone, he smiled. "This is too easy."

"Hello?"

"Mrs. Nicholes?"

"Yes."

"Hi. This is Detective Patricia Marx of the Los Angeles Police Department…"

Linda Nicholes felt her head spin. She grabbed the couch's armrest to steady herself. "Oh my God," she heard herself say. "It's Amy. Is she…"

"No, no. Sorry to startle you like that," Patty said pleadingly. "As far as I know, Amy's fine."

Linda broke down, sobbing into the phone. "Oh thank God," she said. "Thank God. I thought he found her."

"Who?" Patty asked, already knowing the answer.

"Her husband. She left him last week."

"Mrs. Nicholes..."

"Linda. Call me Linda."

"Okay. Linda. Is your daughter, Amy, married to a man named Orlando Price?"

"Yes. Yes she is."

Patty gave Riley and Howard a thumbs-up. "Okay. Can I ask you a few questions?"

"Sure. Is Amy in trouble?"

"Well, not that we can tell. I mean, I don't know. When's the last time you saw her?"

"Last Thursday. A week ago Thursday. She left Orley and came up here. Then he came up here a couple of days ago looking for her. He was pretty mad. I didn't tell him where she was though."

"Do you know where she is?"

Linda froze. *What if it was a set-up? What if Orley paid a woman to call and ask about Amy?* She suddenly regretted saying anything at all.

"Hello? Mrs. Nicholes? Linda?"

"I...I don't know."

"Mrs. Nicholes. It is very important that we find her. Very important."

"How do I know you're who you say you are?"

Patty sighed. "Why would I lie?" she said, closing her eyes and pinching the bridge of her nose between her thumb and forefinger.

"What if you're with him?"

"I'm not. You have to trust me."

Silence greeted Patty as she looked at Howard and then at Riley. She shrugged her shoulders at them. Riley walked forward and took the phone.

"Hello," he said.

"Who's this?"

"My name is Greg Riley. I am a reporter for the *Los Angeles Times*. I am standing in your daughter and Orlando's apartment with Detective Marx and a man named Howard Thorsen. Do you know who he is?"

Patty reached for the phone, but Riley turned his back quickly so she could not get to it.

"No," Linda said.

"Do you know who Dr. Sue is?" Riley twirled three complete circles before Patty gave up her chase.

"Yeah. From the radio, right? The one who they're looking for."

"Yes," Riley said, motioning with his hand to Patty to calm down. "Well, Mr. Thorsen is her producer. We think Orlando may have had something to do with her disappearance. We think Amy may be in danger. We need to know where she is, and we need to know right away."

Again, Linda pondered what to do. A tear popped from her right eye and dropped onto the phone's receiver. "How do I know I can trust you?"

"You don't Linda," Riley said. "You're going to have to take a leap of faith."

Linda thought about the situation and then said, "Can't I drive down and warn her myself?"

"You could," Riley said. "But why put yourself into unnecessary danger? Is she close to you up there?"

"No. She's down south by L. A."

"Mrs. Nicholes. The more time that goes by, the less likely it is this lead may pan out. If you think it would be better to tell her yourself, that's up to you. I am asking you to trust us, and I understand if you don't, but I am asking you for Amy's sake and your grandson's sake and possibly Dr. Sue's sake, so please, just tell us where she is." Once again Riley stood with crossed fingers.

"Okay. Okay. I'll tell you," Linda finally said. She heard Riley exhale.

"We have a cabin in a small town called Green Valley. It's down near Magic Mountain. It's off of San Fransisquito Canyon Road…"

"Yeah. I know where that is," Riley interrupted. "I live like five miles from that road. I've driven it a few times. It's beautiful."

"Okay," Linda said. "Well, Green Valley is about twenty miles up the road. Closer to Palmdale, I guess, than Magic Mountain. We have a cabin up there. She went to the cabin."

"Does the cabin have a phone?"

"No. But there's a small convenience store and gas station up there called Mickey's Mart. You can't miss it. It pretty much makes up the whole town. He has a phone. I called and left a message for Amy after Orley left here. The cabin is up a trail behind a small hill that's behind Mickey's. You can't see the cabin from the road, but it's there."

Riley scribbled as fast as he could into his small notebook. "What's the number to Mickey's?" He copied it down as it was read to him.

"Mrs. Nicholes. Thank you. This is probably nothing, and I am going to ask you to sit tight. We'll call you back as soon as we determine this really is nothing."

"Okay," she said. "Be careful."

"Why's that?" Riley asked.

"Orley's got a temper like nothing I've ever seen."

"Right," Riley said. "We'll be careful. Good-bye." He pushed the red *END* button on his cell phone and closed it again. "All right. Let's go to Green Valley."

Chapter 31

Edward's buzz was growing stronger. He looked at the clock and read it was five thirty-five, and that meant he was already five minutes late for *his* party. Waiting for the phone to ring, he took another sip of Jack and Coke, to help clear his mind. It was his last night in town, and he was stuck at work until God knew when. No one had been to the shop, and no one would stop by either. He knew it, and he knew his Uncle Mickey knew it too. He was just fucking with him, trying to keep him down, teaching him a lesson.

Edward took another sip. The smell of smoke wafted through the store from what he assumed was the bonfire. He knew he should be there, but instead, he was stuck in this little rat hole of a store in the middle of nowhere. He sighed and looked at the clock again. Five thirty-six.

"Come on man, call," he said to the silent phone that sat next to him.

He was about to yell, when he perceived movement near the front door. Glancing up, he saw the door to the store open, and then he watched two young ladies walk in. They giggled and then made their way over to the refrigerator where he watched them each grab a twelve-pack of Coors Light before strolling to the counter.

"Anything else?" he said as they set the boxes on the counter in front of him. He could hear the bottles tinkle against each other despite the nervous pounding in his chest.

"Pack of Marlboro Lights," one of them said.

He reached up and grabbed the tiny, cellophane-wrapped cardboard box. "You ladies twenty-one?" he asked, knowing the answer.

"Of course," they said, giggling.

"Of course," he repeated.

"You going to card us or something," the cuter of the two said, blinking and smiling at him.

"Naw. Wish I was going with you. You're going to the party at the campground, right?"

"Yeah," the cuter girl said. She stared at him for a second before saying, "Why don't you come too? It's gonna be a rager."

"I know," Edward said. "It was my idea."

"You're Eddie?" the girl said with enthusiasm.

"Yeah." Edward suddenly felt flush.

"You're cuter than they said."

He felt his face grow hot as the two girls giggled at each other. His hand shook slightly as he picked up his cup and took another big sip, trying his best to seem cool.

"So, why don't you come with us?" the other girl said.

"Can't. Gotta watch the store until some dude calls. Could take five minutes. Could take two hours."

"You got a machine there. Just let it answer. Or, maybe you're not cool enough to hang with us?"

"I'm cool enough," he heard himself say.

"So why're you still back there then?"

Edward stared into the cuter girl's inviting brown eyes as he pondered his options. An idea suddenly hit him.

"I know," he said. "I'll just leave a new greeting on the machine. I'll tell the dude to go ahead and deliver the stuff on Monday morning, any time. That should work. Uncle Mickey 'll never know. I'll just tell him I talked to the dude directly. He'll never know any difference."

"Whatever," the girl said. "You just seriously need to party tonight. You're cute, but kind of square."

"Square," Edward said, staring at the girls. He downed the rest of his rum and Coke and then walked to the refrigerator. Yanking open the door, he grabbed two more twelve-packs of Coors Light and slammed the door closed with his rear end. "Come on. Let's go," he said. He nodded toward the door.

"But we haven't paid," the girl said, picking up her twelve-pack from the counter. She motioned for her friend to do the same by nodding her head at the sweating silver box.

"Now who's being square?" he asked as he held the door open with his foot.

"Rock on," the girl said. She hurried, with friend in tow, into the cool night air.

Edward let the door slam behind him. He locked it and then stuffed the keys into the front pocket of his jeans. Seeing the girls lower themselves into a convertible Beetle, he heard the radio yell to life. Hurrying toward the open door, he jumped into the passenger seat just before the car tore out of the dirt lot and onto the darkening road. Had the radio not been so loud, Edward probably would have heard the phone ringing through the store's thin door.

Orley could hear the distant sound of music. He blinked the sleep from his eyes, and then his heart jumped in his chest. Quickly leaping from the mattress, he flicked on the light and unlatched the bed. Lifting it, he saw Dr. Sue, still bound and gagged in the same crooked position he had left her.

He stared down at her and saw she had been crying again. She looked pathetic, nearly naked from the waist down. His mission was almost complete. Bringing his index finger up to his lips, he motioned for Dr. Sue to keep quiet but saw no reaction from her one good eye.

"You might survive this, unless you do something stupid," he whispered. "We're almost there. Be a good girl, and I just might let you go home." He knew he was lying, but he also knew he had to take that chance.

He stood up and stretched, staring in the direction from which the music was playing. Yawning, he shook his stubbled head.

"Sounds like they're having a party."

He smiled and rubbed his chest with the tips of his dirty fingers. "May have to go check out the talent. Never know what little treasures may be suddenly dropped onto your lap. Know what I mean?" he said before closing the lid and latching it shut.

As soon as Dr. Sue heard the lock latch, she knew she was safe. Just to be sure though, she waited until she heard the door to the motorhome open and then slam shut, and then she went to work.

Once again, she rolled onto her back and removed the tape from her mouth. She took a deep breath and nearly gagged as the smell was becoming unbearable.

Earlier, while lying in the rancid darkness, she had come up with an idea. Now, knowing he was gone, she finally had the chance to see if it would work.

While she had to admit she was not exactly a voluptuous woman, she did wear a bra, and thankfully, Orley had left the top half of her body clothed.

Reaching behind her, she unlatched her bra and then slipped it off through her sleeve without removing her white silk shirt. Holding the bra in front of her, she felt in the darkness until her fingers found the underwire that gave her the little bit of support her B-cup breasts required.

The wire, she felt, actually seemed to be pretty thick, making her believe her idea might just work. So once again, she used the sharp points of her corner teeth to gnaw at the thread that kept the wire buried in the folds of Lycra.

After a few frustrating moments, she felt the threads begin to give. She pushed the fabric away and unsheathed the wire. It was stiff and thick and felt like it might just do the trick.

Inching her way toward the place where she figured the lock to be, she began to work the wire between the wooden ceiling and the wall, hoping to catch the lock trip with the end of the wire. One of two things had to happen. She would either find the latch, open it, and then finally be free, or she would fail to find it, remain trapped, and eventually die at the hands of a psycho.

There was absolutely no way she was going to let herself die in this hellhole. Not today. Not ever.

Orley stepped out of the motorhome and into the cool dusk. He could smell a campfire burning, and he could hear the sound of music drifting from its direction. The dry, crisp air cleared his head, putting him suddenly in a really good mood. Lighting a cigarette, he decided to mosey down to the party and see if he could score up some action.

As he approached the small gathering, he noticed the group was huddled around a small campfire. He recalled seeing a sign that prohibited such fires due to the dry conditions, and an alarm went off in his head. Since he didn't need a run-in with the cops right now, he debated what to do.

The youthful laughter of a young lady brought him back to reality. He instantly felt the burning sensation in his crotch, and he knew that trying to fight the beast right now was useless. The demon demanded a release, and he knew the crumpled-up flesh of the older woman back in his motorhome wouldn't cut the mustard.

As he approached the group, a younger guy with shoulder-length brown hair turned toward him. Orley smiled. The dude smiled back.

"'s up, my man," Edward said, switching a red plastic cup from his right hand to his left and then extending the empty hand toward Orley.

Orley grabbed the kid's hand and pumped it twice. "Not much," he said after letting his hand fall. He suddenly found himself holding a cold bottle of Coors Light. "Thanks." He raised the bottle in a mock toast and then took a sip.

"No prob," Edward said. "That your motorhome up there?"

"Yup," Orley replied.

"Sweet. Hey man," Edward said, nudging another guy who was standing next to him and talking to a giggling young girl. The guy looked at Edward, obviously annoyed. "That's his ride. That big rig up there." He nodded at Orley. "'s his."

Orley saw the other guy shrug and then direct his attention back to the girl.

"My name's Eddie. Welcome to the party."

"Thanks," Orley said. "You guys live around here?"

"Naw," Edward said. "I live back East. Just out here visiting. Gotta go home tomorrow."

"One last shin-dig, huh?"

"Yup. One last party."

Orley cringed as Edward let out a loud yell, but then he heard the obnoxious call greeted by a female response from across the fire, and for some reason, that made it okay. He took a huge chug of beer and was rewarded with an instant headache. He refused to care.

"Know what though man?" Edward said. It was obvious to Orley the kid was pretty drunk.

"What's that?" Orley asked, eyeing a sweet, extremely young-looking girl that was sitting across from him. She looked innocent and pure, bundled up in an oversized yellow sweatshirt. His groin was aching now, and the denim in his crotch was as tight as it could be.

"I got all these girls here wanna give me a good-bye to remember," he heard Edward say while he continued to eye his next target.

"Yeah," Orley said. "That sucks."

"Naw, man. That doesn't suck. What sucks is the one I want to nail isn't here."

"Too bad," Orley said, finishing the beer. He tossed the empty bottle into a pile of already dead ones. "Want another one?"

"Sure."

Edward reached into a large red cooler and pulled out a dripping brown bottle. He handed it to Orley, who unscrewed the cap and flicked it into the fire.

"Nice shot," Edward said.

"Thanks. So where is she?" Orley asked, not really interested in the response. But, he figured the way into the pants of any of the young ladies here was through the annoying little twerp who was supposedly their guest of honor. So he made do.

"Who?" Edward asked.

"The one who's not here?"

"Oh yeah," Edward said. "Stuck-up bitch wouldn't come. Got a kid. Living in a cabin up the road."

The burn in Orley's crotch instantly fled. He looked at Edward who was staring at the fire. "So why didn't she come?" he said.

"You know women," Edward replied, puffing up his chest and rubbing his belly with his unoccupied right hand. "You lay the pipe in 'em once and they get all bitchy and stuck up."

Orley could feel his ears turning red. "Yeah," he said, using every ounce of strength he had to control himself. He took a deep breath of his own and then chased it with a giant sip of beer. "So you nailed her, huh?"

"Oh yeah," Edward said. "I pretty much nailed all the girls here, but I liked her the best, and she didn't come."

Orley shook his head. "Yeah, but you did," he said, smirking. He wanted more than anything to bash the beer bottle into the young face next to him.

"You know it," Edward smiled. "And I'm gonna come again tonight," he elbowed Orley. "Know what I mean dude?"

Orley smiled. "Yeah man. I know what you mean." He stared at the girl across the fire again but felt nothing except pure rage in his body. "So where is she, I mean the cabin? You said it's around here?"

"I'm not supposed to say," Edward said. "I think she's hiding from the cops." He suddenly stood up straight and looked at Orley. "You're not a cop, are you?"

Orley smiled. "You think a cop can afford a rig like that?" He nodded over his shoulder.

Edward slouched again. "Whew," he said, smiling. "Glad you're not a cop. Not a lot of over-age people here, if you know what I mean. Plus, we're not supposed to have a fire either."

"Yeah. I saw the sign. Looks like you need another beer," Orley said, nodding down at Eddie's empty cup.

"'s not beer, man. Rum. Straight."

"Wow," Orley said. "Where'd you get that?"

"At my uncle's store. You know, Mickey's Mart. The only freaking place in town."

"Oh yeah. That place. I saw it as I blasted through town. Up the road there," Orley said, nodding into the darkness.

"Yup. That's where she is now. Right up the road."

"The girl you want to nail again?" Orley said, blood still boiling.

"Yup. Figure a few more cups of liquid courage and then I'll mosey my way up there. I'm a hell of a lot more eloquent when I'm drunk. Know what I mean?"

Orley finished his beer. "Yeah. I know what you mean. She live in the shop?" Orley asked.

"Naw, man. There's this tiny little cabin up the trail behind it. Can't see it from the road, but guess what?"

"Hmm," Orley said.

"I snuck up the hill one night and saw her naked through the window. She's really hot."

"That before you nailed her or after?"

"Before man," Edward said. "Had to see if it was worth the effort."

"Was it?"

"Hell-fucking-yeah it was. Why do you think my heart's all broken now?"

"Maybe I can help you out," Orley said.

"How's that?"

"I got some stuff up in my rig that'll have her spread eagle before you and purring in your ear."

Edward's eyebrows arched. "Yeah?"

"You bet. Got it in Mexico. Works every time. I freaking swear."

"Spanish fly?"

"Better."

"Dude. Le' me buy some? I got cash." Orley watched Edward nearly fall over as he dug his hand into his jeans.

"Tell you what," Orley said, putting his right hand on Edward's shoulder to keep him from falling down. "You can have it for free. Since it's your last night and all. Come on." Orley nodded toward the motorhome. "I'll give it to you for free."

"Right on, man," Edward said, raising his hand for a high-five. Orley slapped it and then slapped his hand on the kid's back as the two walked toward the distant rig.

"You gonna try and nail her tonight then?" Orley said as they walked away from the music.

"I gotta," Edward replied. "How fast does the stuff work? I mean, am I gonna have time and stuff?"

"It's instant."

As the two rounded the front of the motorhome, Orley saw they were totally blocked from view.

"She won't even know what *hit* her," he said, slamming his fist into the unsuspecting youngster's soft belly while saying the word *hit*.

Edward doubled over, the wind knocked out of him. He tried to cry out but found he could only inhale. Blinking and trying to regain his composure, he attempted to run away, but it was too late.

Orley grabbed the surprised young man by his ears and then thrust the youngster's head down toward the ground while simultaneously raising his own right knee. He felt and then heard Edward's nose crunch against his knee just before he let the younger man crumple to the ground into the fetal position.

"When you *fuck* another man's wife," Orley said, "shut your *fucking* mouth. You don't know who you're *fucking* talking to, you piece of *fucking* shit." He kicked Edward hard in the ribs every time he said the word *fuck*, and he saw the young man didn't move. He was tempted to check for a pulse but decided to just spit on him instead.

Satisfied, Orley sucked the cool crisp air into his lungs before yanking open the door to the motorhome. He was still full of rage, but kicking the crap out of that little piece of shit sure seemed to help. Looking at the empty Jack Daniel's bottle, he felt a twinge in his pants, so he glanced to his left at the dark bedroom.

"Feeling lucky, Doctor?" he asked, loudly. "Old Jack's lonely tonight, and I'm madder than a snake right now." He didn't hear a response, but then he didn't really expect to hear one either. Glancing at the bottle once more, he decided he probably needed to make some distance between himself and that little shit outside before doing anything to the doctor. Plus, now he knew where to go. It was not that far.

He climbed into the seat and started the motor. As he drove past the campfire, he noticed no one seemed to miss Mr. Eddie at all. His suspicion was Eddie never really laid his pipe into anyone at the party, but it was clear to

Orley the little shit still needed to get his ass kicked, and he was more than obliged to have done the kicking.

"Traffic's pretty heavy," Riley said as he picked his way through the slower moving cars on the 5 Freeway.

"Be careful Riley," Patty said. "I was shot and survived. I'm already running on borrowed time."

"Any luck with Mickey?" Riley asked.

"Still nothing except the answering machine," Howard said from the dark backseat. "I'll keep trying though."

"There's gotta be a way to warn her," Riley said, more to himself than out loud.

"What's that?" Patty asked.

"I said I wish we could warn her somehow. You sure we shouldn't call the police?"

"Riley, this is still one of your wild hairs. I can't call the chief with this. Not yet. He'll hang up the minute he hears me mention your name. You know that as well as I do. We need some hard proof. Theories aren't going to cut it on this one."

"Who pissed on your Wheaties?" Riley asked.

"What?" Patty replied.

"I said, what's eating you? All of a sudden you're all quiet and then bitchy. I thought we made up."

Patty stared at Riley for a few moments before saying, "Don't let that little incident outside that apartment go to your head. You're still on my shit list. And you know what? You suck as a kisser."

"What?" Howard said from the backseat.

"Nothing," Riley and Patty said simultaneously.

"Kissing? You guys were making out at the apartment? Here I was with nine and one dialed into the phone, staring at my watch ready to hit the last one and then *SEND* when fifteen minutes *exactly* had passed, and you guys are going at it in some child molester's home. Holy cow…"

"That's it," Patty suddenly yelled.

"What?" Riley replied, surprised at the outburst.

"Let me see that picture," Patty said, digging through the stack of papers and photos that were sitting on the dash. She clicked on the reading light and found the picture of Orlando Price in front of the motorhome. She adjusted her glasses and squinted at the photo.

"What?" Riley said again. "You want me to pull over?"

"Yeah. Pull over for a sec. It just popped into my head. There was something eating at me since I saw that picture, and then suddenly," she snapped her fingers. "It was just there."

Riley pulled onto the soft shoulder of the freeway.

"Are you going to tell us what it is?" he asked after putting the car into park and leaving the motor running.

"You saw the tattoos, right?" Patty asked Howard.

"I'd say I got a pretty good look at one of them after the arm it was attached to shoved me in the chest."

"This one right here," she asked, pointing at his left arm with her stubby, unpainted fingernail. "It looks like a little girl on a seesaw?"

"Yeah. I remember that one," Howard said, leaning between the two front seats to see over Patty's left shoulder. "So?"

"I've been chasing this asshole for a few months," she said, thumping her finger against the picture. "He's been suspected of raping little girls. But, there's never any evidence because…"

"He's the one that wears a condom," Riley interrupted.

"A rapist wears a condom?" Howard asked.

"You'd be surprised at what kind of freaks live in our town," Patty replied. "One of the little girls said she saw a picture of a girl on a seesaw on one of his arms. That's not a common tattoo. I'll bet this son-of-a-bitch is the one I've been looking for."

"You'd better call it in," Riley said. "May be an excuse to get the cops up there."

"I'm not sure I can do that. I mean, technically, I'm on leave."

"Well, we gotta do something," Riley said. "I'm fairly certain that we're not gonna get phone service once we hit that canyon road. It gets pretty sparse if I remember."

"Man, if this is the guy," Patty said "he's supposed to have a pretty bad temper. I mean from what some of the girls have said."

"They're not the only ones to say he has a temper. I mean, Amy's mom seemed pretty scared." Riley slammed his fist onto the steering wheel. "There's got to be some way to warn her. There's got to be."

"I've got an idea," Howard said.

Chapter 32

Amy burst into the cabin, her heart hammering in her chest. She looked around frantically before dashing into the small bedroom.

"What's wrong Mommy?" Joel asked from behind wide eyes.

"We gotta go honey," Amy said, grabbing the suitcase from atop the huge armoire that dominated the tiny bedroom. Yanking it open, she withdrew a second smaller case from inside the larger one.

She didn't know why, call it providence or whatever, but for some reason she decided to go out to the car to listen to the news. She had wanted to go to Mickey's to see if she could pick up a new radio, but her desire to avoid that little shit Edward kept her from doing just that.

As luck would have it, she had only been in the car for a few minutes when she heard the breaking news report. Her heart stopped beating when the woman's voice told the station's listeners the program manager for the Dr. Sue Show wanted to talk to an *Amy Nicholes* about her husband who was coming to see her in *Green Valley* and someone thought *she* somehow knew something about the kidnapping of Dr. Sue.

After that, the rest of the report had been irrelevant. All Amy needed to hear was her husband was coming to see her in Green Valley. For a few seconds, she had stared in disbelief at the digital radio, almost as if she believed that by staring at it, the report would not be real. But it was real, and she knew she had to get out of Green Valley, right now.

Snatching all of their clothes from the dresser and throwing them into the two open suitcases, she reached between the mattress and the box springs and withdrew the large yellow envelope that contained the rectangular lump of cash she had withdrawn from the bank the day prior. She tossed it on top of one of the piles of clothes and then zipped the suitcases closed. Carrying them out to her car, she could smell the hint of a fire, and a chill ran up her spine. He was close. She could feel it. *Run*, a voice in her head screamed. *Run now!*

Opening the car's trunk, she dropped the two suitcases inside, slammed the trunk with a thump, and then dashed back into the cabin to grab her son.

"Why do we have to leave?" Joel asked. "I thought we were going to stay here for a long time."

"Daddy found us," she said between nervous breaths. "We have to get out of here before he gets here." She wiped a tear from her cheek with the cloth that covered her right shoulder.

After buckling Joel into his car seat, she slammed his door, jumped into her own seat, and started the car. The smell of the nearby fire was getting stronger. Leaving the headlights off, she slowly descended the dirt path that led to the lot behind Mickey's Mart.

Why didn't someone call Mickey? Amy wondered until she saw the lights were off in the store. *That's odd*, she thought. *It was usually open until ten. Even on Friday.*

She made her way through the parking lot and around the small store to the highway. Looking both ways, she saw no traffic, so taking a deep breath, she turned right, away from Los Angeles. She figured Orley would be coming from the city so she decided to make her way toward Palmdale and then up to Mammoth or Reno as quickly as possible.

Finally feeling safe enough to turn on her headlights, she pulled out onto the highway and sped off into the darkness, her eyes alternating between the road and the rearview mirror. She saw no other traffic in either direction.

It was not until about two miles into her escape that her heart dropped into her stomach. She felt the panicky feeling of acid rising in her throat as itchy beads of sweat simultaneously formed all over her back. She looked onto the seat next to her and then at the dark passenger floor.

"No," she said, pounding the steering wheel. "Joel, honey, did you move Mommy's purse?"

She saw Joel shake his head as she glanced over her shoulder. She searched the seat and the floor again but still did not see it. "Joel," she said drawing out his name.

"I wanted some gum," he whined.

Amy slammed on the breaks, pulling the car onto the shoulder. "Where'd you put it?" she asked, tears running down her cheeks.

"I'm sorry," Joel said, burying his face into his hands. He started to sob.

"It's okay honey," Amy said, reaching back and rubbing his tiny forearm. "Mommy's not mad at you. I just need to know where it is. Did you put it in the cabin?"

"Uh huh," Joel said, his face still buried in his hands.

Amy quickly pondered her options. She could drive toward her mom's without her purse. She did have a heck of a lot of cash in the trunk, and they could live on that for a long time, but her purse had her driver's license and credit cards as well as Joel's social security and medical cards. She knew if Orley got hold of some of those, he could make some demands that she was unwilling to accept.

"Damn it," she said, slapping the top of the steering wheel with her hand. She leaned forward and rested her forehead on the top of the wheel, rubbing at her temples with the knuckles of her index fingers.

"I'm sorry Mommy," Joel said through a small voice from the backseat.

After a few seconds, Amy, with eyes still closed and head still resting on the steering wheel, said, "It's okay hun. Mommy's just mad at herself. Not you."

Taking a deep breath, she sat up, put the car into drive, turned around, and headed back to the cabin despite the lead weight that sat in her stomach.

As she approached Mickey's Mart, she saw it was still dark. Taking a deep breath, she let out an audible sigh of relief when she saw Orley's car was not in the store's parking lot. She told herself to relax as she made her way back up the dirt road toward the cabin.

"Mommy," Joel said.

"Yes hun?"

"I need to go to the bathroom."

She looked over her shoulder at her son. "Number one or number two?" she asked.

Joel held up two fingers.

"Can you hold it a while?"

She saw him shake his head no.

"Okay, come on," she said as she climbed out of the car and helped her son out of his seat. "But hurry up hun. Okay?"

"'kay."

Amy felt a chill pass through her body as she crossed the door's threshold. *It's just because it's cold out*, she told herself. She didn't believe it though.

"Chief?"

"What? I said I didn't want to be disturbed," Chief Bruggeman said into the intercom box that sat on the front corner of his desk. Still pissed about the failed rescue attempt earlier in the day, he was startled as the door to his office suddenly burst open.

"Quick. Turn on the radio. KKLA. You gotta hear this."

The chief hit the power button on a small radio that sat to his left and leaned back. "What the hell 're you still doing here anyway? Didn't I tell you to scram?"

"Had some stuff to do," Connie, his secretary, said.

The chief nodded and then looked at the radio. His jaw dropped into his lap when he heard the special news broadcast. "Who the hell authorized this?" he yelled.

"I don't know. It just came on." The phone next to him suddenly rang. Connie reached over and picked it up.

"Chief Bruggeman's office," she said into the receiver. "One moment. I'll see if he's in." She covered the receiver and mouthed the letters "F-B-I."

"Crap," the chief said through thin lips. He nodded to Connie who, in turn, handed him the phone.

"Chief Bruggeman," he barked. "Yeah. I just heard it too…no, I did not authorize it. I'm still pissed about the disaster at the Sage house earlier. I think we should pursue the San Francisco lead. It makes sense." He stared at Connie and rolled his eyes. "How the hell do I know where Green Valley is? It's not in my jurisdiction. I'll call the sheriff and see if they can find it. Then *they* can waste their time sending a unit there." He scribbled a few words onto a piece of paper and handed it to Connie. "Look. It's your call. I think we have a solid lead in San Francisco. Like I said, this thing reeks of the gay community and extortion. The M. O. fits…All right…Okay, I'll call the sheriff and have him send a unit over to check it out. It's probably just a prank though, but I'll keep you posted anyway. Okay. Yeah. Good-bye."

Connie appeared with a printout from MapQuest. "Just right up the road, Chief. Between Palmdale and Santa Clarita."

"I knew it. It's out of my jurisdiction. Get me the damn sheriff's office. And get the number for that idiot Greg Riley. He had Dr. Sue's producer with him earlier. I'll bet that little freak is behind this. If he is, I am going to crush his nuts."

"Right away, Chief."

"And Connie?"

"Yes Chief?"

"Thanks for staying late. I owe you."

Connie smiled and dashed back to her desk.

Orley pulled the rig into Mickey's Mart. He saw a large dirt lot behind the building so he maneuvered the lumbering motorhome so it was parked near its center, the nose of the rig facing the small store. He cut the ignition and then turned off the lights.

Looking over his right shoulder, he saw a small trail that looked like it led from the back of the lot, up a shallowly sloping hill, and into total blackness. Although narrow, it did appear to be sturdy enough to hold the motorhome, as long as the trail didn't make any tight turns once it crested, in the area he couldn't see. He decided to check it out on foot just in case.

Popping the door open, he jumped out into the chilly air. He could still smell the campfire, and he wondered if the cops would come to check it out. If so, he needed to work quickly.

Orley scanned the darkness, listening for any sounds that might indicate the presence of another human being. The air was quiet and crisp. He appeared to be alone.

Trotting up the small hill in front of him, he only slowed when he reached its peak. As he rounded the crest, he looked down and saw his wife's car parked in front of a tiny wooden cabin. He could see a light was on inside, so he figured she was there. Testing the road with his foot, he determined it looked like it was sturdy enough to support the motorhome. Plus, he could barely make out a large dirt lot in front of the cabin. *Perfect*, he thought, as he saw the motorhome would be well hidden from the highway. Things were looking pretty good, so he decided to make his move.

Trotting back down the dark dirt road, he revised his plan as he went. He knew Dr. Sue might put up one last fight as he tried to transfer her into the cabin. So, he decided the best thing for him to do was to hit her with the chloroform again. That way he could carry her into the cabin and wait for her to wake up. Then, he would get her to tell Amy she had given wrong advice and that Amy should not have left him. He smiled as he opened the door to the motorhome. Everything would be done by sunrise.

After a dreadfully long time, Dr. Sue gave up picking at the lock. No matter how hard she tried, she simply could not get it to unlatch. While resting in the dark and working on plan B, an idea suddenly hit her. Although simple and risky, she was certain it would work.

When she felt the motorhome come to a stop, she maneuvered herself back into the *bound and gagged* position, but this time with a little surprise of her own. She heard the door to the motorhome open and then close and wondered what had been going on. All kinds of thoughts raced through her mind. She knew she was close to the end, and she knew she was not going to go down without a fight. Although she was sore, thirsty, dirty, and tired, she was ready for anything, and she was ready to do anything to see her family again.

After what seemed like a relatively short time, she heard the door to the motorhome open and then close again. Her heart started to pound in her chest as she heard the muffled thumping of footsteps walking toward her.

Light washed over her when the lid to her world popped open, but other than a few blinks, Dr. Sue lay perfectly still.

"Okay Doctor," she heard Orley say as he stood over her, "your time has come da face the music. We are at Amy's place. She's inside. I'm going da give you a little something to make you go night-night. When you wake up, we'll be inside her cabin. You tell her you gave her bad advice, and then you tell her she should come back da me. You do as I say, and you live da see your family. I'm feeling pretty good right now. You do anything else, you get a dirt nap in the desert that I guarantee you will not wake up from. Nod if you understand."

Dr. Sue nodded her head slowly. She knew it was now or never. Dirt nap or not, she wasn't going down without a fight.

Chapter 33

Orley disappeared for a few seconds and then returned holding a small brown bottle and a rag. Dr. Sue saw him open the bottle and dowse the rag with some sort of liquid. She watched him put the bottle down on the small shelf next to her empty water bottle and then move toward her.

"Don't do anything stupid," he said as he leaned down slowly into the box.

It was difficult for Dr. Sue to judge distance since one of her eyes was swollen completely shut. Nevertheless, after a slow count to three, she made her move.

Swiftly, with a strength born out of fear, anger, and adrenaline, she darted upright and lashed out with her left fist.

Startled, Orley's eyes shot open, and then he cried out in pain as something sharp drove into his right eyeball. Out of pure reflex, he thrust the rag up to his face and winced in tremendous pain. That's when his world began to spin.

Dr. Sue knew she scored a direct hit when she both felt and heard Orley's eye pop after driving the metal wire into his unsuspecting face. She saw him bring the rag up to his eye and then saw him stagger backwards and collapse onto the small floor. She thought she heard a muffled scream as she leapt from her confines, but she wasn't going to stick around to find out if he was okay. Instead, she darted down the small hallway to the first door she could find.

Yanking it open, she was greeted with two lungs full of cold, crisp, smoky night air. It was her first breath of fresh in God knows how long, and it was wonderful.

As she dashed out of the motorhome's door, she felt something catch her shirt. Fearing it was Orley, she jumped out of the doorway and into the darkness, her silk shirt ripping from her body during the process. Nude from the waist up, scared, and full of adrenaline, Dr. Sue rushed around to the front of the motorhome where she spotted a small convenience store. Pulling the duct tape from her mouth, she yelled as loud as she could.

"Help! Helllp!" She ran toward the small building. "Somebody please help me!"

Reaching the store's door, she yanked on it, but it was locked. She peered inside, through one of the door's small windows, and saw the building was empty. Something sharp dug into the bottom of her right heel when she stepped away from the door. Looking down, she saw a tiny piece of green glass hanging from her foot. She pulled it out and immediately noticed a trickle of blood drip from what looked to be a small cut. Pressing the tiny wound with her thumb, she looked away from the building, wondering what to do next.

After a few seconds, Dr. Sue let go of her heel and then followed the side of the building until she reached a payphone that pancaked the wall near a locked bathroom door. She yanked the receiver from the cradle and dialed *9-1-1*. Nothing. She repeatedly banged on the lever that would have held the receiver had she not been holding it, but there was still no dial tone. Leaning forward, she squinted in the gray light and read with her one good eye she needed to deposit thirty-five cents in order to get a dial tone. She also saw someone had cut the aluminum tube that would have encased the chord had there actually been one.

Her heart sank. She slammed the receiver onto its holder and fought the urge to cry. *Why is there nobody here? Why will nobody help? Why is the world against me?*

Looking across a dimly lit parking lot, she could see a dark highway so she made her way toward the road in the hopes of flagging down the first car she saw. She was beginning to shiver wildly now. The crisp air against her bare chest and back, although refreshing at first, was becoming unbearable. She dug her hands, still braceleted in plastic straps, into her scratchy armpits and squatted down on her haunches to keep warm. *Where are the damn hot flashes now?*

Once again Dr. Sue looked around in the darkness, praying for a car to drive by. But all she saw was black, all she smelled was smoke, and all she heard was silence. After what seemed like an eternity, she decided she needed to act. She would freeze to death if she waited much longer, and she had come way too far to let that happen. She wiped a stream of tears from her right cheek with her shoulder and considered her options.

Rising slowly, she made her way back toward the store. She figured Orley might be looking for her so she made sure to be quiet. Although she was certain there was a jacket inside the motorhome, returning to it was completely out of the question. She would find another way to get warm.

She traced the perimeter until she once again found the front door. Peering inside, she spotted a telephone next to the cash register, and she could see a little red light blinking on what appeared to be an answering machine. Her heartbeat picked up its pace.

She looked around on the ground for something she could use to break the glass. All she needed was about a minute to make a quick call. After that, if Orley came, she would only have to hold him off for a few more minutes until the police arrived. She was confident she could find something in the store to use as a weapon. Plus, she was almost certain she had wounded him pretty badly.

Trotting back toward the road, she searched the ground for something hard enough to do the job. After a few quick seconds, she spotted a good-sized rock, grabbed it, and then slinked back toward the store.

Orley's spinning world finally slowed. He tried to recall what had just happened, but his mind was nothing but a series of flashes, and his right eye was killing him. Keeping it closed, he glanced at his hands with his left eye and saw they were covered with blood.

Needless to say, he was completely confused. Sniffing at a wet rag, he winced at its smell and then tossed it onto the bed. He needed to get into some fresh air or else he was going to throw up all over the place.

Making his way to the motorhome's door, he saw it was already opened, so he staggered out into the cold air. His head instantly cleared, and he saw a white piece of cloth lying on the ground at his feet. He grabbed it and brought it up to his face, holding it firmly against his painful right eye. After a few seconds, he realized he was holding Dr. Sue's blouse, which stunk pretty badly.

Orley felt his head begin to spin again, and his legs gave out from underneath him, causing him to fall. The blouse fell from his face as he struggled to break his fall. Resting on all fours, he dry heaved into the dirt below him. *What happened*, he thought, shaking the drool from his lips and the cobwebs from his head.

The sound of rustling leaves on the other side of the motorhome drew him out of his funk. Anger and frustration refocused his senses, and he immediately remembered where he was and why he was there. Fighting the stinging pain in his eye and the nausea in his stomach, he willed himself to his feet and staggered toward the back of the motorhome.

Peering around the corner with his good left eye, he saw a shirtless figure trot away from the store, in the direction of the highway. He moved quickly toward the small store, hoping to catch her before she could flag someone down, but she moved too swiftly. Plus, he was having trouble seeing straight. He leaned against the wall of the building to catch his breath and to steady himself. His right eye continued to throb, stinging to the rhythm of his heartbeat. A cough from the other side of the building froze him in place. Squeezing himself flat against the wall, he held his breath and waited.

A noise near the corner of the building caught Dr. Sue's attention. Shivering, almost beyond control, she convinced herself her mind was playing tricks on her since she heard nothing else for a good twenty seconds. She was finding it difficult to move in the paralyzing cold, and her breathing was becoming labored. She coughed into her empty left fist before heading toward the corner of the building so she could break a window and then open the store's door.

But before she knew what was happening, she felt a large hand slap against her mouth and pull her chin toward her left shoulder. She tried desperately to scream, but everything happened too fast. Falling hard onto the ground, she felt sticks and small rocks jab into her naked back, but that was nothing compared to what she felt next.

"Stupid, stupid bitch," Orley said, kneeling on top of Dr. Sue's sternum. He both heard and felt a rib pop and then he saw her face wince in pain. Feeling her trying to scream against his hand, he refused to let go. "Look what you did to my eye," he yelled, uncupping his right eye with his right hand. "Look."

Dr. Sue, tears careening down her cheeks, forced herself to look away. After an eternity of pain, she felt her body being lifted as her arms dangled behind her. She wanted to scream and fight and yell, but she couldn't. He had literally crushed the will right out of her, and now all she wanted was to die.

She felt him carry her into the motorhome, not bothering to resist as he rolled her onto her stomach so he could wrap duct tape around her wrists. Once he had secured her wrists behind her, she felt him roll her back over so she faced him.

The slaps came, but she heard them more than she felt their pain. *Slap. Slap. Slap.*

He continued smacking her with both sides of his hand, but she refused to care. The last thing she remembered before blacking out was seeing the picture of her family and asking God to protect them after she was gone.

Chapter 34

"Okay Mommy. I'm done," Joel said as he walked out of the cabin's bathroom.

"Feel better?" Amy asked, walking toward the cabin's front door.

Joel nodded.

"Did you wash your hands?"

Joel nodded again.

"Good. Put your jacket on, and let's get the heck out of here." She looked down at her watch. Fifteen long minutes had passed since they returned to the cabin.

Joel slipped his tiny body into his dark blue jacket and walked through the door as his mom held it open. He climbed into the backseat, and then she closed the car door for him. Falling into the front seat, she started the car, put it into gear, and then put it back into park again.

"I'll be right back honey," she said as she jumped out of the car and ran back inside. Thirty seconds later, she darted back out to the car and threw her purse onto the passenger seat. "Almost forgot it again," she said, smiling at Joel. She saw him smile back.

Amy put the car into drive and then turned it around on the large dirt driveway. Leaving the lights off again, she slowly made her way up the cresting, winding trail. As she neared the top of the small knoll, she saw what looked like another set of lights approaching from the opposite direction. She slowed the car, and then her heart leapt into her throat.

"Oh no," she whimpered as she saw the large motorhome crest the hill. She felt like she was going to throw up.

Trapped between the oncoming vehicle in front of her and the dark cabin behind her, she put the car into reverse and slowly backed down the dirt hill, careful not to stray too far from the center of the trail as it fell away quickly into a deep valley to her right.

As she inched her way back into the driveway, she saw the motorhome was coming at her faster than she was backing up, rapidly eating up the distance between the two vehicles. Quickly accelerating in reverse, she promptly found herself in the exact spot from which she had only moments ago departed.

She watched the motorhome come to a standstill, and then she saw the driver's door open. Orley jumped from the door, staggering when he hit the ground. *He's drunk*, Amy thought before noticing he was covering his right eye with a towel. Instantly, her motherly instinct took over.

"Run Joel!" she screamed as she saw Orley approaching in the darkness. "Run and get Mickey!"

Without missing a beat, Joel opened the opposite rear door and darted out into the darkness.

"Joel!" Orley cried when he saw his son dash out of the car and then disappear. He trotted toward him but was intercepted by his wife.

"Let him go you bastard," she said, blocking Orley from chasing her son.

"Joel!" Orley called again, pushing Amy out of the way. "I'll deal with you later you bitch," he whispered as he slid past her.

"Run Joel," Amy yelled into the darkness. "Don't worry about Mommy. Just run."

Orley stopped moving toward his son and instead turned toward Amy. He saw her back away as he approached.

"You little cunt," he said, grabbing her arm with his left hand, his right hand still holding a towel to his right eye. "You think you can leave me? Take my son?" He pulled her toward the motorhome. "Well, I got something I wanna show you. You're gonna love this. You'll see you made a huge mistake."

Amy stepped into the dark motorhome and immediately winced at the smell. "Quit pushing me," she said when she heard the door close behind her. "It stinks in here." She squinted when the light suddenly clicked on.

"I don't believe you two have been formally introduced," Orley said.

Amy turned around slowly and then stifled a small scream by quickly bringing an open palm to her mouth.

"Is…is that Dr. Sue?" she said, blinking tears from her eyes.

"In the flesh," Orley said, smiling. "And when she wakes up, she has something to tell you."

Amy stared at Dr. Sue who, except for what appeared to be a large diaper, lay naked on the motorhome's tiny couch. Her hands were tied behind her back. Her right eye was a bruised and swollen slit, and Amy could see both sides of her face were beginning to swell up and darken as well. She was covered in dirt. Amy noticed a line of unusually dark blood had seeped from the corner of her mouth and slowly traced its way toward her chin.

"What did you do to her you monster?" Amy said, stepping forward to slap Orley. He caught her forearm and threw her backward where she stumbled and then fell between the motorhome's small table and one of the benches that sat beneath it.

"Now, now, now," Orley said. "Let's not do something we're going to regret here." He stepped toward Amy and saw her cringe slightly. "The good doctor here knows she has made a mistake. She knows she gave you some really bad advice, and when she wakes up, she's going to tell you what she really meant to say." He looked down at Dr. Sue. "Isn't that right Doctor?"

"There is nothing you can make her say to make me feel any different about anything Orley. It's over between us. I'm leaving you. I want a d..."

Amy heard the slap before she actually felt it, but when the pain came, it arrived with a force she had never felt before. She doubled over sobbing, trying to protect herself from the blows that thankfully never came.

"Get up," Orley said.

She remained seated, face in her hands, and cried.

"I said get up bitch." Orley reached down and grabbed Amy's left arm, yanking her onto her feet.

Amy could feel the sting on the left side of her face increase to a raging burn, and her eyes began to water uncontrollably. She reached down with her right hand to steady her spinning world by resting it near the edge of the tiny wooden table. "Sorry," she said meekly.

"I know," Orley replied. He reached forward and wiped a tear from her cheek with his left thumb. "When she wakes up, you'll see everything 'll be all right."

Amy looked up at Orley and then yanked her arm from his grip. "What happened to your eye?" she said, wiping her wet cheeks and then rubbing her left arm.

Orley turned his face slightly away from Amy, enough so he could see her with his good eye while simultaneously hiding his wound. "Nothing," he said. "Don't worry about it." His eye was killing him.

"Can I go find Joel?" Amy asked. "It stinks in here, and it's cold out there."

"No way," Orley said. "I've come too far to have you slip away again. In fact, why don't you come over here and sit next to Dr. Sue?"

Amy contemplated dashing for the door, but she knew it was hopeless to resist right now as Orley was in one of his moods. She had learned long ago the best thing to do during times such as this was to just ride it out and hope for the best. She took two short steps toward the sleeping Dr. Sue and then turned around and sat down next to her on the couch.

"Slide your arm in behind her," Orley said. He ripped a large piece of duct tape from a roll that suddenly appeared in his hands.

Amy slid her left arm in between Dr. Sue's bruised right upper arm and small, naked breast, her own sweatshirt-covered arm brushing against Dr. Sue's erect, right nipple.

"Now, put your other arm behind you."

Amy did as instructed.

"Don't try anything stupid," Orley said as he reached behind Amy and quickly bound her hands behind her back by wrapping the large strand of duct tape four times around her tiny wrists.

Orley glanced down and admired his work. Satisfied, he walked over to the small sink and filled a cup with cold water.

"No thanks," Amy said, sniffing wet air into her dripping nose. She wiped her left cheek with her shrugging shoulder. "I'm not thirsty."

Orley smiled a quick chuckle. "Don't worry honey," he said as he stepped toward the two bound women. "It's not for you."

"There," Riley said, pointing to the small convenience store whose lighted sign suddenly announced its presence on the right side of the dark road. Riley slowed and maneuvered into the area containing the station's only two gas pumps. He stopped the car.

"Looks closed," Howard said from the darkened rear seat.

"Yeah," Riley replied, squinting into the darkness. "I don't see anyone in the store. He looked over at Patty. "Wanna go take a look?"

Patty surveyed the dark area before pulling her cell phone from her purse. She pushed one of the keys, and then read the words NO SERVICE on the tiny screen. "Anyone getting service out here?" she asked weakly. She was greeted with silence from the two others who suddenly found themselves staring at their own small phones.

"I wish I had some sort of backup," Patty said. She looked up at Riley and noticed a surprised look on his face. "Just in case, you know." She quickly glanced down at her phone again.

Riley popped open his door, the inside of the car suddenly awash in light. "C'm' on," he said, stepping out into the cold night. "I'll be your backup."

Patty took a deep breath and then opened her own door. Her heart was racing. She forced herself to calm down.

"Don't go making out in the woods you two," Howard called from the backseat. "I'm all alone here."

Riley smiled. "Don't worry Howard. We'll be right back." He slammed the door.

"I heard that one before," Howard said as he leaned back into the dark and stared, impotently, at his cell phone.

"I got a weird feeling about this Riley," Patty said as the two made their way toward the store's front door.

"You wanna drive back down the hill and call for backup. I'm sure Chief Bruggeman is going freaking bananas after Howard's call to the radio station right about now."

"Naw," Patty said, wanting desperately to drive back down the hill and call for backup. She kicked herself for having let Riley talk her into this. "Maybe there's a pay phone around here," she said. "You know. Just in case."

"Maybe," Riley said, sensing Patty's nervousness. "Let's check the back. See what we can see."

"Go ahead," Patty said, following Riley around the building's small perimeter.

Joel was freezing. He withdrew the hood of his tiny coat from its small zippered compartment and pulled it over his head. After he jumped out of the car, he ran straight toward the darkness behind the cabin just like his mommy told him, and he didn't stop even though he heard his dad yelling at him. He was definitely going to be in big trouble because his dad would be very mad at him, but he was pretty scared so he chose not to think about that right now.

After making a wide arc through the creepy darkness, he ran toward the little store as quickly as he could, but when he got there, he saw no one was inside. He was cold and alone and very scared so when he had seen the strange car pull into the gas station, he had done what any kid in his or her right mind would have done; he ran back to his parents.

From the tree line in which he now found himself, he had a pretty good view of his dad's big motorhome and the front door of their new cabin. He didn't know whether anyone was in the motorhome or in the cabin so he decided to just stay put for a while to see if his mom would come to get him when it was safe.

But then he saw the motorhome's side door open, and then he saw his dad walk down the small, metal step. Unconsciously, he twisted his fingers into knots as he kept watching to make sure his mom was okay. What he saw next scared him to death.

Although it was dark, light from the inside of the motorhome provided enough brightness for Joel to see his mom was somehow tied to a small, naked woman who was walking and stumbling behind her. His mom seemed to be holding the naked woman up, basically carrying her along the short path to the cabin, and his mom wasn't even that big.

He continued to watch, crouched in the darkness, as the three of them slowly made their way to his new cabin's door. Only after he heard that door slam shut did he slowly make his way to the rear of the small building.

He slinked as quietly as he could to the darkest area behind the cabin so he could peek in through the kitchen window. Although the drapes had been pulled closed, he could still see underneath the frayed bottom hem, and he could clearly see his mom and the naked woman were sitting in chairs, their backs to him. He couldn't hear what his dad was saying, but he could see him pacing back and forth, and he could tell he was very mad.

Joel backed away from the window. Even though he was scared, he was beginning to feel angry since he could see his mom was crying. He really hated his dad, especially for making his mom feel bad, and he decided he needed to help her and the naked woman get away from him.

Bending down, he picked up a rock, but he knew the small rock in his hand would not be enough to stop his big dad. Besides, he also knew he was not that good at throwing rocks anyway so he would probably just make his dad even madder at him. That's when he thought of a better idea.

Tiptoeing as quietly as he could, exaggerating each giant step as he went, he sneaked around to the front of the cabin and peeked at the giant motorhome. He could see the big door to the inside was still open, and craning his head around the corner of the cabin, he saw the door to the cabin was still closed.

Taking a deep breath, he ran as fast as he could across the short distance to the motorhome and then darted quickly up the steps and into the safety of the inside.

Once inside, he nearly gagged. The smell of dirty diapers reminded him of the daycare where he had grown up while his dad was still in jail. He looked around the motorhome. The small area was a mess. There was blood on the floor and furniture, but it was warmer than it was outside, and that was good because he had begun to have the shakes.

Teeth chattering despite the motorhome's warm temperature, he made his way toward the driving compartment. Once there, he climbed up onto the driver's armrest and pulled open a small wooden door that covered a small compartment over the driver's seat. Pulling himself up so he could barely see over the bottom shelf of the tiny cabinet, he glanced inside and spotted the item for which he had been looking.

Riley stuck his left hand behind him, indicating to Patty that he wanted her to stay back as he peered around the corner. "Oh my God," he said as he suddenly drew his head back.

"What?" Patty said, eyes the size of saucers.

"It's…it's…a parking lot." He stood up and smiled at her.

"You son-of-a-bitch," she said, slapping his arm. "You scared the living shit out of me asshole."

"Sorry," Riley said. He rubbed his left arm. "Just trying to relieve the tension."

"I'll relieve your tension with my foot in your ass if you do that again dickhead."

"I think I'd like that," Riley said. "Come on. Let's see what's over there." He nodded toward the rear of the convenience store.

As the two made their way around to the back, they noticed it led to a large dirt parking lot. They also saw that a dirt trail, probably a firebreak, wound its way up a small knoll into the night's darkness.

"Probably parking for trucks over here," Patty said, motioning toward the lot.

"Or motorhomes," Riley said, arching his eyebrows. "Hey, what's that?" he said as he walked toward the center of the lot. Patty followed him.

"Looks like a rag," Patty said as she saw Riley pick a white piece of cloth from the dirt.

"Not a rag. It's a silk shirt," Riley said. "Got a flashlight?"

"It's in my purse," Patty said. "In the car."

"There's a light over there." Riley nodded toward the store.

The two trotted toward the one small light.

"Looks like it's covered in blood," Riley said as he flipped it around in his hands. "What was Dr. Sue wearing when she disappeared?"

"Red-skirted suit," Patty said. "Could have had a blouse like this one under it though." She reached out and took it from Riley. "Le'me see that."

She flipped it over in her hands until she could see the tag on the back. "Holy shit," she said. "Look right here."

"What's that? *S-K-S*," Riley said as he read the initials sewn into the shirt beneath its tag.

"Susan Kimberly Stein," Patty said. "It's gotta be."

Riley whipped his cell phone from his coat pocket. "Shit!" he said. "No damn service."

Patty glanced over her shoulder and saw the pay phone hanging on the store's wall. "There," she said. The two darted the quick six feet to the phone. "I'll call nine-one-one."

"Looks like blood drops on the ground." Riley bent over and touched one of the many drops and then rubbed his fingers together. "Still wet," he said as he stood back up. "Did you call?"

"Damn chord's cut," Patty said, holding the end of the wire that used to connect the phone to its receiver.

"Well what do we do now?" Riley asked, his usual clueless look on his face.

Patty thought for a moment. "Howard," she said and then quickly darted back around to the front of the building.

Riley watched her disappear, and then felt suddenly alone. "Wait up," he said before dashing around the building. Patty jumped into the driver's seat, and Riley climbed into the other side.

"Recognize this?" Patty asked as she clicked on the car's interior light and handed the torn blouse to Howard.

He stared at the blouse and then said, "Yeah. It's hers. Those are her initials. She has them on all of her clothes. Man, that thing really smells."

"I think we've found her," Riley said. "Can you believe it? I think we've really found her. So now what?"

"Why don't we call the police?" Howard said. "This store's got to have a phone."

"Store's closed and the phone isn't working," Patty said. "Neither of us has cell coverage out here."

Howard yanked his phone from his pocket and stared at it. "Me either," he said.

"Figured," Patty replied.

"What now?" Howard asked, throwing his phone onto the seat next to him.

"Wait. I have an idea," Patty closed her eyes and then paused for a few moments. "Okay, here's what we do." She opened her eyes. "Howard, you take the car and drive as fast as is safely possible back down the hill until either you get cell phone service or you see a pay phone. Call the sheriff. Call the CHP. Call the freaking National Guard for all I care. Just call for backup. Tell them an officer needs assistance at Mickey's Mart in Green Valley, California. Tell them we found Dr. Sue and we need help. And tell them to hurry."

"Got it," Howard said, opening the back door and scrambling out of the car.

"What about us?" Riley asked, getting out of the passenger side.

Patty grabbed the flashlight from her purse and stuffed it into her coat pocket. She climbed out of the driver's seat so Howard could jump in. "Go," Patty said. "Go, Howard. Go, go, go."

Riley and Patty watched the car speed off into the darkness.

"What about us?" Riley asked again.

"Well," Patty said, withdrawing her service pistol from the holster that rested comfortably next to her left breast. "You go stand by the road and wait for the cavalry to come. I'm gonna go take a look up the trail."

"Up the trail," Riley said incredulously. "You mean the dark trail behind the lot?"

"Yep," Patty said. "I just wanna take a look."

"Why don't we *both* wait by the road for backup?" Riley said weakly.

"I'm just gonna take a look Riley. Dr. Sue may be in danger. We don't know what we're dealing with here."

Patty made her way toward the back of the building. Stopping, she turned around and looked at Riley who was obviously concerned. "Don't worry man," she said. "I'll be okay."

Riley watched as she disappeared around the corner. He suddenly felt vulnerable so he made his way to the road, as instructed, to "wait for the cavalry to come." He wanted to believe everything would be okay, but somehow he knew things were going to be very, very bad.

Chapter 35

The sudden shock of ice-cold water pulled Dr. Sue back toward consciousness where her world became a constant twirl of light and dark, feeling and numbness, heaviness and weightlessness. Unable to focus, she felt herself being lifted to her feet and then heaved, toes dragging on the dirt, through the cold night air and into the warmth of the place in which she now sat.

Although thoroughly confused, she could tell she wasn't sitting alone, and knowing someone was next to her comforted her. The warm body beside her, its softness and protectively fragrant scent, reminded her of her own mother. She found herself unable to resist resting her head on the bony yet comfortably padded shoulder directly to her right.

"Well, don't you two look sweet sitting there?"

Dr. Sue heard the familiarly frightening voice and instantly recognized its owner. With her one good eye, she blinked Orley into focus, and this caused a chill to run down her spine, despite the warmth of her present surroundings. He stood in front of her, smiling, his evil and wicked grin burned into her psyche.

With every ounce of strength she could muster, she lifted her cheek from the soft fleshy pillow next to her and turned her head to see its owner. Since her right eye was swollen completely shut, she had to twist her head as far as it would go to the right to get a hazy look. The desperation on the face of the young girl sitting next to her moved her. She tried to speak, but her swollen tongue wouldn't let her. The coppery taste of blood dominated her senses. Clearing her throat and swallowing, she coughed weakly and then tried again.

"Amy?" she whispered.

Dr. Sue saw the girl nod in reply, and then she noticed a pair of tears fall from two innocent, round eyes onto two dirt-streaked cheeks. "I'm sorry Amy," she said and then slowly swiveled her head back so she could rest it on Amy's shoulder once more. She was so tired and so weak. All she wanted to do was snuggle up to the warm body next to her, close her eyes, and go to sleep, forever.

"There we go," Orley said, walking closer to the two women who were seated, arms intertwined behind their backs, on a pair of wooden chairs in the middle of the cabin's tiny front room. "I guess there's no need for introductions now. But come on. I've had this planned out in my mind about how things were going to go. So, if it doesn't bother you two too much, I'd like to go through the motions anyway.

"Dr. Sue, this is my lovely, young, innocent, gullible, stupid, childish, irresponsible wife. Her name is Amy." He pointed to Dr. Sue with his left hand while holding a wet dishtowel against his right eye. "Amy, this tiny, wrinkly, lump of wasted flesh is Dr. Sue. That would be the same one whose arrogant, stuck-up face you see on the billboards and buses all over the damn place. Not so royal now is she? Just a normal, quivering, shit-stinking little cunt like everyone else."

Orley pulled the rag away from his eye but immediately replaced it as the light from the cabin caused the sting to increase. Wincing, he took a couple of deep breaths and then said, "So, now that you two have been reacquainted, I think the good doctor here has something to say to you. Isn't that right Doctor?"

Orley could tell Dr. Sue was starting to withdraw again. He stepped forward and slapped gently at her right cheek with his left hand. "Come on Doctor. I need you here with me. Hello...Dr. Sue?" He saw her eye flutter back to life and then stare at him at half-mast. "You with us Doc?" he said.

"What?" she managed to mumble. "I jus' want to sleep."

"Oh, you'll get some sleep. Don't worry about that."

"Just leave her alone," Amy said. "She's sick. Just leave her alone."

"Well," Orley said, straightening up. "Old faithful here has something to say, huh? You hear that Dr. Sue? My beloved, devoted wife here says you're sick."

"Orley," Amy said. "Stop..."

Before she could say anything else, Orley backhanded Amy across the face. "Shut up," he said, hand cocked and ready to strike once more. "The doctor here is going to tell you something, and I want you to listen to her and do exactly what she says."

Dr. Sue twisted her head again and looked at the tear-stained face next to hers. Amy looked young and innocent and scared despite the hell she surely endured living with this monster. During that quick moment, Dr. Sue was able to stare into the girl's deep sad eyes and clearly see the pure and innocent soul of someone who just wanted to protect and be protected. This moment of clairvoyance enabled her to gain one last bit of inner strength as she felt an overwhelming need to protect and shelter this girl from the beast that stood before them.

Although Dr. Sue knew she was on her last leg, a sense of clarity descended upon her like a warm, soft blanket. She knew she was dying and the odds were stacked against her she would actually make it through the night alive, and for that reason, motherly intuition, human compassion, and every other basic instinct took control of her being. She felt herself lean her face close to the little girl's next to her and gently kiss its wet cheek before turning to face their aggressor.

"Wow! I can't believe I just saw that. I think I'm going to jack off," Orley said. "Do that again. I think I may have stumbled upon gold here."

"Go to hell," Amy said.

"Ooh. Feistiness turns me on. You know that." He looked at Dr. Sue, suddenly serious again. "Now, Doctor, the reason we are all together here is because I believe you have something to say to my wife."

Dr. Sue stared at Orley and then slowly twisted to glance at Amy again. She knew what she had to do to save the young girl's life. Clearing her throat, she said, "Amy. P...P..." Her lips were suddenly dry, and she found herself having trouble speaking. Her feet and fingers were growing cold, and her tongue, heavy and numb, felt oddly out of place, like an arm that's fallen asleep or a hunk of not yet chewed food inside of her mouth. A doctor, she knew the significance of this, but she forced herself to ignore it.

"Go ahead Doc," Orley spat. "Tell her damn it. Tell her."

"P...P...Protect your son from this monster," she mumbled. "Protect him."

"No!" Orley shouted, backhanding Dr. Sue across the left side of her face with all his might. He heard Amy scream after Dr. Sue's head ricocheted off of Amy's left cheek. "Shut up," he yelled at Amy before grabbing Dr. Sue's drooping chin and pulling it up so his face was inches from hers. "Bad advice, Dr. Sue. Tell her you gave bad advice. Tell her you were wrong. Tell her you made a mistake."

Dr. Sue pulled her head back so her chin slipped from Orley's grasp. "Go to hell, you son-of-a-bitch."

Orley cocked his arm and then backhanded Dr. Sue repeatedly. Amy shouted for him to stop, but the blows were relentless. About three slaps into the onslaught, Dr. Sue felt herself once again slip from her body and stand next to the scene as it unfolded in front of her. Although she felt no pain, she could hear the never-ending slaps of flesh on flesh. But she was no longer scared as she knew the end was near.

Out of breath, Orley stopped slapping her. The back of his hand was throbbing so he shook it and wriggled his fingers in an effort to stop the pain and to allow the blood to begin to flow again. He flexed his fist a few times as he paced in front of the two women.

"Leave her alone Orley," Amy said between sobs. "Just leave her alone. I'm not coming back to you. It's over. I'm never coming back to you."

Orley rubbed his hand through his short hair and then scratched at the stubble on his chin. He let out a quick series of giggles. "You're right," he said. "Fuck it. It was a bad plan." He shrugged. "I tried, you know, but I guess it never would have worked." He turned and walked to the door.

"Where are you going?" Amy asked, scared out of her mind.

"Got a gun out there. Gonna go get it. Shoot you guys, find Joel, shoot him too, and then I'm going to Mexico. Start over down there. Find me some youthful señoritas. Fuck every last one of 'em. No one cares down there. Think about that for the rest of your five-minute life."

"No Orley. Wait," Amy said, but it was too late as she watched him slide out of the cabin's door.

Patty, gun at the ready in front of her, slowly made her way up the dark dirt path. She could feel her heart pounding in her chest as her senses were alive. When she was about halfway up the hill, she heard a faint scream and quickly dropped to a knee. Holding completely still, she strained to hear against the silence of the night.

After what seemed like an eternity, she quietly got back to her feet and cautiously continued up the hill. She felt herself sweating now, fear suddenly driving the cold from her body. She wiped her forehead with her left sleeve and proceeded into the darkness.

From her blurred vantage point, Dr. Sue could barely see through the cabin's open front doorway and into the motorhome. As soon as she saw Orley disappear into the coach's door, she twisted her head toward Amy and said, "Come on. Let's get the hell out of here."

Shocked, Amy instantly stood.

"Is there another door?" Dr. Sue asked.

"What?"

"Is there another door?"

"No," Amy replied.

"Well, let's go then. Hurry."

Like Siamese twins, conjoined at the elbow, the two women managed to dash, as best they could, through the cabin's front door and into the cold night.

"That way," Amy motioned toward the darkness to the duo's left. She felt Dr. Sue pull her in the opposite direction.

"Where?" she said. "I can't see too well."

"Here," Amy replied, swinging around into the lead. "Follow me."

The two women quickly and quietly hurried toward a dark line of trees that sat at an elevation slightly above the cabin. Once inside the darkened area, Dr. Sue whispered, "Wait, Amy, wait. I gotta rest." She could feel her world begin to tilt again.

Orley could not remember a time when he had been so mad. The decision was obvious now. He slowly made his way to the motorhome devising his plan as he went.

An area as isolated as this was probably no stranger to gunshots. He would simply take Amy and Dr. Sue out back and shoot them. He'd just leave the bodies for the coyotes. It would be a nice treat for them. After that, he'd find Joel and then take him to Mexico where he'd raise him into the man he needed to be. He had enjoyed lying to Amy about shooting his son, especially recognizing the terrified look in the bitch's eyes.

Reaching the motorhome, he pulled himself inside. He had purposely left the door open, hoping the smoky smell from the campfire would continue to waft its way into the motorhome and eventually drive the smell of shit and blood from the inside of the coach. He was going to have to live in this rig for a long time, and the sooner he could air it out, the better.

Orley grabbed a quick swig of Jack Daniel's and sighed as the warm liquid burned a familiar trail into his stomach. Setting the bottle onto the table and then making his way up to the front of the rig, he froze in his tracks when he saw the cabinet door above the driver's seat was open.

Leaping toward the compartment, he stood up onto his tiptoes and looked inside. Panic flooded his being as he fought to comprehend the fact his pistol was not there. He scanned the inside of the motorhome, kicking over the small piles of clothes that littered the floor, but he didn't see anything.

"That bitch," he said, dashing back to the door. "That bitch stole my fucking gun." He jumped down from the motorhome and sprinted through the cabin's front door. "No!" he yelled before dashing back out of the cabin and into the dark.

He could feel his heart beating in his eye. The pain was becoming unbearable. He sprinted around to the back of the cabin, but it too was completely black. "I'll kill you!" he yelled into the dark. "You can't get away from me! I'll fucking kill you both!"

After a few deep breaths, Orley staggered back to the front of the cabin. He was fucked, and he knew it. He had no weapon, no doctor, no wife, and no son. His right eye was destroyed. His plan was down the tubes, and he was broke. It was over. He'd blown it.

Sighing, he rubbed a shaky palm through his short hair and took a step toward the motorhome. A rustle near the back side of the rig froze him in place. Remaining still for a few seconds, he slowly bent down and picked up part of a thick, short branch that had fallen from one of the tall trees that dotted the cabin's surroundings.

It's not over yet, you bitches, he thought as he made his way toward the rear of the coach. *I know where you are.* He shook his head defiantly. *Oh no. It's not over yet.*

The sudden yell in the silence had startled Patty back into reality. It was clear that whoever was in the cabin, the roof of which she could now see peeking above a large motorhome that sat parked directly in front of it, was in danger. So as soon as she heard a male voice shouting, she quickened her pace to the top of the small knoll. Once over the crest and not wanting her body to be outlined against the light of the dark sky's half-moon, she rapidly descended the backside of the hill toward a sufficiently dark shadow directly behind the large motorhome.

Reaching the nearly pitch-black area, she stopped to catch her breath and listen. She was greeted with silence. Inhaling the smoky, cold air, she took a step toward the rear of the motorhome so she could get a better view of the cabin and its surroundings, but the total blackness of the area hid a small bush in front of her, causing her to trip and fall onto her right side which in turn caused her glasses to fly from her face.

"Crap," she whispered. Everything was a blur.

Rising to one knee, she held her weapon out in front of her with her right hand as she swept the ground around her with her left, blindly searching for her glasses.

After a few moments, she located them and then slid them back onto her face. She worked her way toward the end of the motorhome. *Come on Howard. Don't let me down,* she thought. Grasping the white steel bumper, she slowly peered around the corner, and that's when her already dark world went completely black.

Chapter 36

The unmistakable sound of a man's voice echoed through the cold, crisp night. Riley, pacing next to the dark highway and trying his best to keep the cold air from completely overtaking his shivering body, looked out into the darkness toward the back of the mini-mart.

Although it had been faint, he had definitely heard it, and then after a few seconds, he heard the man's voice again, this time more clearly. It was unmistakable. The anger, the threat, and the cold air made Riley shiver with fright.

"Patty," he said to himself before walking toward the back of the mini-mart. He rounded the corner, expecting to see something besides the dirt lot, but between deep breaths and amidst a thumping chest, he saw nothing unusual at all. Just a large dark lot in front of a small hill. Everything remained quiet and cold, and the isolation made him shiver harder than he thought possible.

It was then he realized he was completely alone, not to mention scared shitless. He glanced at his surroundings, searching helplessly for an object that would bring him comfort or security, some sort of weapon. He patted his pockets. Nothing. He searched the ground near his feet and then near the store. Nothing there either. He had nothing with which to defend himself, and he was terrified. *What the hell am I doing here?*

Another shiver ran up his spine, and then it hit him. He did have a weapon. His protection, his comfort and security had just undauntedly inched her way ever so cautiously up the dark trail which now unwound before him into the blackness of uncertainty. A trail *he* would never have thought to go "check out" without an army surrounding him, especially in the search for a deranged kidnapper with a bad temper.

She is *a hero*, Riley thought, suddenly feeling small. He wondered how she, a woman, could be so brave in such a frightening situation, and how he, a man, so scared.

"I *am* a pussy," he whispered to himself. *I do justify my own sense of importance by reporting on others' misfortunes or misery*, he thought. *Patty was right. I do suck.*

At that moment, he gained a newfound respect for Patty not to mention all the other cops who risked their lives for him. That was why he had never made it as a police officer. He was a coward.

Patty was brave. She was willing to lay it all on the line, to go deliberately into harm's way in order to let other cowards like himself live in a world where he could throw rocks at those who so selflessly gave for others.

A lump formed in his throat as he finally grasped why that newspaper article had offended so many people, especially Patty. It was clear why he was hated so much, and he couldn't blame those who hated him. It was easy. He hated himself.

He had to make it up to her. Right now. The only problem was although he understood what he needed to do, he couldn't command his feet to move. Not a single inch. Nothing. Rather than rushing up the dark knoll to help, he just stood and stared. He could not garner the intestinal fortitude to do what he had to do. He was a coward, end of story. He knew it, and there was absolutely nothing he could do to change that fact.

Orley fingered the cold steel of the pistol he had taken from the woman. When he had stood near the back of the motorhome, arm cocked, ready to strike, the last thing he thought he would have seen sticking its head around the corner was some strange woman with a gun. But he wasn't picky. He had no idea who she was, and he didn't stick around to find out. He took the gun and ran because whoever she was, he was quite certain she wasn't alone.

Orley trotted around to the back of the cabin. In the half-moon's light, he could make out a narrow trail that led up a shrub-covered finger, and he could discern, in the loose dirt, definite footprints, though he could not tell if they were new or not. His options limited, he decided to follow the trail. Who knew? Maybe the footprints would lead him somewhere useful.

His eye socket had its own heartbeat, and the cold air drove the pain to the next level. Using his rage to shove that pain aside, he forced himself to concentrate on the task at hand. He was on a hunt for revenge, a hunt that would not stop until he found his target or was killed in the process, and he didn't plan on dying tonight.

From a tree line near the front of the motorhome, Joel watched his dad disappear into the darkness behind the cabin. After he had barely made it out of the smelly motorhome before his dad had unexpectedly shown up, Joel had snuck into the woods, near the front of the cabin. He was both frightened and happy when he saw his mom and the naked woman run out of the cabin, but the happiness left when he watched his dad run out and yell the swear words at them. He had wanted to run to his mom so she could hug him and tell him things were okay, but he saw his dad was really mad, and he knew if his dad caught him, he would definitely get into trouble for taking his gun. Instead, Joel stayed back for a few minutes before deciding to quietly follow his dad's trail.

Holding the heavy pistol in his right hand, and inching his way toward the back of the motorhome, he froze when he saw a woman lying on the ground. She wasn't moving, so he quietly made his way closer to her body. *Maybe she was taking a nap*, he thought when he saw tiny clouds of breath coming from her nose and open mouth. Stepping past her, he silently slipped to the back of the cabin where he could still see his dad's lumpy silhouette slowly moving up the dark hill toward the place he and his mom had their picnic earlier that day. He was about step forward so he could follow his dad up the hill when he heard a tree branch break and then his mom scream. Tears flooded his eyes as he helplessly watched his dad's shadow dart toward the sound. Standing still, he strained to hear if she was okay. That's when he heard his dad's voice, and he could tell his dad was definitely mad.

The woman's scream forced Riley into action. Throwing caution to the wind, he sprinted up the dark trail, his gangly legs propelling him into the unknown. He could feel the adrenaline coursing through his veins. His vision seemed to tunnel, so he aimed for the point where the trail crested the small hill. He was scared and excited and out of control.

As he reached the low summit, he looked down and saw a large motorhome parked in front of a small cabin. Nearly sick from the short sprint, he made a quick promise to get back into shape if he made it through the night, and then he noticed the body lying near the rear of the rig.

No, he thought before running down the path. He could feel an anger rising inside of him. Recognizing it was Patty from about fifteen feet, he sprinted to where she lay and knelt down beside her.

"Patty," he whispered, holding her delicate face in his hands. "Patty. Come on. Wake up." He patted her soft, cold cheeks. "Don't die babe. I'm here."

His heart jumped when he saw her eyes flutter slightly and then open. He grinned before bending forward and kissing her tiny nose.

"Riley," Patty said, her world still spinning. "What happened? Where am I?"

"It's okay babe," Riley said. "Just relax. Help's on the way." Riley could hear the faint sound of sirens in the distance and hoped that meant the cavalry was coming.

He cringed when he heard the now familiar male voice yell from a distance. "There you are, you bitches! I'll kill you! I'll kill you both! You can't get away from me!"

Patty craned her neck to see, but flinched at the pain on the right side of her head. "My glasses," she said. "I can't see without my glasses."

Riley picked up the pair of smashed spectacles and held them in front of Patty's squinting face. "Not going to do you much good tonight," he said.

"Riley," Patty whispered, leaning forward, reaching toward her leg. After a few seconds, she lay back down, a small caliber pistol in her right hand. She thrust it into his midsection.

"What?" Riley said. "Where'd that come from?"

"I always keep a spare in a holster strapped to my leg."

"I thought you always wore pants 'cause your legs were so damn hairy, not 'cause you were packing heat."

"You can never be too careful." She thrust the pistol at him again. "And, I'll *start* shaving my legs when you *stop* shaving yours. Here. Take it."

Riley stared at her, dumbfounded. "I...I can't," he said.

"Not now Riley," Patty said angrily. "Don't go to soup on me now. Those women need your help. I can't see. You go do your job."

"My job is not to shoot people. I just write about it afterward, remember? I can't Patty. I'm a pacifist. I can't kill anyone."

"Riley, look at me," Patty said. She was seething with anger. "That monster is going to kill them and then kill me. If he finds you here, he's going to kill you too. Take the gun, and go get him."

"Can't you hear the sirens?" Riley pleaded. "They're on their way. The cavalry's coming to help. They'll be here in a few minutes."

"We may not have a few minutes," Patty yelled. "Go do it. Now!"

Riley stared into Patty's angry eyes and then looked down at the gun. He had not shot a pistol since he was in the Army nearly twelve years ago, and he hated doing it back then. He didn't like loud noises. It took every ounce of will to reach forward and grab the small weapon.

"Take it and go Riley. Go. Go now."

"You don't have a second set of glasses babe? In a leg pouch?"

"Riley, if you give me back that gun, I swear, I'm going to shoot you with it. And stop calling me *babe*. I told you I freaking hate that."

Riley stared at the pistol and weighed his options. *Maybe I can just scare him*, he thought. *Or delay until the cops got here. Yeah. That'll work. That's what I'll do.* He slowly stood and looked toward the back of the cabin, from where the yelling had come. Taking a deep breath, he looked back down at Patty who managed to sit up, though definitely still in pain.

"Be careful Riley," Patty said. "I've been chasing this guy for a while now. He's a real psycho."

"Thanks," Riley said. "That helps a lot."

Amy had begged Dr. Sue to keep moving, but she could see the woman was in tremendous pain. She kept complaining about her ribs, and she would not stop coughing. Amy remembered the dark liquid dripping from the corner of Dr. Sue's mouth, and she knew, from movies, that wasn't a good sign. Both of the women were shivering fiercely, Amy fully clothed, Dr. Sue completely naked except for the large diaper.

"Where are we going?" Dr. Sue asked through wheezes. "I'm not going to make it. I'm too cold. I need to rest."

"We have to keep moving," Amy said. "He'll find us if we stop." Although it was dark, Amy kind of knew where she was going. The problem was there were so many steep drops in this wooded area, and it was so dark she had trouble seeing what was good ground on which to walk, and what was not.

Unfortunately for the two of them, Amy chose poorly. The two suddenly found themselves tumbling down a dark ravine, the fall preempted by a loud scream from Amy. When the two hit the bottom, they lay still for a few desperate moments covered in leaves and dirt. Dr. Sue started to cry.

"Come on," Amy said when she heard Orley yelling he was going to kill them. "Come on Dr. Sue. Don't quit now. Mickey's is just over there."

"'s no one there. No one will help me," Dr. Sue whimpered. "I tried, but no one will help me." Amy could tell Dr. Sue was fading away.

"Dr. Sue we need to keep moving. Come on, or he's going to kill us." Just then, she heard sirens in the distance. "Listen Dr. Sue. Listen. You hear that? Help's on the way." She stood up and pulled Dr. Sue to her feet. "We need to keep moving until help arrives. We need to keep moving Dr. Sue."

Amy froze.

"You need to shut the fuck up is what you need to do," a man's voice said. Its owner was unmistakable. "Now, let's go back to the cabin and try this again."

"Fuck you Orley," Amy said between sobs. "The police are coming. They'll get you."

Orley heard the sirens as they grew louder. He pointed his gun at the silhouettes of the two women. "Well, I guess the jig is up then, isn't it?" he said, moving the barrel toward Dr. Sue and cocking the hammer. "Oh well." He took a deep breath. "It was nice knowing you Doctor. I guess I'll see you in hell."

Riley heard the rustling of leaves and the low muttering of voices over the comforting sound of the distant sirens. He slowly and quietly made his way toward the hushed conversation. He was almost to the group when he felt a tap on his right elbow. His heart stopped. He was a goner for sure.

"You better hurry the hell up," Patty said in a whisper behind him. "I can crawl backwards faster than you can freaking walk."

"How the hell 'd you get here?" Riley said. He thought he was going to vomit. He was scared out of his mind.

"You're noisier than a freaking chainsaw. You know that?"

"You take it then," Riley said, shoving the tiny pistol into Patty's chest.

"I can't freaking see."

"You found me."

"Quit being a pussy Riley. Jeez."

"I'm going to kill you when this is over," Riley said, regaining his bearings after nearly passing out from fright. "You hear that?"

"Yeah. Whatever. You see anything?" Patty asked, squinting. The right side of her head was still throbbing with pain.

"Naw, it's too dark," Riley whispered. "Wait. There," he said. "Come on." He hurried across a moonlit patch of earth toward a position where he could clearly see three shadowy figures.

As he silently approached the group, he could see the dark outlines of three people standing in a clear patch of woods at the bottom of a small hill. From the dim light of the moon, he could make out a man and what looked like two women handcuffed together.

"There they are," Riley said. "He's got 'em."

"What are they…"

"Wait," Riley said, raising the pistol up and pointing it at them. "He's going to shoot 'em. What do I do Patty? Oh shit. He just cocked the pistol. What do I do? What do I do?"

"Shoot him," Patty spit. "Shoot him Riley. Kill him."

"I…I can't," Riley said, still pointing the shaking gun at the target.

"Shoot him now Riley. Before it's too late!"

Riley noticed the man must have heard Patty. In slow motion, the dark figure turned his head so he was staring directly at Riley. The sound of the sirens suddenly vanished, and everything in Riley's world decelerated. In fact, all sounds were instantly replaced by the thundering of his heart in his ears as he watched the man slowly swing his extended arm in his direction.

Riley saw the light of the moon glint off of the silver barrel of the handgun as its muzzle made the slow, agonizing journey toward him. Trying to recall his marksmanship training in the Army, Riley forced himself to squeeze the tip of his index finger as it shook on the trigger. His eyes began to blur. He squinted at his target.

A deafening explosion rocked the night air. Riley didn't even feel his pistol kick, and he thought it weird to see the man in front of him fall forward. He let the pistol drop to his side.

Slowly, his vision expanded, and his ringing ears began to differentiate between the noise of the sirens and the voices that came toward him in the dark.

"Nice shot Riley," he heard Patty say. "I didn't think you had it in ya."

Riley forced the bitter bile back into his stomach by swallowing as hard as he could. Holding the pistol in his right hand, he felt his body for holes but didn't find any.

"I...it wasn't me. I didn't fire."

"What do you mean?" Patty said. "He's down. You got him."

"No," Riley said. "It's still cold. Feel it. The barrel's still cold."

Patty reached forward and felt the gun. "Well, who?" she said.

"Joel!" Amy yelled when she saw her son walk forward.

Riley saw, in the distance, the shadowy figure of a child stagger into the clearing. In his hands he recognized the unmistakable shape of a rather large pistol.

"Don't shoot," Riley said as he stepped into the clearing. "We're here to help."

Chapter 37

A loud explosion shattered the twirling night. Ears still ringing, Dr. Sue felt herself being dragged, once again, across the dirt floor. Her feet were numb with cold, and she was shivering wildly. The world was spinning out of control, and she was ready to let go.

As if in a dream again, she found herself standing outside of her body watching the entire scene unfold around her. She saw herself, still bound to Amy, stoop down toward a young boy who suddenly appeared in the woods. She heard words being said, but could not decipher them.

Next, she saw a man and a woman rush toward the three of them. The man was yelling something, but she couldn't decipher what he was saying either. The woman with the man suddenly produced a flashlight and swept its beam across the three of them. Staring at herself, Dr. Sue could see she was terribly cold. As the beam of light moved across her face, she saw her own deathly purple lips and a pair of hollow cheeks. Atop her head lie a nest of tangled brown hair, and she could see her right eye was completely swollen shut. Thick, black fluid dripped from the right corner of her mouth. She looked like death, and she suddenly became afraid.

The man snatched a pocket knife from the woman with the flashlight and cut at the duct tape behind both her and Amy's backs. Feeling free at last, unshackled from the abyss in which she had existed for what seemed like her entire life, Dr. Sue saw herself mouth the words "thank you" before falling forward into the startled arms of the male stranger.

Her world instantly became warm, a bright light shining upon her. It seemed so perfect, so wonderful, so pure. She fought to open her one working eye, straining with every muscle in her body, but it would not budge, and she didn't care.

As if suddenly a feather, she felt herself floating away, understanding it was finally over for her. She had met her destiny, and she was willing to accept it. She heard the pleasant sound of motherly voices hovering around her, and she felt her feet being lifted, heated, rubbed. The laughter of children floated through the air. In all of her imagination, she had never dreamed heaven could be so wonderful.

The warmth only a mother's touch could provide suddenly smothered her left wrist. It was the softest and sweetest touch she had ever felt, and she clutched onto that feeling as the light around her dimmed into a warm, gentle blackness.

"Is she gonna make it?" Amy asked Patty as she reached out and grasped Dr. Sue's bony wrist.

"Paramedics are on the way," Patty said. "All we can do is keep her warm until they get here."

"Want my jacket Mommy?" Joel asked, holding his tiny coat out toward his mom. "It's really hot in here. I don't need it anymore. Maybe you can put this on top of her too."

Amy smiled, and taking the jacket from her red-faced son, she placed it atop the huge pile of blankets in which Dr. Sue was encased. "Thanks honey," Amy said. "It's just what she needed."

"Detective Marx," a man's voice said from behind the two women.

"Yes," Patty replied as she turned away from Dr. Sue's body and walked toward the small fireplace to where Riley and a young deputy sheriff were talking.

"How's your head?" he asked, squinting to get a better look at the long red welt that extended from the top of her tiny ear to the bottom of her right cheek.

"I'll live," she said.

"You're very lucky I saw Mr. Thorsen when I did," he said, nodding toward Howard who had taken Patty's place next to Amy. "I was just about to go get a bite when he came screaming around a dark corner, hellbent for leather. I thought I had a madman on my hands."

"Is his body still out there?" Patty said.

"It is. My partner's guarding it. LAPD and FBI forensic personnel are on the way, and the paramedics should be here any…"

Before he could finish his sentence, the door to the small cabin burst open, and two men and a woman rushed in with a gurney. And then before Patty could say anything, she saw the small team thrust an I.V. into Dr. Sue's right wrist. The trio then lifted her lifeless body onto the gurney and wheeled her out of the door and into the darkness. The whole evolution took less than a minute.

"Wait," she yelled, running past the deputy. "Where you taking her?"

"Chopper's on the way. Gonna land in two minutes in the parking lot on the other side of that small hill, by that small store. It's taking her to a trauma center in Palmdale."

"She gonna be okay?" Howard asked, moving in next to Patty.

"Let's pray," the paramedic said, rushing toward her partners who were struggling to push the cart up the small trail.

Patty could hear the rotor blades beating the crisp air as the helicopter approached.

"Wonder if they have room in the chopper?" Howard said.

"Maybe. Why don't you go ask?" Patty could see, through the one cracked lens of her broken glasses, that Howard was tired. Large bags had formed under his already drooping eyes, and he looked drained. She could only imagine what she looked like to him.

"Right," he said and then dashed up the hill toward the gurney that was carrying Dr. Sue.

"He left in a hurry," Riley said, walking toward Patty as she turned to close the door.

"Gonna try to catch a ride in the chopper. I think he really helped tonight. The deputy said the sheriff told him to come out this way because of the announcement from the radio station. Good idea on his part."

"Yeah." Riley reached out and put his right hand on Patty's left shoulder. "You did good too babe," he said looking into her eyes.

"Thanks Riley. So did you."

Riley stood and stared at her welted face. He had never seen her as beautiful as she was right now.

"What, Riley?" Patty said. "You look like you got something on your mind."

"Well, it's just that...there's something I've been meaning to tell you for a long time." He could feel his heart thumping in his chest, and his face was getting hot. He didn't know if it was the heat from the fireplace, the excitement of the night, or the presence of the one who he finally realized was the part of him that had been missing in his life, but he knew he needed to tell her what was on his mind. It was now or never.

"Patty. I..."

The door to the cabin opened again with a whoosh, and Chief Bruggeman followed by a uniformed LAPD officer and two men in expensive-looking suits hurried into the cramped cabin. Patty and Riley turned as the four men walked up to them. They were not so much surprised at seeing the chief as they were at seeing the smile on the chief's face. When he reached the duo, he thrust his arm out and shook both of their reluctant hands with genuine gusto.

"Nice job Detective, Mr. Riley. Nice job," he said. He slapped Patty on her shoulder, and she cringed as it was still tender from the gunshot wound she had suffered what now seemed so long ago.

"Chief," Patty muttered, rubbing at the pain. "I guess I'm surprised to see you here."

"Rode in on the chopper," he said. "Couple agents from the FBI wanted to take a look around. Ask a few questions." He put his arm on her tender shoulder and spun around so he was standing beside her. "Agent Daczkowski, Agent Pease, I want you to meet Detective Marx who cracked the case." He squeezed her next to him, causing her head to bobble on her skinny neck.

One at a time, the two agents shook her hand.

"One of the best detectives we got," Chief Bruggeman said before finally releasing her.

"Actually, Riley here deserves all of the credit," Patty said. "Had you listened to him earlier Chief, none of this would have happened."

Chief Bruggeman smiled hard. Riley could see sweat beading on his forehead.

"Yeah, well. We had a lot of leads to chase down at the time. You know how it is." The chief felt himself getting hot. He wiped his forehead with the back of his right hand and then wiped that hand on his dark blue pant leg. "Ah hell. Nice job Riley. I wish I had listened to you in the first place. You don't know how much it pains me to say it, but thanks. And nice shot by the way. I didn't know you had the onions to do it."

"Actually Chief, I didn't…"

"Chief," Patty interrupted, "why don't you guys go take a look at the scene? It's right up the hill, behind the cabin. Bunch of lights in the woods. Can't miss it."

"Good idea," Chief Bruggeman said. "We'll talk tomorrow."

With that, the chief and the two other men disappeared into the dark night.

Patty turned to Riley. "So you were saying," she said, looking up into his dumb dopey face.

"What was that all about?" he said. "What'd he mean *nice shot?*"

"Come on Riley. That poor kid's been through enough. Let's let it end for him tonight."

Riley stared at Patty for a long moment before grasping what she meant. He smiled and then said, "You're right. It was a nice shot."

"So, what were you saying?" Patty asked again.

Riley put his hands on her shoulders. "You know you really look like shit," he said.

Patty shrugged her shoulders from beneath his large hands. "Go to hell." She turned to walk toward the door.

Riley reached out, and grabbing her by the waist, spun her back toward him and planted a firm, semi opened-mouthed kiss on her surprised lips.

For a split second Patty felt like resisting, but the inkling passed, and instead, she went limp in his grasp.

"Excuse me," a deputy sheriff said, clearing his throat.

Riley broke his lip-lock and turned toward the voice.

"The press is starting to arrive. They're wondering if they could get a statement."

Patty looked at Riley and then at the deputy. "Tell them I'll talk to them in the morning. I gotta do another interview right now." She smiled up at Riley.

"Guess I'm getting an exclusive," Riley said, winking at the blushing deputy.

"Guess so," he said before turning and walking toward the door.

"Wanna go?" Patty asked.

"I think we're through here," Riley replied. He slipped his hand around Patty's waist and the two walked out of the door and into the night.

Seven Months Later

Chapter 38

Dr. Sue slipped her headphones onto her head. As the soft cups covered her ears, a smile came over her lips. She finally felt complete again.

It had been a long seven months of recovery. Her doctors told her she had been literally minutes from death. Her two broken ribs that probably occurred when Orley assaulted her outside of the motorhome had punctured her liver, and she nearly bled to death.

She had permanent damage to her right eye resulting in the loss of nearly thirty percent of her vision on that side. Over the past seven months she'd had to endure six surgeries and many long sessions with a therapist to help her get through the shock of what she endured. During those long sessions, she realized how lucky she had been to have been loved by those around her.

"Good day ladies and gentlemen. It's great to be back on the air, finally." She took a deep breath and a quick sip of Dasani water. "First off, I want to thank all of you out there for the flowers and the cards of encouragement. You guys are wonderful, and it is wonderful to know you would take the time out of your busy days to show such support.

"I am fine," she said. "In case you are wondering. I still have nightmares about the ordeal, but it helps me to deal with those nightmares if I talk about them, so bear with me.

"I wish I could put into words the experience I had to endure, but the only word that is even close to doing it justice is *evil*. *Pure evil*. I never thought pure evil existed in the world until my time in the hell of that man's box. I was exposed to a world in which children, small children, are bought and sold into sex in our own country. I was defiled, raped, beaten, tortured. I gave up hope many times. I wanted to die almost every other minute. It was a dark, heinous time, and it was an experience I would not even wish on my worst enemy. Not even Orley, who put me there."

She took another sip of water and a deep breath. "But, through all of that evil, and hopelessness, and despair, I could not stop thinking about my family. The love for my family is what let me endure such a terrible time.

"I learned many things lying there in my own feces, arms bound behind me and nailed to the floor, mouth duct taped shut most of the time with nothing to eat or drink except for a small tube through which I could sip stale, plastic-tasting water. I learned the human spirit is strong and resilient. I learned evil exists all around us, and it's up to us to take a stand against it. I learned evil people can do whatever they want in this world when good people do nothing.

"I don't remember my rescue, but I do know I owe my life to those who sacrifice all for others. People who I had never met went out on a limb for me, and I owe them a huge debt of gratitude for that. Patty and Riley. If you guys are listening, thank you. I hope your life together is joyful, and I am still expecting an invitation." She chuckled, wiping a tear from her right cheek.

"I guess what I am trying to say is I'm sorry for having been a little arrogant in the past. But, don't expect my standards to drop because of it. There is a right way and a wrong way to live out there, and now I have a benchmark from which to advise.

"That being said, I am pleased to finally take my first caller in a long, long time. So here we go.

"Josh, thank you for calling the show. How can I help you?"

Author's Biography

J.P. Pellegrino was born and raised in Southern California. He attended the United States Naval Academy, graduating in 1994 with a BS in Economics and was commissioned an officer in the United States Marine Corps. For 20 years he flew KC-130 and Gulfstream aircraft (in peacetime and war), worked at the Pentagon, commanded an air station in Hawaii, studied strategy at a DC think tank where he published articles on ethics and defense strategy, and worked as an Inspector General. He has been happily married since 1995, currently resides in Mayo, Maryland, and thoroughly enjoys spending time with his family. He thanks you for purchasing his book and hopes you have enjoyed its contents.

Made in the USA
San Bernardino, CA
25 March 2014